I had to do this for Liam, because of my love for him.

To protect him.

I snapped my whip out, cracking a grey-skinned ogre in the face. He fell back, screaming as though hot acid had been poured onto him. And the result of the whip was more than a little like that. The ogre fell, his skin bubbling and breaking in huge pustules that exploded spraying those around him. A shimmer of darkness oozed from where my whip had cracked him and then the demon was free. For a split second it stared at me, then with a screech, an opening appeared behind it, and the Veil seemed to suck the demon back to where it belonged.

All of that happened in two strides of Nikko's long legs. His horn flashed as he drove it through the thigh of an ogre who stepped in his way. Over and over again, I sent my whip out, desperate to get to Liam. I was afraid to Track him, afraid of what I'd find. I couldn't see Erik; the red unicorn no longer carried him. The fool had dismounted. Things were going downhill fast and about to get even faster. As my fear for Liam rose, my effectiveness against the demon-possessed ogres fell.

The ogres are circling us.

Sons of bitches. By the time Nikko's words hit my brain, he was already wrong. They weren't circling us. We were surrounded.

PRAISE FOR SHANNON MAYER AND THE RYLEE ADAMSON SERIES

"If you love the early Anita Blake novels by Laurel K. Hamilton, you will fall head over heels for The Rylee Adamson Series. Rylee is a complex character with a tough, kick-ass exterior, a sassy temperament, and morals which she never deviates from. She's the ultimate heroine. Mayer's books rank right up there with Kim Harrison's, Patricia Brigg's, and Ilona Andrew's. Get ready for a whole new take on Urban Fantasy and Paranormal Romance and be ready to be glued to the pages!"

—*Just My Opinion Book Blog*

"Rylee is the perfect combination of loyal, intelligent, compassionate, and kick-ass. Many times, the heroines in urban fantasy novels tend to be so tough or snarky that they come off as unlikable. Rylee is a smart-ass for sure, but she isn't insulting. Well, I guess the she gets a little sassy with the bad guys, but then it's just hilarious."

—*Diary of a Bibliophile*

"I could not put it down. Not only that, but I immediately started the next book in the series, *Immune*."

—*Just Talking Books*

"*Priceless* was one of those reads that just starts off running and doesn't give too much time to breathe. . . . I'll just go ahead and add the rest of the books to my TBR list now."

—*Vampire Book Club*

"This book is so great and it blindsided me. I'm always looking for something to tide me over until the next Ilona Andrews or Patricia Briggs book comes out, but no matter how many recommendations I get nothing ever measures up. This was as close as I've gotten and I'm so freakin happy!"

—*Dynamite Review*

WOUNDED

Books by Shannon Mayer

WOUNDED

A RYLEE ADAMSON NOVEL
BOOK 8

SHANNON
MAYER

TALOS

New York

Talos Press books may be purchased in bulk at special discounts for sales promotion, corporate gifts, fund-raising, or educational purposes. Special editions can also be created to specifications. For details, contact the Special Sales Department, Talos Press, 307 West 36th Street, 11th Floor, New York, NY 10018 or info@skyhorsepublishing.com.

Talos Press® is a registered trademark of Skyhorse Publishing, Inc.®, a Delaware corporation.

Visit our website at www.talospress.com.

10 9 8 7 6 5 4 3 2 1

Library of Congress Cataloging-in-Publication Data

Names: Mayer, Shannon, 1979- author.
Title: Wounded / Shannon Mayer.
Description: First Talos Press edition. | New York : Talos Press, 2017. | Series: A Rylee Adamson novel ; book 8
Identifiers: LCCN 2016039145 | ISBN 9781945863028 (softcover : acid-free
paper)
Subjects: LCSH: Missing children--Investigation--Fiction. | Paranormal romance stories. | BISAC: FICTION / Fantasy / Urban Life. | FICTION /
Fantasy / Paranormal. | GSAFD: Fantasy fiction.
Classification: LCC PR9199.4.M3773 W68 2017 | DDC 813/.6--dc23 LC record available at https://lccn.loc.gov/2016039145

Original illustrations by Damon Za www.damonza.com

Printed in Canada

ACKNOWLEDGMENTS

To those who have made this journey an adventure; thank you.

To my readers who love Rylee, Liam, and the rest of the gang; thank you.

To my team who keep me and Rylee on the right track; thank you.

To my fellow authors who commiserate and make me laugh; thank you.

To the two brightest lights in my life, who love me despite all my flaws; thank you.

CAST OF CHARACTERS

Rylee Adamson: Tracker and Immune who has dedicated her life to finding lost children. Based near Bismarck, North Dakota.

Liam O'Shea: Previously an FBI agent. Now he is a werewolf/Guardian as well as lover to Rylee.

Giselle: Mentored Rylee and Milly; Giselle is a Reader but cannot use her abilities on Rylee due to Rylee's Immunity. She died in *Raising Innocence*.

Millicent: AKA Milly; witch who was best friend to Rylee. Now is actively working against Rylee for reasons not yet clear.

India: A spirit seeker whom Rylee Tracked in *Priceless*.

Kyle Jacobs: Rylee's personal teenage hacker; human.

Doran: Daywalker and Shaman who helps Rylee from time to time. Located near Roswell, New Mexico.

Alex: A werewolf trapped in between human and wolf. He is Rylee's unofficial sidekick and loyal companion. Submissive.

Berget: Rylee's little sister who went missing ten years prior to *Priceless*. In *Raising Innocence*, Rylee found out that Berget is still alive. In *Shadowed Threads*, Rylee discovered Berget is the "Child Empress" and a vampire.

Dox: Large pale blue-skinned ogre. Friend of Rylee. Owns "The Landing Pad" near Roswell, New Mexico.

William Gossard: AKA Will; Panther shape shifter and officer with SOCA in London. Friend to Rylee.

Deanna Gossard: Druid, sister to William. Friend and help to Rylee.

Louisa: Tribal Shaman located near Roswell, New Mexico.

Eve: Harpy that is now under Rylee's tutelage, as per the Harpy rule of conduct.

Faris: Vampire and general pain in the ass to Rylee. He is in contention for the vampire "throne" against Rylee's little sister, Berget.

Jack Feen: Only other Tracker in existence. He lives in London and is dying.

Agent Valley: Senior in command in the Arcane Division of the FBI.

Blaz: Dragon who bonded (reluctantly) with Rylee in *Shadowed Threads*.

Pamela: Young, powerful witch whom Rylee saved in *Raising Innocence*. She is now one of Rylee's wards.

Charlie: Brownie who acts as Rylee's go-between when working with parents on all of her salvages. Based in Bismarck, North Dakota.

Dr. Daniels: AKA "Daniels"; a child services worker and a druid Rylee met up with in *Raising Innocence*. Rylee and Daniels do not like one another.

"A wounded deer leaps the highest."
~ Emily Dickinson ~

1

All around me was silence; but under that silence was a brooding tempest of fear. Doran's home and courtyard had never been so fucking quiet, though the calm hid the dread flowing around us. The four horsemen of the apocalypse would soon be upon us, thanks to Orion, the demon I was supposed to stop, according to the prophecies. We were in trouble, and as the truth set in, a literal explosion occurred within the council. Chaos. Total and utter madness ripped through the group, driven by fear, by the announcement Faris had made, and by the sight of his missing arm.

Faris was a powerhouse, a vampire who not many could take on and survive. Yet he'd been nearly killed by Orion's demons, the ones *preceding* the four horsemen, who were, for all intents and purposes, stronger and more deadly.

The four generals of Orion were upon us.

There was a slam of hands on skin, roars of anger and fear. Yelling, pushing, and shoving. I watched as one of the ogres tripped over a zombie that rose under his feet; another zombie erupted out of the ground next to Faris and grabbed his legs. Faris ripped the zombie's head off and tossed it behind him, inadvertently hitting a unicorn on the ass. The equine kicked out and nailed an ogre in the guts. Turning my head didn't improve the view. Doran and Berget used their phenomenal strength to toss those who were closest to them backward, creating a space the zombies kept trying to push into.

All because no one had thought it would come this fast. No one thought they would really have to deal with the demons. Not with me here. Understanding dawned.

They'd said they would stand with me against Orion, but they hadn't really believed they would have to. I could see it in the way they looked at me, their gazes sliding over me. Hope and fear lingered in their eyes, along with a healthy dose of recrimination. Like I should have already stopped this by now.

They didn't think demons were truly something they would have to face. They thought there would be other supernaturals, or maybe humans they would each have to battle. But demons? No, that realization had only now sunk in. And it scared the ever living shit out of them. As it should.

In a matter of seconds, the council, so newly formed, was about to incinerate into tiny, dangerous shards that would leave us standing on our own against Orion and his demons.

Through it all, I sat, unmoving. Liam stood behind me, Alex sat at my feet, and Pamela sat to my left. Against the edge of the house, my uncle Erik, last of the trained Slayers, leaned, watching. Surreal, the scene seemed to push me out of myself. I needed a moment; I needed distance. So I sat and did nothing to stop the fights breaking out. In that moment I needed calm and the only way to get it was to withdraw.

I needed to think, to remember why I was doing this.

Had it only been months ago that I'd gone after India, the young spirit seeker? It felt like years. That had been the first case I'd worked with Liam, though I'd known him as O'Shea then. The first case where I'd ever faced a demon. From that moment forward, my life had gone into overdrive. I'd been stung by a Hoarfrost demon and nearly caused an apocalyptic winter. I'd faced down a necromancer raising children from the dead, her blind attempt to fill the void her long deceased daughter had left.

My best friend Milly had alternately turned on me and saved me and now she was lost to the deepest Veil, captive of Orion once more, and there was nothing I could do to save her or the child she carried. I'd found Pamela, a young witch who was fast becoming a power to be reckoned with. I'd lost Giselle, my mentor and mother of my heart. I'd fallen in love with Liam and chased him across Europe to prove it, to bring him back from the brink of losing his humanity.

I'd lost one of my best friends—Dox, an ogre and ally I could never replace. I'd lost Jack, someone who could have been a great mentor, a Tracker like me. I'd gained back my little sister Berget, who I thought was gone forever. Blaz and Erik had come into my life, giving me two someones to lean on as I faced what was on its way.

All of those things, both good and bad had brought me to this moment.

The current through everything in the last five months was a sense of urgency, a fear that drove me and those around me. Orion was coming, a demon sent to take the world into his hands and claim it for his own.

I was to stand between him and the world with nothing more than the memory of the books of prophecy I'd read before they'd been destroyed by Deanna and her druids.

I leaned back in my chair, watched the supernaturals around me yelling and roaring at one another, the noise distant in my ears. In some ways, I wish I didn't need their help. The days of Tracking a child on my own seemed so far gone, and so simple.

A missing child to find, bring them home no matter what—what had seemed difficult at times in the past now looked straightforward. Almost easy compared to what loomed ahead of me.

Yet here I was, supposedly the only person who could save the world.

Something in me clicked into place. Saving the world would save more than one child; it would save many, many thousands. This was my fate; this was my place in the world.

This was what I'd been born for, even if it scared me worse than anything I'd ever faced. There was no greater cause than stopping Orion, no matter how much fear the task gave me.

Enough daydreaming of the past and how I wished things were as they'd been. We needed someone to lead, someone to pull the reins on this runaway carriage or we might as well give Orion our souls on silver and golden platters.

Fucking hell.

I'd already known, but still, a small part of me hoped Doran or someone would have stopped the hemorrhaging of this open wound, the council falling completely apart. Nope, looked like it was going to be me to pull this together.

"Are you all about done with your pissing and moaning?" I barely raised my voice. Didn't yell, didn't scream. Booyah for me, acting all calm and cool. Leaderly-like, even.

The silence that dropped over the outside courtyard was more than a little cool. It was downright icy. Or that could have just been the late January wind whipping through and around us, teasing at the spray of water over the koi pond. Everything stilled, zombies included.

Ogres, vampires, necromancers, witches, were-wolves, and unicorn. All turned to me, and more than one was a little . . . ticked.

Blaz's voice whispered through my mind, and I stared at him on the edge of the courtyard, his eyes on mine. *They are afraid. Be careful not to drive them away, Rylee. Orion has planted the seed of fear well and it grows with a violence that will cut down those in front of it.*

The dragon was on point, of course, and I knew they were afraid. Could almost smell it, even though I was no shapeshifter.

They were not the only ones who thought facing down demons called "the four horsemen of the apocalypse" was a very bad idea.

Yeah, if I were a betting gal, I wouldn't bet on us, either.

I lifted one hand, palm up, and wiggled my fingers at them. "Look, this is what Orion *wants*. He wants us fractured and freaking the hell out, because he knows if we are too busy fighting each other, he can swoop in and kick all of our asses. So everyone calm the fuck down."

Liam hadn't move from his position behind me. Nor had Pamela or Alex shifted away from me. Okay, Alex as making faces at the crowd, his long tongue flapping at them, but he stood by me. My heart swelled. Even if everyone else walked in that moment, I wouldn't see this through alone. I had my family.

Nikko, the black unicorn was the first to nod, his voice projecting much like Blaz's, inside all our heads at once.

You are right, of course. There is no sense in fighting one another. We will do the demon's job for him if we kill each other now. I will listen to what you have to say, Tracker. We have promised our help, and we will stand by our word. He lowered himself to the ground, then tucked his legs underneath his body, his golden horn glinting even in the starlight.

One by one, each of those in the council found a seat or at least put their weapons away. On each of them I saw tightened lips, narrowed eyes, twitching muscles, sweat-dripping skin in the cold winter night air—marks of fear. I wasn't sure I could convince them all to stay, and we desperately needed them to stay.

Without the numbers, I wasn't sure we would have any way of stopping Orion and his demon hordes. Because even if it came down to me and Orion, one-on-

one, I was pretty sure I would have to battle through his demons to get to him. Or at least, I was assuming.

Doran and Berget stood side by side, unmoving, looking as if they hadn't just been ready to toss everyone out. This was, after all, Doran's place we'd invaded. I wouldn't blame him. But he looked at me and gave me a slight nod of encouragement.

I stood, felt the world sway, and locked my knees. Fuck me if I was going to pass out in front of all these powerful supernaturals.

First thing's first.

"Faris, tell us exactly what you saw." I paused and fought to say the next word without a hint of sarcasm. "Please."

Faris pushed himself away from a shadow that held tight against the house, his eyes flicking to Thomas, then back to me. He didn't cradle the stub of his missing arm, though his good hand twitched as though he'd like to. "I went, at Doran's bidding, to check on the state of the castle. We wanted to know for sure that all the doorways were indeed destroyed and there was no way through those left into the human world."

His eyes went to Doran, who gave him a nod.

"There was nothing at first; I didn't see anything or smell anything. Then a woman stepped out of a third floor balcony—"

I lifted a hand to stop him. "What did she look like?"

He took a breath before answering. "Long white hair, but young in the face. I didn't get much more from her than that."

"Did she give her name?" I suspected who it would be, but I wanted to be sure.

Faris shot me a look, his eyes puzzled. "No, she didn't."

"I'll bet it was Talia," I muttered. Who else would it be, really?

Apparently, I didn't mutter so quietly. Thomas sucked in a sharp breath. Of course, he would recognize a fellow necromancer. Maybe he'd even trained her. I'd only met her once, and I knew she worked for Orion, albeit reluctantly. Orion needed a necromancer to open the gateway to the deep Veil and he'd been training Talia against her will for some time. At least, according to what she told me.

The vampire went on. "She did something to the last doorway, the one that leads to the deep Veil. The one that leads to the demons. I don't know how, but she opened it. And then the pack of demons was in the castle and I was fighting them."

He shook his head, his lips tightening, his fangs peeking out between them. "I thought I could take them, but there seemed to be nothing I could do. I fought my way free far enough to open the Veil to escape. As I fell backward through the Veil, I saw them leave through the gate in the courtyard. The broken doorways seem to have slowed them, but not by much. Whoever broke the doorways has done us a favor."

There was silence for a few heartbeats, nothing but the sound of the wind and the trickle of the fountain splashing.

"You're welcome." Erik pushed himself from the wall and stepped forward, drawing everyone's eyes to him. "Rylee, if I may address this?"

My eyebrows had never climbed higher, but I cleared my throat and managed to answer. "Yes, say what you've got to say."

He nodded as I gave my permission. "I broke those doorways and sealed the final two, making them traversable only one way, because I ran out of time. That was when I was grabbed by Talia and her little helpers. They hunkered down and waited for you while Bert took my spot." He must have seen the question in my eyes. How the fuck did someone take out a Slayer like Erik? He gave me a wry twist of a smile, "They hit me from behind."

"Blaz, tell Bert we want to speak to him. Maybe he can enlighten us on what the fuck Orion is up to." Bert was still an unknown to us in many ways. He'd started out as my Uncle Erik's doppleganger, sent by Orion to get close to us and take out our two dragons. But we'd caught him in time, and now he'd sworn fealty to my uncle. It was that or die, and he'd chosen wisely. Strange to think, though, that a demon was on our side.

He's coming, Blaz said, loud and clear so everyone heard him.

While we waited, Faris handed me two pieces of paper. One was handwritten with no signature; the other was a picture. I looked at the photo first, memorizing the kid's face. It was a young boy, maybe sixteen years old, with the name Simon scrawled across the back. Faris dropped his voice to a low, quiet pitch. "The necromancer slipped this to me before the fight. Said it was all she could do to help and asked me to give it to you. Likely it is a ruse, but I don't know for sure."

I stared at the picture, the dirty blond hair, and skin so dark I wondered if it was his heritage or if he just tanned that way. But it was his eyes that caught me, made me hold my breath. Eyes that seemed to have blue, green, and aqua swirling within them. Shit, a Tracker? Another one?

Suddenly, my place as the so-called "chosen one" was not as solid as I thought, and a tiny part of me was really, really happy. But this Simon kid, he was just a boy. A child who likely didn't even know what he was, and there was no way I would want to put this burden of saving the world and facing down Orion on him. Hell, the kid probably didn't even know how to Track yet. The ability to Track didn't come until late teens, well into puberty and, according to Jack, most often not until something traumatic happened. Then there were the prophecies. They referred always to a "she." Lucky me.

I opened up the folded sheet of paper, scanning the words.

Four packs precede the four you should fear above all others. Kill the packs and seal the doorway with the blood you cherish above all else.

There was no signature, but the handwriting was feminine, and I didn't doubt Talia had written it. I folded and tucked it into my back pocket, choosing to not think too much about "the blood you cherish above all else."

Faris let out a breath, and tapped the picture. "They will try to kill him, take out any possible successors for you. Just to be sure. Assuming, of course, he is a Tracker and this isn't a trap of some sort."

I nodded and tucked the picture into my inner jacket pocket. Fuck, this complicated things in a way I didn't really want to address right now. Could I not have just one problem at a time?

There was some muttering amongst the council, the tension rising with each minute that passed, but it stilled as Bert stepped into the courtyard. As a doppelganger, he could have chosen to look like anyone. What he decided to project was a weak imitation of Bruce Lee. After we realized what he was, he told us how he'd fooled us so completely. He'd apparently taken possession of a very minor witch, one whose skills were miniscule enough that they could be easily passed off as other things. Like the skills of the so-called Slayer he'd tried to impersonate. The little bit of magic he'd had, he used to making us believe he truly was my Uncle Erik so he could get close to us and kill Blaz and Ophelia. The only thing that stopped him was his true affection for Ophelia. That hadn't ended well and Ophelia left us, for gods only knew where.

Now, Bert was bound to my true uncle, forced to serve him.

Bert wrung his hands and looked sheepishly from me to the others in the courtyard and then back to me. Raw sneered at him and stepped back, as if just by being close to the demon he could somehow become infected. Not good.

I crooked a finger at Bert. "Come here."

He swallowed hard and shuffled across to me, cringing as if expecting a blow. "I've done nothing wrong, Master."

Oh shit, that was not going to fly. "My name is Rylee. Use it. Or if you can't, call me Tracker."

He bobbed his head and I wondered again how he'd been able to keep up even a small sliver of believability as my uncle. Looking back, though, I'd never fully connected with him, or trusted him while he played that role. He always seemed . . . off. Now that he'd been "outed" as a demon, he was a damn sniveling weakling.

"Bert, the four demon packs preceding the four horsemen are loose. Where are they headed?" I was going to give him the benefit of the doubt, and allow him to answer before I asked Erik to put pressure on him.

He shook his head and stared at his feet. "I don't know."

I leaned in close to him, so my mouth was next to his cheek, though I wasn't quiet with my words. "Demon, perhaps you forget who you are dealing with. I'm not like most women. I will fucking pull you apart by the seams and not even blink while you scream for mercy if you don't tell me. I know you're lying. I suggest you think hard before you answer me."

Swallowing several times, he fought to suck in a breath, but he said nothing. I stepped back and pulled my whip free, snapping it out, holding the tip in one hand and the handle in the other. "You have ten seconds before I start unstitching your skin to find out what a makes up a demon from the inside out."

Bitchy? Hell yes. But we didn't have time for polite chatting and dodging the issue. Big, bad, nasty, ugly demons were loose on the world. Bert was the least of my concerns at this point.

His eyes lifted to mine, glimmering with tears, and I almost felt bad. Almost. There was nothing I wouldn't do to keep my family and friends safe. Bert was nothing to me but a weak-assed demon I would use as I saw fit.

"Orion wants the humans to love him because he knows people will fight him if he comes in with guns blazing. But if they love him, revere him, they will willingly do as he wants, they will do as he pleases. So he'll stir up the wars and . . . and strife, and *then* he will come and 'save' the world." Bert took a deep breath and as he spoke the words seemed to come easier, like a weight was being lifted off him. And maybe it was. "The packs, and later the four generals, their jobs are to stir the fear and the panic amongst the human population; they are to convince the humans the end days are upon them. It is at that point Orion will come through and 'vanquish' the evil in the world. The evil, of course, will be the supernatural world."

That was exactly what Milly had thought. She'd explained that one of Orion's plans had been to stir up the humans, but not that he would want to expose the supernaturals as "evil."

"And the humans would help him wipe us out?" Erik asked the question on the tip of my tongue. Bert nodded furiously.

"Yes. That is the plan."

Berget stepped up, her brows drawn over her bright blue eyes. "Why did only the packs come through? Why not the generals or Orion himself?"

Erik answered her before Bert could even process the question. "Because the Veil is not truly opened to the demons, not yet. There are things that must happen. Signs that must be fulfilled before the hordes can come through. The four horsemen are second only to Orion in strength. The generals will need to possess strong bodies, supernaturals that will be difficult to take, but also have a great deal of inborn power. The necromancer will have to help them with that. And maybe even your friend." He looked at me when he said "friend." Of course, he meant Milly. She'd stayed behind, bound once more by Orion.

I wasn't so sure Talia had the strength to force people through the Veil and make them prisoners. But Milly did. My heart twisted, knowing she was trapped there. She was due to give birth in a couple of months, and we had no way of getting her out. Bound to Orion, she would be dangerous to have near us, as dangerous as she was away from us. I pulled myself together, though by Liam's glance, he was the only one to notice my mind wandering.

"Answer Berget's other question," I said. "Why doesn't Orion come through?"

Bert gave a little laugh, though there was no true humor in it. "Didn't you hear me? He wants the humans to love him. He has to save them to do that. Of course, he doesn't have the body he wants, or needs yet, either. That's coming as soon as the witch gives birth. He needs that body if he wants to fulfill the demon prophecies. Once he has it, he could take another body. But he must start with the child. A child of great power."

His words stabbed through me. He was talking about Milly and her unborn baby. Liam's hand was on the small of my back, subtly supporting me, his words quiet and only for my ears. "You could do nothing more. Milly made her choice to save you so you could stop Orion."

The words that flowed out of me were words I'd read out of the grey-skinned book of prophecies what seemed like eons ago. Before I'd truly understood what we were facing. "Orion shall twist the magic of the Great One, and shall bring her to her knees with his lies. For when he possesses the heart of her soul, salvation shall fall to one bound by oaths to stay his hand of death over the world. The Tracker must break her oaths to save the world, or we will all be doomed."

The courtyard was very quiet; everyone was looking at me. I didn't even blink, though my eyes burned with unshed tears. "Milly, she's the greatest witch the world has seen. And the heart of her soul, that's her baby. That's what the prophecy meant, what it means. She asked me to do what I had to do. She meant killing her child if I had to. That would break my oath to protect children." Why, oh why did I have to understand that prophecy now?

Nikko stood and he walked solemnly to me, his horn lowering to touch one shoulder.

All the prophecies will be fulfilled, Rylee. But we cannot always see in what way until they are upon us.

Erik cleared his throat, drawing everyone's eyes to him. "Be that as it may, we still have the four packs to deal with. I believe Bert here."

Bert stood a little taller as Erik clapped a hand onto the smaller man's shoulder.

"But that doesn't mean Orion's plan hasn't changed."

Bert slumped. "I don't think he knows yet, that I've . . . umm."

Okay, it was damn weird to see a demon stumble and stutter over his words. But I knew what he was getting at.

I lifted an eyebrow. "Orion doesn't know that you've defected."

"Exactly."

"Well," I said. "I guess there's only one thing to do."

All eyes swung my way once more. Probably was going to have to get used to that.

I gave them a smile that I knew was easily as cold as the wind tugging at us. "Time to go demon hunting."

2

While the council argued over the best way to take out the demon packs, Liam found his way to Berget's side.

She blinked up at him and gave him a soft smile as her eyes searched his face. "You save her, you know that, don't you?"

"What do you mean?"

"She doesn't have your patience, or your ability to hold back when she needs to. Of course, it is more than that. You are her heart. Without that, she would be far crueler than she needs to be."

He thought about her threats to Bert. "I don't know about that. She seemed plenty cruel with the demon. As she should be."

Berget shook her head, blonde hair tossing lightly in the wind. "No, that was necessary. She needs to make a strong impression, and while she might not understand it, her instincts to lay into him run true. It was good, not only for him, but also for those who follow her, to see she will do what she must, no matter how gruesome. Too many leaders fail because they are afraid to do what is right because it is hard, or they are afraid of how it will make them look."

Her eyes flicked to his face and she shifted so they were side by side, looking out over the courtyard. "But that is not why you stand with me, is it?"

Liam thought for a moment. Though Berget was only sixteen, there was a huge part of her that was older, knowledge she'd gained only by living amongst vampires before she herself was turned. On top of that, carrying around the souls and memories of two ancient vampires had aged her, and made her wise far beyond her years. "No. It isn't. She told me you were searching through your memories, and those of your parents, for the key to the Veil, to the things that had to be done to close it off."

From the side, her face went carefully blank. "Yes, she did. But I see no need now—"

He lifted one hand, stopping her. "We already know it has something to do with the guardians, that their blood can somehow close the doorways. What have you learned?"

They didn't look at one another; instead, they watched the council argue.

"The blood of a guardian can close a tear in the Veil; it is not the same as the Blood of the Lost, but it is strong enough to do the job for a time. Taken by force, that is all it will do," she said softly, so softly her words were less than a whisper.

The image of Eagle, sprawled out, blood-soaked in Rylee's bathtub, slid to the front of his mind. The demons who'd taken Milly and Pamela had used Eagle's blood, forcibly, to close the doorway behind them. To wipe clean their own escape and prevent anyone from following through the tear in the Veil they'd created.

Berget kept speaking, which jarred him out of his memories. "The blood of a guardian freely given, a sacrifice, can shut the Veil for a period of time, putting the entire system in stasis. No one can cross in either direction."

"How long does it give, this sacrifice?"

"You cannot, Liam." She turned to face him, grabbed his hand. Cool, dainty fingers clutched at his. "You cannot leave her. My parents have lied to me before. I do not know for sure this would even work."

He gently squeezed her hand, grateful Rylee had Berget back in her life, even if it was somewhat on the peripheral. "I don't plan on it. There are other guardians, and we need to know how and where they can help. The loss of a little blood is not too much to ask of them to give us time to plan for Orion, is it?"

Berget closed her eyes, the blue veins along her eyelids sharp in contrast to her pale skin, even in the dim light. "That is true."

The sharp scent of her lie bit at his nose. Acrid and tangy, he blew it out.

"Berget. What aren't you telling me?"

She shook her head and took her hand from his. "Nothing you need to know."

He stared down at her, as if he could will the truth from her. But he knew better. Tiny though she was, there was nothing he could do to make her spill her secrets before she was ready. Even if she hadn't been a vampire, she was a woman—that alone meant she wouldn't say anything if he pushed her, and she wasn't yet ready to talk.

He let out a sigh. "Will you tell me at some point?"

Her shoulders sagged and she closed her eyes. "Yes, Liam, I will. But not today."

There was a large part of him, the wolf in him that wanted to grab Berget and shake the truth from her. Mostly because he had a feeling it would impact him in ways he didn't want, and he hated not knowing.

For now, though, her promise that she would tell him would have to be good enough.

Across from them, Rylee looked up and he gave her a wink, immediately pushing back the frown he knew had been on his face. Her lips didn't move, but he could see the smile in her eyes, her face, the way her head tilted. No one else would see it.

And that was fine by him.

Until we had more information, there was no point in continuing to hold the council together. Doran dismissed everyone, nicely of course, asking them all to come back after we'd had some time to discuss the possibilities with Bert. No point in riling everyone up without just cause. The ogres and unicorns headed off together. Their camps had been set up so the ogre's camp was a larger circle around the unicorns, in a defensive measure. Having the smaller contingent, and having brought their only foal with them, the unicorns had agreed that was best. Just in case things got ugly.

Once the courtyard cleared, it was just me, Liam, Erik, Bert, and Faris. I sent Alex and Pamela to bed since it was nearing three in the morning and they were both yawning like crazy. Pamela frowned, but didn't argue. A sure sign she was exhausted. Even Doran and Berget backed out of the mini council.

Doran tried to swat me on the ass as he left. "There are so many things that need to be attended to and you don't need me. Faris will fill me in later." I managed to dodge his hand impressively, considering how fast he was. Of course, there was a chance he'd let me dodge him, too.

In the relative silence that followed, I listened to the spill of the fountain for all of about three seconds before diving in.

"Bert, you're up. What can you tell us about these bastards we're dealing with?" I stared hard at the wimpy demon, but he didn't flinch, seeming to gain some confidence from the fact we were actually listening to him.

Bert stood in front of us, his hands clasped together behind him. A frown settled over his face before he started to speak.

"Well. I don't know for sure what packs have come through. There are seven kinds of demon packs."

Erik stopped him. "There is precedence to this, though. This is not the first time a powerful demon has tried to take over the world." He had everyone's attention with those words.

"Wait, what?" I blurted out, my eyes widening. "What do you mean?"

"You don't think that all of the disasters that humanity has faced were all natural, do you? The bubonic plague is a good example. It was blamed on a number of things. Rats, the Jewish people, punishment from God. It all led to a cleansing of anything unusual.

Mostly supernaturals who were trying to blend in, and in that process, the humans wiped out many of their best defenders against the demon population, which then went on to spread the plague across the world. But that is just one example."

"What was the point, though? Wouldn't the demons have wanted people to be alive so they could possess them?" Liam asked.

Erik gave a ruthful smile. "Yes and no. The bubonic plague wasn't so much about killing people off, as it was infecting them. Making them weak and easier to possess. The plague compromised their immune systems, allowing them to be taken over. Especially the young."

Something about what Erik said sent a twang through my brain. I struggled to put the pieces together, but they floated just out of reach. Damn it. Liam touched my arm. "What?"

I closed my eyes and pressed my palms into them, blocking out any light. "Let me think for a minute."

The feel of the night air and the sound of the fountain filled my ears as I looked at the pieces one by one.

Demons escaped in London who bred fast.

Minor supernaturals were being possessed by lesser demons and evil spirits.

Packs of Orion's demons were free to cause chaos.

The only thing we were missing was a plague, and then Orion would have access to all the young people he wanted. The urge to vomit swelled up through my stomach and burned the back of my throat.

"Children are normally hard to possess, aren't they?" That was why it had taken a full pentagram when the black coven was trying to have India possessed so many months ago. At least, that was what I understood.

Bert bobbed his head. "Yes, it can be very difficult to possess a child. There is a natural protection over the young when it comes to demons, something the elementals put into play." He grimaced as he said "elementals" and again I wondered at these particular supernaturals that I'd only just been hearing about. "But when the small humans are ill, that protection goes into keeping them alive, rather than keeping them from being possessed."

Feeling like a bully, but not really caring, I leaned in to Bert. "How did the bubonic plague really start?"

An interesting thing happened. Bert paled and shook his head. "I can't tell you."

My eyebrows shot up and I glanced at Erik. "You want to make him talk, or do you want me to make him talk?"

Erik shrugged. "Either way is fine. I haven't interrogated a demon in years. I've missed it."

Bert paled even more and his lower lip trembled. "I can't tell you. I can't. Tracker, Slayer, both of you have to trust me. Please."

"Begging will get you nowhere, little demon," Erik growled. He had a short, serrated knife in his hand that he'd pulled from somewhere within his robes. It was curved, like a skinning knife, and if it hadn't been for the rough edges, that's what I would have called it.

"Track demons and evil spirits," Bert blurted as he fell to his knees. "Proof I am on your side, that I truly want to help, but cannot tell you about the plagues. Track them; you'll see it isn't me fooling you."

Erik paused and looked over at me. "Up to you. Personally, I'd just as soon dice him up."

"Fuck, why not? Tracking will take me two seconds," I grumbled.

I send out a thread to Track demons as a whole, paired with a thread for evil spirits, just to satisfy—

Holy. Fucking. Hell.

I swayed on my feet and went to one knee, the overwhelming wash of pings I got back seriously making me re-think getting out of bed the day before.

We were surrounded by Orion's minions.

Hundreds of them.

3

Liam helped me to stand. "We have a problem," I whispered, as I turned to look up at him.

"How bad is it?"

"Hundreds of very big, very bad uglies."

Faris's eyes searched the darkness around us. "I don't sense anything out of the ordinary. Wolf, what are you picking up with that nose of yours?"

"Ogres, unicorns, only what we already have here."

Bert whimpered. "I told you I wasn't fooling you."

I didn't look at him, just clung to the threads as a horrible, horrible idea bloomed. Carefully, as if they would be able to tell, I Tracked Raw, hoping I was wrong. His threads lit up inside my head, overlapping one of the pings from the demons.

"It's the ogres; they're possessed." Oh, we were in shit. There was close to a hundred ogres out there, pretty much surrounding Doran's home. And we'd invited them.

Unclenching my jaw, I strode forward. "We have to move on them, before they know we know. Otherwise, there is no way we can take them all out."

You would discount me?

"No." I shook my head. Blaz had a point.

Liam burst that bubble. "If you go after them, how are you going to get the unicorns out without Blaz frying them? They are in the middle of the ogre camp; they'll be slaughtered before we can even get to them." His silver-golden eyes searched the darkness. "I think I can get some local wolves to help buffer us. But you're right, Rylee. We have to get the hell out of here."

Hanging onto the threads of the demons and evil spirits around us (I couldn't call them ogres any more), I knew we were about to be in serious trouble. "Faris, go tell Doran what's going on, jump the Veil, get Thomas or Frank to help, whatever you can do. Get everyone out."

He didn't argue with me. "Where are we meeting?"

There was only one logical place. "Jack's. It's far enough away." And maybe we could get Will and Deanna to finally help."

Faris gave me a tight smile and then strode into the house. For the moment, I could trust him.

"Erik."

My uncle turned his head to me. His eyes narrowed. "There are too many. Even if we extract the unicorns, there are too many to deal with. Between the ogres' natural strengths and abilities, and the drive of demons and dark spirits in them, they will be power-houses. Our best option is to get the hell out of here before they are on to us."

That was not what I wanted to hear. "We have to get Nikko and his crush out. I can't leave them."

Liam put a hand out. "Let me try something." He closed his eyes, let out a slow breath. The world around us stilled and then suddenly, from the outside perimeter of Doran's home and land, the eerie howl of a wolf broke the clear night air.

"What are you doing?" I grabbed at Liam's arm. "We don't want them to know we're on to them!"

He gave me a grin and shifted right there, his clothes going with him for the first time. Shit, he'd finally managed it. That surprise stuck with me long enough for him to lope off into the darkness, leaving me standing there, slack-jawed.

I took two steps and Erik stopped me. He stood with his back to me, his arm barring my way. "This is not a rush job, Rylee. Let your man do what he can to get the unicorns to safety."

"I'm not rushing in," I snapped. Liam was going into a fight without me, and I was just standing there. Doing nothing. It ate at my insides.

"No, you rush in because you don't know any better." His expression changed, looking almost sad. "I wish I'd known you'd lived, Rylee. I would have raised you myself. Taught you some patience."

His eyes met mine and behind them I saw he was telling the truth. But it was a bitter gall and I spit out the one thing that had been bothering me about Erik since I'd met him.

"I read my mother's journal. She said you were always causing trouble with her and my father. Why would you want to raise me?" I asked the question, but I was listening hard for another howl, another sound from whatever was going on out there. I'd read my mom's journal while Liam and I were in Europe, at Jack's actually, and it had answered a lot of questions about my past. Mind you, it had also left a bunch of new questions rolling through my head.

Erik gave me a small smile, his eyes crinkling. "Because I loved them both. One was my older brother; the other was the one who got away."

I stared at him, my eyes popping wide. "Wait, you and my mom were an item? That was *not* in her journal."

"It wouldn't be. It wasn't her style to kiss and tell. And it's not a story I'm going to share with you in detail, either, but yes, I loved her." Erik's smile faded. "I saw her first and I was angry when she chose my brother over me. The things I said and did … lashing out at them both. I'm not proud of it. Worse, I never got to say goodbye, to either of them." He shook his head and I found myself totally mesmerized by his words. And it was in that moment I realized he'd done it on purpose. He'd totally distracted me from the fight going on outside.

"You sneaky son of a bitch. You knew you'd be able to—"

"Keep you from the fight? Yes." He grinned at me again, totally unrepentant. "Because you, my niece, need to learn when to hold back. And this is one of those times. Let Liam do his job, let him protect you."

With my teeth gritted, I stared into the darkness where Liam had disappeared. Fuck, I hoped Erik was right.

He bolted toward the sounds of howling and wondered just how long it would take before Rylee was right behind him. But there was no sound of her heartbeat or even the steady pound of her footsteps, shocking him. At the same time, he was pleased. Maybe she would finally let him do what he had to do to protect her.

The howls ahead of him were those of werewolves, and if there was one place his instincts and Peter's training came in handy, it was dealing with other wolves. Not to mention he'd called them in, asked them to attack the ogres.

Harry them. He sent the thought to the wolves who'd quickly come to his call. A damn nifty trick Peter had taught him, but it was the first time he'd actually had the nerve to put it in play. Controlling other werewolves was a gift and one he didn't want to abuse.

The closer he got to the ogres, the more the sounds of the fight filled his ears. Ogres swung their wicked-sharp, heavy weapons and the wolves around them dodged blows while inflicting devastating bites, but he could see they had listened to him. Even their lead bitch, who snarled as he loped by.

Between one step and the next he shifted back to human form.

His wolf surged forward again, though, and he used the power in his voice as Peter had taught him, blending the word with a command, with the very essence of what he was. Guardian, wolf, and alpha.

"ENOUGH!"

It was like a switch had been thrown, and the wolves fell to the ground, cowering. The ogres seemed about as stunned as the wolves.

"What is the meaning of this?" Came a soft, purring voice from somewhere within the mess of ogres and wolves.

Slim and tall, with legs that seemed to go all the way to her chin, a woman slowly rose from the ground and walked toward him. Long dark hair flowed around her, partially hiding her nudity. She had Asian features, sharp and pristine, like a doll come to life.

He ignored the woman's question as he drew in deep breaths, scenting the wolves around him. Trying to pinpoint them and where they fit in. What he found shouldn't have surprised him, but it did.

These weren't just any wolves, though some of them may have been local by their scents; no, the majority of them were from Rylee's territory. Yet they were here.

This was Beauty's pack. He'd run into them more than once when he'd first been turned and had been staking territory around Rylee's home.

Which meant the woman walking toward him, the woman he knew only by the power radiating off her, was Beauty herself.

"Why are you here, Beauty?" He all but growled the words, but they were for the ogre's ears, really. He only hoped she would play along. Overconfident as she was, she played right into his plan.

She rolled her shoulders. "We roam where we wish."

He doubted that. He infused his next words with power. "I want the truth. Why. Are. You. Here?"

She blinked and spoke almost without seeming to realize it. "The Great Wolf commanded us to travel here. That we would be needed." A breath escaped her and then she glared at him. "Oh, dear, you think you can boss us around? You think you can run this pack, or," she laughed softly and put a hand to the hollow of her throat in a delicate gesture, "take it from me?"

Taking the pack from her wouldn't be *that* hard, not really. Peter had shown him how. Interesting, though, that the Great Wolf had commanded it of them. Could it be because of him? He had a feeling it was.

Before he could say anything, Raw stalked over to them, his feet sending up splashes of muddy ice water. This was what Liam had been waiting for.

Fury lit the red ogre's features, carving it into a mask a devil would balk from dealing with. He held a pike over his shoulder, the tip gleaming with what could only be blood. "Are these your wolves, Liam?"

"No. Not yet. Were any of your people seriously hurt?" Time to play the part, though he couldn't help scenting, trying to pinpoint the demon in Raw. Three breaths and he had it, a smell of swamp water lingered, though there were no swamps in the vicinity.

Raw shook his head. "No, these are werewolves, but not like you." Raw's eyes didn't look like he believed Liam. He looked more inclined to keep fighting. Not a good sign.

Beauty let out another laugh, but under this one he could hear the nerves, and in her eyes there was a flicker of uncertainty. She was right to be nervous. "What do you mean, we are *just* werewolves? We are at the top of the food chain, ogre."

Liam shook his head. "Not anymore."

Of course, in that moment, he thought things were going to go peacefully, or at least as peaceful as possible.

He was wrong. Not that he should have been surprised; he'd commanded the wolves to start this fight, and now he had to look like he had nothing to do with it. Apparently, Beauty didn't like that.

Beauty leapt at him, shifting midair, a flash of tawny fur and fangs. He dodged her, slamming a fist into her head and still managing to keep his wolf in check. The wolves around them started to rise from the ground, growls sliding along their throats. Beauty lay on the ground, shaken from the blow that would have killed a normal wolf.

"I said enough," Liam bit out between his teeth and the wolves froze, lowering themselves the few inches they'd come up.

Raw laughed. "That's it, hit the bitch."

He ignored Raw and moved to stand over Beauty. "Either you submit, or I'll kill you."

She snarled up at him, blood trickling from her pale nose, golden eyes glittering with hatred. Even for her life, she wouldn't submit, and he knew it a split second before she lunged at him, her teeth sinking into his right thigh. Right over the wound that had brought on his own change.

Her teeth sunk in deep and he gritted his jaw. Killing her was the only option, but that didn't mean he had to like it; not when he'd asked her pack here.

He slid his hands around her neck and she glared up at him, but didn't move. She knew what was coming.

No, there had been enough death, and they needed strong allies. Beauty might not have been the nicest bitch in the book, but she was strong. With every ounce of power in him, with everything Peter had taught him, he spoke to her.

"Let go and submit."

Her teeth withdrew from his leg and she sat back on her haunches, a look of consternation passing over her eyes. She shifted into her human form, panting for breath.

"That's not possible. I am an alpha; you can't force me to submit."

A look of confusion passed over Raw's face. "Are we going to kill them or not, Liam?"

Liam shook his head slowly, the wound in his thigh closing up already. "No. Not today."

Raw let out a heavy sigh. "Then keep them far away from us. My ogres will not be controlled as easily as this." He swept out the pike in a circle, encompassing the area.

With a grunt, Liam flicked his hand, beckoning the wolves. They slithered on their bellies toward him. Not submissive like Alex, but not such strong alphas that they could take on Beauty for leadership of the pack.

He scrubbed a hand through his hair as Beauty stepped up beside him, pressing her naked body against his, her shift in tactics not surprising him at all. "You are the one I've been waiting for. I will share my pack with you . . . amongst other things." Her hands slid down his back to his ass, massaging him hard.

Liam stared at her, let her see the wolf in him. "You aren't sharing anything with me, Beauty. I am taking this pack. Defy me again and I will let the ogres have you."

Beauty paled and her eyes glittered with fury. Well, at least he knew she was no longer interested in him; she just wanted to kill him now.

Wrong again. She puckered her full lips and blew him a kiss, then slid her tongue along the edge of her mouth.

Irritation flared in his gut. "Go. Wait for me there." He pointed at Doran's house and the pack moved off as a unit, Beauty snarling, but doing as he said.

Raw thumped his pike into the ground. "That was relatively well-handled. For a wolf. Will you stay and eat with us?"

"No, I want to check on Nikko, make sure none of the wolves got through to them." Last thing he wanted was to remind Raw about the fact that Nikko's daughter was the *only* young unicorn—the only one born in the last fifty years and a potential tool to bring Orion across the Veil. He wanted to avoid that almost as much as he wanted to avoid putting himself alone in the middle of a nest of demons.

"They are fine, we are watching over them," Raw said, his eyes glittering, his pupils dilating and then elongating horizontally. His hand gripped his pike, knuckles turning a faint pink. This was not good.

"Rylee's instructions. I don't disobey her. You know how she gets." He held up his hands like he had no choice and started to walk deeper into the camp. Hell, they should have known something was up when they saw how the ogres had gladly offered to be the outer ring of protection for everyone.

Yet, if they couldn't trust their allies, who could they trust?

Raw's eyes followed him; he could feel the anger from the ogre burning into his shoulder blades. It took everything he had to not to spin around and challenge him right there. Erik was right, though; there were too many. A very loud part of him, the suspicious FBI agent who he would always carry around, wondered why the ogres had waited. Raw didn't make him wait long on that count.

"When will the harpies be here?" Raw called out after him and Liam knew in a flash of understanding why they hadn't attacked.

They were waiting to take all of them by surprise, to wipe out every ally Rylee had.

"Not sure. Eve thought a day or two at most." He lied, knowing the harpies were supposed to be showing up in the morning. They were so screwed if they couldn't get everyone out before then. He picked up his pace, putting some distance between himself and the perimeter where Raw stood guard. As he stepped around a tent set up by the ogres there was a whimper from inside. He stopped in his tracks and took a breath.

It was Mer, the green ogre that had been sharing Raw's bed. He glanced around, gritted his teeth, and made a quick decision. Shit, he was getting more and more like Rylee with each passing day. Without fully thinking it through, he scratched on the tent with one finger and called softly, "Mer?"

The whimpering eased and the tent flap slid open. Her eyes were dark and heavy lidded, and not just from tears. One eye was swollen shut, the other right behind in that department, her lip was split in three spots, the piercing in her cheek had been torn out, and the few fingers he could see were bent at the wrong angle.

"What?" she managed to mumble and still sound a bit snotty. It was her temperament, but that didn't bother him. He took a long breath, the scent of the ocean and hot sand filling his nose. No scent of demon.

He crooked his finger at her, taking a chance. "Come with me." With great care, she emerged from the tent, the rest of her body not looking any better than her face.

"He will beat me for leaving the tent."

"Not if you're with me." Liam had to fight to keep the snarl from his voice. Even though there was no scent of demon curling around her, he would still have Rylee Track her when they got back to Doran's, to be on the safe side. "We are checking in with Nikko, then you'll stay with us."

Her lip trembled and that broke open the cuts making them drip down her green skin. "Why?"

"Because that isn't how anyone should live."

They said nothing more as they carefully made their way to the unicorns. The unicorn crush was smack in the middle of the ogre camp. They were sleeping standing up, heads hanging low, except for a few on the perimeter who watched the darkness.

Nikko saw them coming and trotted out to meet them, Calliope at his side. His young daughter pranced lightly, tossing her head, her black mane blending with the night as much as her snow-white body stood out like a sparkling gem. She was young, only seven months old, but already she had a strong place in the unicorn crush as the future leader.

Wolf, has the council already come to a decision? Nikko's voice rang in Liam's head. He lifted a hand to the stallion. How was he going to warn them without setting the ogres off? He didn't want to take the chance they would be overheard, even this close to the unicorns. So he played it safe and couched his words, hoping Nikko would understand.

"Rylee wants to set up a perimeter on the other side of Doran's house. Would you be willing to move your crush?"

Nikko bobbed his head. *Of course. When?*

"Right now."

Mer started, her eyes narrowing. "The ogres are capable."

Again, Liam lifted his hand. "I know. But this is what Rylee wants, and she's running the show."

Nikko's eyes met Liam's and he wished he could send thoughts like with Blaz. Instead, he held the stallion's gaze, flicking his eyes once toward the ogres who stood twenty feet away. He could only hope it would be enough.

The stallion didn't question him, but instead gave a soft nicker that floated in the air, his eyes never leaving Liam's. Almost as a unit, the herd woke, heads and horns lifting into the air. Liam did a quick count. There were less than thirty unicorns, and that was including Calliope in the mix.

Take my daughter with you. We will circle around.
There was an edge to Nikko's voice that Liam caught. The savvy unicorn knew something was up, and he knew better than to come right out and ask.

"Of course. Come on, pretty lady, let's go see Rylee."

Calliope trotted over to them and put herself next to Mer. Without hesitation, the ogre dropped her hand to the filly's withers. Calliope gave a snort and butted her nubby horn against Mer's thigh.

Mer gave a soft gasp and Liam glanced over to see her face healing. "Don't forget to thank her."

The green ogre bent and kissed the tiny unicorn on the nose. "Thank you, precious one."

Of course. Calliope's voice was a tiny echo of her father's; the power was there, but not the iron hardness. At least, not yet.

Liam started them across the long walk to Doran's home, each step ratcheting up the tension along his spine. Something bad was coming and he was pretty damn sure he knew it would be in the form of ogres trying to kill them. Mer's back straightened as they walked, but he noted she didn't offer to stay now that the worst of her wounds were healed.

"He wasn't always like this. He'd never hit me until after the ceremony with Sas to break ties with the rest of the ogres." Mer glanced at him.

"Not here. We can talk about it later." He bit the words out. Calliope turned her eyes to him.

Is something wrong?

Many eyes were on them as they walked, and not one was kind, or even just curious. Hatred flowed through the air like an overwhelming perfume. Someone had heard what Mer had said, and it was going through the ogres like a wildfire.

"Mer."

"Yes?"

"Protect the foal at all costs."

He counted the moments in heartbeats. When he hit six and they were forty feet from the ogres' perimeter, Raw stepped in front of them. He lifted his massive hand, a flame appearing above his fingertips.

"Going somewhere, *precious*?"

Liam put himself between Mer, Calliope, and Raw.

"She's coming with me, sweetums."

Yeah, he had truly begun to take on some of Rylee's lesser qualities. Like pissing off the bad guys when he shouldn't. Raw's face dipped into a shade of red that was almost purple.

"Mer." Liam put his hand out, pointing at Doran's, but didn't take his eyes off Raw, "Take her and go."

Mer didn't hesitate, just scooped up Calliope and bolted the last forty feet past the ogres who reached for her. She managed to dodge them all and then she was in the clear. Good enough.

"Our master doesn't care about a unicorn foal and an ogre whore," Raw said, laughing. "But you, you are important to him. He will be so very pleased when we hand him your head. Do you know that this knife"—he pulled out a dull, copper blade with a wooden handle—"is cursed? It is the knife that killed the last guardian." Raw's grin was feral, madness oozing off him.

Liam didn't wait. This was not a time to fight, but he needed to buy himself some time. He leapt toward

Raw as he shifted into his wolf form. Startled, Raw stumbled back, but not before swinging with the copper knife. It hit Liam in the chest, slicing through his muscles, stuttering his heart. He let out a howl as he hit the ground, calling the wolves to him, even though he'd just sent them away.

It wasn't his time yet. He knew it was coming, but he'd be damned if he let some piddly-ass demon take him out.

4

Waiting on Liam was one of the hardest things I ever had to do. So I didn't wait. I ran inside, Tracking Doran. He was in his herb room and I skidded to a stop in the doorway. "Tell me you can exorcise evil spirits."

He didn't flinch. "Maybe. But we are leaving, are we not?"

"Liam is out there, trying to get the Tamoskin crush clear."

Doran closed his eyes for a split second. "Are you willing to donate to the cause? Your blood makes me stronger."

I tipped my head and pulled my shirt down, baring my neck. "Do it."

No need to ask him twice. His lips were on my neck, his teeth pushing through the skin with a soft pop. For Liam, I would give up anything, and a little blood was not too much to ask as far as I was concerned.

Doran drank deep, his hands circling around my waist, holding me tight against his body. I stared at his right ear, and noticed the new gold cuff circling the top of it. Wondered if it signified anything.

"Berget, take her."

Doran handed me off and I was going to protest, but I could barely open my mouth. Shit, how much had he taken?

"A lot. I took a lot to make this happen, Rylee." He breathed, his eyes sparkling with power. Without another word, he was gone, like he'd disappeared into thin air. Then again, I might have just closed my eyes for a second or two. Berget held me against her side and I didn't remember her even being there, or taking me.

"That was not smart; he took a lot of your blood. Each time he does, it ties you more to him." She brushed a hand over my neck and the skin tightened, the two pinpricks healing over.

"Mm frothing bhmmd." Damn, the words wouldn't come out. I tried again. "Liam is worth it."

She let out a little sigh and helped me stand. I was wobbly, but already a little strength was coming back. "Faris?"

"He's trying to get Thomas to work with him to open up a double doorway, one the unicorns and harpies can easily go through."

"The harpies are here?"

"Eve, she's gone to meet them, stall them if she can." She helped me walk and tried to pull me to the back of the house. "Faris is out here."

"But Liam is this way," I grunted and slid out of her hands, using the wall to support my steps. Berget let out a sigh and came around to help me.

"I could just pack you out there, you know."

I snorted. "Yeah, I know."

But she didn't try to, and for that I was grateful.

The courtyard was a seething mess of supernaturals by the time we got there. No one had listened to me. Apparently, everyone wanted to stay and fight. Fucking hell. I'd almost prefer they were still afraid enough to run. A part of me, though, was secretly pleased. When push came to shove, they would fight and work together. That was a good sign at least.

Standing on top of the fountain, Doran chanted, his deep baritone taking me back to the first time Liam had held me tight as the hoarfrost poison had been drawn from me. Doran's words swirled through the air, creating a fog that cut through the night, silvery and sleek.

As it condensed, wolves slunk toward us through it. Correction, werewolves. They were all easily as big as Liam, their backs bristled with hair that stood on end and their teeth were bared. Shadows of the night, it was a fucking eerie scene, straight out of a horror movie. Their eyes glowed gold in the scattered light around us. The wolf at the front shifted, her body emerging from her wolf shape in a smooth wave as she stood in the fog.

Buck naked, she'd obviously never been taught to shift with her clothes. Straight black hair and porcelain skin accentuated her ballerina body.

Alex was suddenly there, putting himself between me and the woman. "Beauty bad," he snarled, snapping his teeth, his tail stiff in the air.

She laughed and put a hand to her throat. "Oh my, is this Alex? You escaped us many times." She sneered. "Impressive. For a submissive."

From my hip, I took my coiled whip and slowly let it unwind. "Who the fuck are you?"

She flicked her hair back so her body was totally exposed; her nipples didn't even pucker bad in the cold air. Bitch. Her eyes flashed gold as her wolf rose for a brief second.

Yeah, she really *was* a bitch.

"You may call me Beauty. I am the leader of this pack." Her eyes narrowed. "I do believe you have thwarted me in the past, when I tried to kill the submissive." Her golden eyes flicked to Alex suspiciously, but he didn't cower, instead stiffening even more as a growl trickled from his lips. "But, he does not seem so submissive now."

"Aren't you supposed to be out there, helping Liam?" I was guessing as I pointed with my whip; I'd assumed the howls earlier had been because Liam had called them. Beauty casually looked over her shoulder and then shrugged.

"He sent us to wait for him here. Which means we will wait until he comes."

Alex didn't seem convinced of her sincerity. "Bad. She is bad."

I Tracked demons and evil spirits, just to be safe. The pack was clear—there was nothing coming off them that worried me. But the sudden clatter of hooves steered my mind away from the werewolves.

Nikko came snorting up behind us, his crush strung out in a "V" formation.

What is wrong? The wolf sent us away in a hurry and I sensed there was more than your wish for us to move.

"The ogres are not our friends." I tried to think of a way to say it so nothing would be given away to Beauty and her pack. "They are friends of Orion."

Nikko reared up, sending me back a few steps. He came down so hard he cracked the tile at his feet. *They meant to take us by surprise? To come down on us as we slept?*

"Most likely."

"Who is this Orion? I have heard his name," Beauty said, her eyes narrowing.

There was no chance for me to answer. A howl ripped through the night air and there was only one wolf who wasn't standing in the courtyard.

Liam.

The wolves turned as a pack, bolting into the darkness. I started to follow, knowing there was no way I could keep up to them.

I will carry you; he saved us. Nikko went to one knee and I didn't think, just leapt on his back. A second unicorn with a coat so red it looked liked fresh spilled blood joined us and Erik leapt astride as though it were nothing.

"Niece, where you go, I go."

My heart twanged a little, but I had no time to think on it, other than a fleeting thought of, "this was what it meant to have blood relatives stand by you."

"Faris, get people out of here!" I yelled as Nikko leapt forward into the fog Doran created, toward the sounds of ogres roaring. The wolf pack ran at our side, their howls answering Liam's.

My hands curled tight into Nikko's mane as he galloped toward the fight. But his steps faltered as we came across a green ogre running toward us, Calliope in her arms.

I Tracked demons and evil spirits again, and got nothing back, and by then I could see who it was. "She's clean! Mer, get to the house!"

Mer nodded and continued to run.

Be careful, the demons have a cursed knife. Calliope's voice was soft, but there was no fear in her, only confidence.

Nikko picked up the pace again, catching up with the rear guard of the werewolves, the red unicorn and Erik at our heels. The wolves slammed into the first line of ogres like a wave hitting a rock wall. They were rolled back, their bodies flung by magic and weapons. But that didn't stop them. Nor did it stop us.

"Run parallel the front line." The two unicorns moved in tandem.

Nikko spun on his haunches and launched himself to the left. Whatever power I had as a Slayer depended on my heart. I couldn't destroy a demon when I was afraid or angry. I had to kill them for the right reason.

I had to do this for Liam, because of my love for him.

To protect him.

I snapped my whip out, cracking a grey-skinned ogre in the face. He fell back, screaming as though hot acid had been poured onto him. And the result of the whip was more than a little like that. The ogre fell, his skin bubbling and breaking in huge pustules that exploded spraying those around him. A shimmer of darkness oozed from where my whip had cracked him and then the demon was free. For a split second it stared at me, then with a screech, an opening appeared behind it, and the Veil seemed to suck the demon back to where it belonged.

All of that happened in two strides of Nikko's long legs. His horn flashed as he drove it through the thigh of an ogre who stepped in his way. Over and over again, I sent my whip out, desperate to get to Liam. I was afraid to Track him, afraid of what I'd find. I couldn't see Erik; the red unicorn no longer carried him. The fool had dismounted. Things were going downhill fast and about to get even faster. As my fear for Liam rose, my effectiveness against the demon-possessed ogres fell.

The ogres are circling us.

Sons of bitches. By the time Nikko's words hit my brain, he was already wrong. They weren't circling us. We were surrounded.

"Pamela, where are you going?" Frank called to me, but I ignored him.

I wanted to see what was happening. That was the problem with being a kid. No one paid attention to you. No, that wasn't fair—Rylee never ignored me. She depended on me to help her, and that much I could do. What would she be doing if our places were reversed? I had a feeling we were going to be making a run for it and I knew there were things we needed to take with us. Rylee would want those things, maybe even need them.

I ran into the house, bolting toward Rylee and Liam's room. Under the mattress were the papers Milly had given Rylee before we'd come back to this side of the

Veil. I'd seen her stash them there, though I didn't think Rylee had ever read them. Milly had risked her life to get the papers to Rylee, so I knew they were important. I grabbed them, and stuffed them inside my shirt. Next, I grabbed Rylee's fire opal Doran had given her and tucked it into my pocket. It wouldn't activate unless it was right against the skin. I searched around the room, grabbed one of Rylee's knives, and couldn't think of anything else. I had the short sword Rylee had given me for my birthday, but I didn't have any other weapons. I hoped I wasn't forgetting anything.

After being kidnapped not once, but twice, I had learned to be ready for anything. No way was I was letting anyone get their hands on me again. Even though Liam and Rylee had both asked me to restrain myself from killing, I'd had enough. If I had to, I would kill to keep me and my family safe.

I ran back to the courtyard, breathing hard.

"Pamela, what are you doing?" Frank bumped up against me. Like he was fooling me into thinking it was an accident. I tucked a loose strand of hair behind one ear and stepped away from him.

"I want to help."

Doran looked down from the fountain. "How are you at controlling wind?"

"Better than anyone else here." Blushing, even though I was being honest, I crawled up the edge of the fountain and took the hand Doran offered me.

"Rylee said we should go," Frank called after me.

"I'm not leaving without her or Liam. They're my family." I didn't look back at him. It wasn't that he was a bad guy; he was just needy and naïve.

With a seemingly effortless tug, Doran pulled me up to his perch on the top of the fountain. He wrapped an arm around my waist to steady me, but I couldn't help the heat in my face. I tried to cover it, but Doran gave me a wink, only making it worse.

I looked out toward the ogre encampment and tried not to think about his arm around me. Focusing on the task at hand helped. I knew I could blast the ogres, even at that distance, but I didn't know how that would help when we had friends out there. "What do you need me to do?"

"Blow the fog faster. The sooner we can expel the evil spirits, the faster we can get Rylee and Liam back."

That I could do. I lifted my hands and centered my being like Milly had taught me. Picking through the elements, I touched the third one, wind. Breathing evenly, I pulled the element through me and to my fingertips. Wind was not my strongest ability, but it still listened when I asked it to come forward.

From behind us, the cool night breeze turned into a roaring wind that tugged my hair out from my braid, wrapping it around my face and obscuring my vision. But that didn't matter; the fog was moving faster now.

"Good job, little witch," Doran murmured and I looked at him. He wasn't looking at me, but out where the battle had started. I lowered my hands, feeling like it wasn't enough. What I could do was never enough.

"Come on, now. We need to go or Rylee will have both of our asses."

He hopped down and held a hand out to me. I took it, focusing on my footing on the slippery fountain. "Yes, that's true. But one of us would like that very much." His green eyes popped wide and I slapped a hand over my mouth mumbling past my fingers. "Sorry, I didn't mean to say that out loud."

I should have known, though, that Doran of all people wouldn't be bothered. He threw his head back, laughing. "Truer words were never spoken, little witch."

Frank slid in between us, frowning at Doran. "Come on, Faris has a doorway open and there's nothing you can do now."

That wasn't true, and I dug my heels in. "You go ahead, Frank. I'm waiting for Rylee."

I folded my arms over my chest and did my best imitation of Rylee, even tried to lift an eyebrow, though I'm pretty sure the damn thing didn't budge.

Doran chuckled still, though whether it was over what I'd said to him, or what I was saying to Frank, I wasn't sure.

"Frank, go. I'll look out for her," Doran said and Frank reluctantly backed away.

Doran put a hand on my shoulder. "Don't worry, Rylee will come out of this."

"How do you know? Can you Read her?" I asked, hoping that was the case.

"No, I used up everything she gave to make that fog. But I know her. This will just be a bump in the road."

I looked out, saw the explosions of magic, heard the cries of the wolves and the ogres and wasn't so sure. This was a battle and we needed to be in it with them. Not just stand back.

Doran's hand tightened. "Don't. It isn't time for you, not yet, little witch."

The way he spoke made me turn toward him. "Not my time?"

His lips tightened. "Your time is coming soon, when they will need you to be stronger than both of them. Which means you need to be there. Not diving into a battle here that will get you killed. That much I *can* see."

Stronger than both Liam and Rylee? Was that what Doran meant? His eyes never left mine until I nodded. Though in my heart I wondered how I could ever be stronger than Rylee.

He squared off against Raw as the ogres tightened the circle around him. There was no way to run, no way to get out of this.

He'd just have to kill Raw and hope it would give him enough time to make an escape. The red ogre lunged at him, the copper knife swinging out, screaming through the air. Liam shook his head. He had to be hearing things. Nope.

Another swing and the blade screamed again, coming even closer. The muscles in his chest seemed to echo the scream, demanding he lay down and rest.

He snarled and tried to shift back into human form. Nothing happened. Panic clawed at him behind the pain in his body. No, he wasn't stuck; it had to be something to do with the knife wound.

"Silly wolf, you're going to die; why not just lie down and be a good doggy for once?" Raw swung a kick at him, grazing his hip. Whatever the copper blade had going for it, it had already slowed his reflexes.

Which meant if he was going to end this, it had to be now.

Liam went to the ground, hoping to draw Raw in close. He let out a whimper and lowered his head, panting. But from the corner of his eye, he watched the ogre approach.

Raw lifted his hands, talking to his minions. "Orion will rule this land; it is said in the book of prophecy that the great wolf would bend knee to a demon, and here it is." He pointed at Liam with the hand holding the copper knife. Better yet, he looked away from the wolf at his feet.

Liam exploded from the ground, his teeth snapping down over Raw's wrist, taking the ogre's hand off. He spit it out without pause, not even giving Raw time to be surprised by what had just happened.

Digging his claws in, he drove himself up Raw's body until he could get his teeth around the green neck that beckoned him. This demon would go after Rylee, and that alone was reason enough to kill him. One less enemy for her to face once he was no longer able to protect her.

Bones and skin burst under the pressure of his jaws, the hot blood spurting out and steaming in the night air. With his back turned, he heard the approaching ogres, but he couldn't get out of the way. Three blades drove through him at the same time, cutting deep into his body and neck, but none were the copper blade. That was likely his only saving grace.

A gurgled whimper rolled out of him as Raw's body fell and he went with it. They hit the ground hard, but Raw didn't move. Liam crawled on his belly to the hand he'd removed. The copper blade still sat inside the now limp fingers. That knife was deadly, and the demons couldn't have it. The other ogres laughed behind him and one called out, "No, don't finish him. Let him suffer, let him see his people cut down as they try to rescue him."

With the last ounce of his strength, he lay down by the hand and scooped the handle of the copper knife gingerly in his mouth.

He closed his eyes, praying that he was right, that this wasn't his time.

And that Rylee would come for him.

We were fucking surrounded. Erik was on foot, and wherever he went, the demons were driven out of the ogres' bodies. The ogres didn't survive the expulsion, but it still wasn't enough. We'd taken out at least two dozen of the hundred or so in the gang.

I trusted Nikko to keep me safe and finally Tracked Liam. Everything in me froze. He was hurt bad, his heart beating so slowly I wasn't sure we'd make it in time.

"BLAZ!" Fuck them all, they could roast, but not until Liam was out of the way.

The dragon had been waiting for me and dropped from the sky like an avenging, big-ass angel. He swooped low, teeth and claws snapping ogres in half, following the thread I'd tied to Liam. When he launched back into the air, I could see the limp form of a black wolf in his claws. "Get him help!"

Pamela can help him?

I nodded, knowing Blaz could sense my intent, as well as words unspoken. Liam was out of the way, but we were still in trouble. A flash of light drew my eye and I turned to find Erik had worked his way back to my side.

"Rylee, you truly have a knack for diving in, don't you?"

Erik parried with a green ogre who was small, at least as ogres went. Erik ducked inside of the ogre's guard and put his hand against the skin over his heart. The ogre fell, screaming as the demon ripped free of its body. Twenty-five down, seventy-five or so to go.

Piece of cake. Perhaps not so much.

Three arrows shot through the air, two driving through Nikko's side, and one through the red unicorn's neck. The red unicorn went down with a gurgling cry, his eyes rolling up and showing the whites as a group of ogres leapt forward, slashing and hacking him. Nikko let out a piercing scream that ripped through the night. I looked down and realized one of my legs was pierced through with the arrow, sealing my fate with Nikko's.

It has been an honor to know you, Tracker. Blood of the Lost, you will save us all.

His head whipped around and, with a sharp yank, he grabbed the arrow pinning us together, then gave a mighty buck, sending me flying through the air.

"That won't save us!" I yelled as I fell from the sky, only to be snatched up before I hit the ground by a familiar set of talons.

"Rylee, I see your lizard has left you alone again," Eve said as she tightened her grip on me. I twisted in her claws.

"Erik, we can't leave him!"

"We won't," she said, flipping me into the air and then diving underneath me so I landed on her back.

"Slick moves," I gasped out as I clung to her back.

"They have to be, to keep up with you."

I turned to see a blur of greyish silver wings dive and scoop Erik out of the melee, much to the roaring and consternation of the ogres. I couldn't see Nikko any more and my heart tore at the loss of such a pure spirit and a great ally. But like every other loss in my life, there was no time to dwell on it.

Life was about to get real ugly for the demon ogres; at least, that was what I was hoping. Fog rolled in around them and where it touched, ogres froze. Not all of them, but enough that I could see the fog was doing something to them. An undertone of screaming, faint echoes of voices trapped and now freed curled up through the air, tangling with the fog.

Those ogres possessed by evil spirits and not actual demons were no longer controlled by Orion. Doran had come through.

I opened my mouth to yell to tell them they'd been fooled and their friends could not be saved. But I didn't need to.

Those ogres released from the evil spirits fell on those who were truly possessed.

"I don't understand what's happening, why are they fighting now?" Eve called out. Erik answered her.

"Evil spirits can be expelled, they don't attach to the soul of the creature they possess like a demon does." Simple, yet still horrifying to think of a soul being latched onto by a demon.

Madness, total and complete, erupted as the ogres attacked one another. My heart sank as I watched the bodies pile and the number of the dead rise, and it was not on the side of those who'd been freed.

Erik and his ride, an odd-looking, silvery grey harpy, caught up to us. "The weak ones are free, but they will be dead soon. We have to get the hell out of here."

He was right, this was a lost cause and we had to give way, much as it sucked shit.

"Eve, how far behind are the rest of the harpies?"

"They are on their way to London."

Her words stuck in my brain and I struggled to speak. "How could they have known?" Were they in on it? Shit, was I going to have to check every person who came within our close-knit circle?

"They have seers." She turned her head so I could see the chagrin in one eye. "I argued with them, told them they were needed here but they insisted they would meet us in London."

"Don't feel bad." I put a hand on her neck. "I would have done the same thing, argued 'til I was blue in the face."

The silver harpy swept in close, his baritone startling the shit out of me. "She made a good argument."

I cranked around in my seat to stare at the first male harpy I'd ever met. Now that I was looking at him, I could see the differences. He was far thicker in the legs, body, and neck, and his face didn't have the feminine lines Eve did. His eyes were pale, a grey blue that would have disappeared if not for the black feathers around them like a mask.

"Zorro, how are you?" I blurted.

The male harpy chuckled, surprising me. "I see where Eve got her sass. My name is Marco."

The two harpies banked at the same time as we dropped from the sky, right into Doran's courtyard. Pamela was crouched over Liam's body. Everything in me tensed, even though Tracking Liam I knew he was still alive. But barely.

I jumped from Eve's back before she had fully landed and ran to Liam's side. The werewolves had retreated and were pacing around, whining. Beauty stood to one side, buck naked and leaning against Faris.

"Faris, get them all out of here. NOW," I said, doing my best to not let my voice break.

"They wouldn't go—how would you like me to deal with them?"

"Make them." I curled my hands into the thick fur around Liam's neck, trusting Faris would do as I asked. "Pamela, how bad is it?"

She lifted her eyes to mine for a split second before looking back at Liam, her hands cupping his muzzle. "Bad. It's very bad. I can heal all the wounds except the one on his chest."

The sound of footsteps running told me people were finally listening and going to safety. Which was good because I suspected it wouldn't be long before what was left of the ogres was over run and we'd be dealing with some pissed-off demons.

Sooner than you think. They are on their way to end us now.

"Blaz, can you stall them?"

On my way.

A whoosh of wings and the dragon let out a roar that shattered the air, pierced my ears, and made my heart pound. His battle cry stirred my own bloodlust. Seconds later, the sound of flames roaring across the open field reached us. A fire line would buy us a little time.

"Doran?"

"Nothing I can do, at least, not on my own. The blade was cursed. I'd have to have more of your blood and you have given too much as it is." He crouched beside me and held out a copper knife with a serrated edge, fresh blood on it. Liam's blood.

I leaned forward, Tracking Liam. Yeah, he was right there, but by Tracking him I could get a better idea of how bad it really was.

His heart beat at a strange cadence, and his soul was slipping. I could push some of my strength into him. We'd done it before, when we were in Europe, but it had mostly been me drawing from him. But what if I could give him some of my Immunity, enough to fight off this poison, or the fucking curse or whatever it was he was dealing with?

"Rylee, what are you doing?" Doran whispered as I drew on my own strength and gave it over to Liam. The energy flowed between us, the bond we'd made stronger than death, and his heart started to beat faster, became steadier.

There was a moment where I thought someone was trying to pull me off, to stop me, but nothing could come between us. Liam didn't shift under my hands, but his threads were stronger.

I pulled back, my vision doubling as hands caught me.

"You keep passing out like this and I'm going to think you like the head rush," Doran grumbled.

"He'll make it."

"What the hell did you do? You aren't a healer, Rylee." Doran didn't take his arms from around me and I didn't care. I could barely keep my eyes open.

"I'll explain later. Blaz, take Liam to London. Please."

Tracker, you gave him a lot of energy. Too much.

"Please, don't argue with me, I have a fucking headache." Which was the truth, my head was pounding, the sound of my own heartbeat felt like a bongo drum inside my skull.

You are coming with me.

"I'll go through the Veil."

Fine.

Damn, that sounded suspiciously like a woman would say "fine." Like "fuck, I'm not excited about this, but I'm doing it anyway."

Blaz winged over us, and scooped up Liam. *He'll survive the flight?*

"Yes. But he'll be out of it, probably the whole way," I said, feeling Doran's eyes on me. No one knew the bonding that had taken place between Liam and me. Though I suspected Doran was on to us.

Get through the Veil, Tracker. Blaz called back to me as he flew into the last of the night.

"Going, we're going!" I snapped. Of course, that was the plan. Problem was, we didn't quite make it.

At least, not all of us.

5

Blaz was gone and Eve was about to leave with Marco when the ogres swarmed into the courtyard. Doran dragged me toward the Veil where Faris stood on the other side, his face grim.

"Hurry up!" Faris beckoned with his one hand. Like we didn't fucking well know we needed to hurry.

The problem was, I *couldn't* hurry; my legs were leaden. Between donating blood to Doran and giving Liam my strength, I was done in.

"Come on, Niece, let's get you out of here." Erik scooped me up into his arms. Pamela ran beside him, Alex beside her, and Doran led the way. We were only twenty feet from the slash in the Veil when an ogre got in our way. Or more accurately, it got between Doran and us. Big and blue, it hurt me to see him. He looked so much like Dox, yet was obviously possessed by a demon.

"Rylee!" Doran yelled and his feet stopped (the only part of him I could see past the ogre) and then he was yanked forward.

My stomach sank. "Faris, you'd better have that fucking door open!" I screamed from Erik's arms, already knowing something was very, very wrong.

Pamela snapped a hand out and flipped the ogre out of our way, sticking him to the side of the house like a fly trapped in honey.

The house was in front of us, but there was no opening through the Veil.

Faris had fucked us over.

"EVE!" Pamela screamed and Erik spun back the way we'd come. Eve and Marco were above us, but between the house on one side and the amount of ogres flooding the courtyard on the other, there was no way they could get to us.

Alex kept tight to Erik's side. "Killing demons time."

"No time today," Erik said. And then out of nowhere, Bert was at our side.

Fuck, I'd forgotten about the doppelganger. "Follow me, I can get you around them."

We had no choice but to trust him, and since his life was tied to Erik's, I had to believe he wouldn't put us into harm's way.

Following Bert, he led us into the house. Pamela brought up the rear. I could see her over Erik's shoulder, sending out blasts of fire to keep the ogres from us. Damn, she was a witch to be proud of. At fifteen, she was taking everything that happened completely in stride. Like it was an everyday event. And maybe for her now it was just that.

Erik ducked around a corner, banging my knees into the wall as we ran (and I use that loosely since I was doing no running) through the kitchen. "You know, you could stand to lose a pound or two."

"I love you, too, Uncle Erik," I mumbled, my head fuzzy as I bounced in his arms.

"This way, quick!" Bert shouted and we didn't question him.

We should have.

He led us into the back of the house, the morning sun peering over the horizon, highlighting the row upon row of ogres waiting for us. The prick had turned on us; I don't know why I was surprised.

"Bert," I said and wormed out of Erik's arms, my hand going to a sword on my back.

His eyes watered as he looked up at me. "I can't help you, I wish I could. I am bound; my mouth is literally unable to speak the words. It is a curse placed on all the demons Orion uses, so we cannot turn on him."

So he would take death over dishonor. If he hadn't been a demon, I would have thought better of him for that choice. Honor I understood, but coming from a demon, I wasn't so sure about it. Besides, he'd just admitted that he would have spilled his guts if he'd been able to.

The ogre closest to us was red-skinned and, for a second, I thought it was Raw. He chucked a spear at Bert, pinning him to the ground. The doppelganger's eyes went wide and then slowly the image he'd projected faded, leaving the bare husk of a body I didn't recognize. Whoever he'd possessed hadn't been a large person. Hell, I couldn't even tell if it had been a woman or a man.

"Rylee, you know we're in deep shit?" Erik asked as he slid my feet to the ground and put himself between me and the ogres we faced. Pamela put her back to me and faced the way we'd come. Her hands flung out and the adobe house crumbled to the ground, the earth shaking beneath our feet.

"Yeah, deep shit is a place I know well," I said. "Pamela, when you're done there, think you can make a hole for the ogres to sleep in?"

I hated to ask her to be so violent, mostly because I knew what it was like to lose the childish side of your soul to fighting and surviving at such a young age.

The thing was, the ogres weren't actually doing anything to us. Which freaked me out. It reminded me of being in the deep Veil where the demons all lived and yet, for a huge chunk of the time I was there, I hadn't encountered one. The whole thing was unnerving.

Above us, Eve and Marco circled, screaming obscenities at the ogres, who mostly ignored them. A standoff between the two sides and yet, I wasn't sure why the ogres hadn't attacked.

As Pamela raised her hands toward the ogres, I stopped her. "Wait a second."

Erik choked, but didn't turn to look at me. "We may not have a second, Niece."

I pushed past him, carefully so I didn't lose my balance. "Why aren't you attacking us?"

The red ogre who'd thrown the spear sneered at me. "You are wanted by the master, alive and in one piece. All four of you."

Oh, that did not bode well. "Pam."

"Yes?"

"You want to work for Orion?"

I didn't need to say anything else. Her hands were a blur as she whipped them out in front of her. The ground didn't begin to shake, didn't roll or heave. There was no warning.

The ground fucking well exploded beneath the ogres. Bodies flew through the air, twenty feet up before being flung outward, clearing a perfect path for us. Screams and moans rose in a cacophony that would make any horror film buff happy.

"Time to go!" I yelled, though I really wanted to duck and cover. Erik took my arm and Pamela led the way, flinging bodies left and right, her lips tight and eyes narrowed. Yeah, pissing off the powerhouse witch was a bad idea.

"Glad she's on our side," Erik said as we hit the open space. There was no question of that, but I agreed with him. The look in Pamela's eyes was more than a little spooky.

Eve swooped down, landed, and I scrambled onto her back. Erik climbed on with me, and Pamela leapt on Zorro—I mean, Marco—with Alex. Three seconds and we were in the air while Pamela rained down fire on the remaining ogres who stood and waved their weapons at us.

None of them were dead though; it wasn't that easy to kill demons. And Pamela was too filled with rage to actually do more than push them away.

"If she could learn to channel her emotions more clearly, there would be no need for us," Erik said, his body adjusting to Eve with ease.

"What do you mean?"

"Witches: their emotions run hot and cold, and finding the balance for them to fight from a place of their heart is nearly impossible. They can help Slayers, but most of the time they can't actually kill demons."

That made a weird sort of sense. All the years with Milly and I'd certainly seen the proof of her emotions being all over the map. "If anyone can figure out the balance, Pamela can."

Erik shrugged. "If she can, she could help save us all."

No pressure at all. I heard what Erik said and dug my hands into the silver harpy's feathers.

"Do you have a name?" he called back to me—wow, wait, he?

"Aren't you a harpy? I thought all harpies were female?"

He snorted and dipped his wings, making me shriek as I slid to one side, even though it was only a few inches. He righted himself and glanced back at me, a twinkle in his eyes.

"What, do you think harpies come from eggs?"

My jaw dropped and then he winked. "The males tend to be unheard of. We are the mellow half of the species; we have to be. The ladies get all the press because of their stellar dispositions."

"Oh." Harpies didn't tend to be mellow at all, fighting and shrieking at every opportunity. I was completely thrown by the fact that he was male. "I'm Pamela and this here is—"

"I is Alex," Alex barked out. He clung to my waist, not that I had that much better of a grip than he did.

His tongue hung out, flapping in the wind. "I am werewolf."

The harpy bobbed his head, the same way Eve often did. "My name is Marco. Do you have an idea which direction we should head?"

That was a good question.

"Rylee," I yelled to the other trio, "where are we going?"

She turned toward me, her skin pale and sickly looking, and her eyes dull. "London. But we'll need to stop first."

I waited, wondering if she was going to tell us where. Nope, she leaned forward and whispered to Eve.

"We're going to a place called Bismarck," Marco said.

"You could hear that?"

"Easily. But I do understand the caution. No need to go shouting it to the sky and let all those who seek us know where we will roost for the day."

Eve led the way, and while I was afraid for Rylee, I was glad this time we weren't separated.

I directed Eve to head for a little motel on the outskirts of Bismarck. We all needed a few hours sleep and a chance to decompress from the battle. The wind was icy cold and though Erik did his best to keep me warm, he didn't run hot like Liam. Thinking of him, I found myself reaching out to Liam through the bond between us, rather than Tracking him. He slept and his heart was steady, if a bit on the slow side. I could live with that, as long as he made it.

"That vampire, how sure of him are you?" Erik asked as we drew close to the motel.

"Faris? Fuck, he can be trusted one day, and not the next. I trust Doran, though. And he deals with Faris."

"Doran will be pissed with him for shutting the Veil."

I let out a sigh. I didn't want to say I understood what Faris had done, but I did. He was protecting Doran, the vamp king; that was his job. Even if that meant leaving us behind. Stupid fucking asshat.

"Yeah, he will. But there is nothing any of them can do now." Shit, that wasn't true. Alex had a tie to Faris; we used it in the past. I explained quickly to Erik and he nodded, though his hazel and green eyes were troubled.

"I hope you're right. It would redeem him somewhat."

The rest of our flight passed in relative silence, other than the instructions I gave Eve. Late in the day found us over the motel and the harpies landed on the roof. The flight had given me time to heal, though I hadn't been able to rest, or even nap. I'd been hoping to maybe get a chance to contact Berget, let her know we'd made it out.

Erik, Pamela, Alex, and I shimmied down a fire escape to the back of the motel. We made our way around to the front office. Shit, I hadn't been here in months. I hoped John and his wife were still here. They were old enough that it was a valid concern. I pushed the door open and peeked inside. John snoozed in his regular chair, cowboy boots up on the front desk and hat pulled down over his eyes.

I couldn't help but smile. "John. Sleeping on the job, really?"

He snorted and sat up, grabbed his hat and blinked at me. "Ry! What the hell, girl, you've been a long time between visits. Find any kids lately?"

My smile faltered. "Not enough. Big stuff coming, though."

"Yeah?" He waited for me to say something out-of-the-world goofy. Typical human would think I was fooling him.

"Well, thought I'd try to save the world from demons. Then maybe take an honest-to-God vacation before anymore hunting for kids."

He slammed his hat back on his head as he laughed. "You've got the imagination for telling stories, girl. You need one room or two?"

I knew he still had my credit card on file. Which was good since I had no money on me.

"Just one. For a few hours to get some sleep."

"On the house. Just don't bust up any doors this time." John tossed me a key I caught with ease.

I thanked him and we headed out.

"He didn't say anything about Alex," Pamela noted.

"She has a point. You sure he thinks you are just a human?"

I shrugged. "Don't know. Doesn't matter. He's known me for years." I looked down at the key John had given me.

Lucky number 13.

The room was fixed up, no reminder other than a few scratches here and there of Alex's last visit to the place. That had been when we'd gone hunting for India.

On a whim, I Tracked her, fully expecting her to be back on the east coast where her parents were. She was fucking terrified and I fought back the bile rising in my throat. I Tracked her parents, barely able to recall their names, but I managed.

My jaw dropped and I sank onto the bed. They were both dead.

Erik crouched in front of me. "What is it?"

"Someone took a kid I salvaged months ago. Killed her parents," I whispered, as I struggled to put it together. Why would someone take her? She was a spirit seeker, someone who called spirits to her whether she wanted to or not. Giselle had even spoken through her to get a message to me after she died.

"Could someone be going after your people? Friends and the like?" Erik didn't have to say who the "someone" might be.

I hung onto India's threads. Who else could be taken and used against me? Only one person I could think of. I Tracked Kyle, my personal hacker, who was barely an adult himself.

Shit, he was with India. That was not a good sign. Who else could they have? I wracked my brain, but came up blank. Not that it really mattered . . . wait. I pulled the picture out of my pocket that Faris had given me of Simon, the young Tracker.

I Tracked him while hanging onto the two other threads, hoping I was wrong. Nope, I wasn't. Kyle, Simon, and India were all together. What the fuck was going on?

"Someone is baiting a trap for me with at least three kids I know," I said. Again, the "someone" we knew was not Orion, but who he was using to make this happen was anyone's guess.

"So are you going to call on Faris, or are you going after the kids?"

Something in Erik's voice brought my eyes up to his. "You know the answer, don't you?"

He smiled and leaned forward, putting his elbows on his knees. He stared at the floor while he spoke to me. "You and your mom are the same in this. Heart of a lion, you'd take on anything to protect a child, even more so for one you know and care for. So yes, I do know what you're going to do."

I put my hands over the back of my head and stretched. "It's a trap, and more likely than not, a bad one."

Erik reached over and put a finger under my chin. "Your life as a Tracker, and now a Slayer-in-training, have brought you to this. What does your heart say?"

I let out a slow breath. My heart said what it always did. Protect and save those who couldn't save themselves. Yet there was a bigger picture now, one I couldn't ignore. "How will this help stop Orion, though?"

"It might not. But you have to live with the decision for the rest of your life. Can you do that, knowing you gave up on three young kids?"

"They could still die," I said.

Pamela sat on the other side of me. "But you could save them too."

Alex lay on the floor at my feet and stared up at me with his liquid golden eyes. "Rylee saved me. Saved Pamela. Saved Erik."

What they were saying was true, only there was an exception here. Would I give up the safety of the world to save three children, one I didn't even know?

I stood and wobbled to the bathroom. "Call on Faris. See if you can get him to respond to you, Alex."

I didn't turn around as Alex howled Faris's name because I already suspected we were on our own. It had been too long since Faris had fed from Alex, and that was the only connection we had. If the feeding had been recent, Faris would have a strong connection to Alex and would be able to find us. Doran had fed from me, but he didn't have Faris's ability to travel through the Veil, so that wouldn't do us any good, either. This time, there would be no quick and easy way to get to London; we were going to have to fly up the coast as far north as we could and then island hop to the European continent.

I shut the door behind me and leaned against it. A sudden urge to vomit gripped me and I fell to my knees, losing what little food I had in my belly. I heaved until nothing but bile and water burned my throat and tongue. Yeah, that was unpleasant.

"Rylee, are you okay?" Pamela knocked on the door as she asked.

"Yeah. Just give me a minute." I scooted back from the toilet and lay on the cold floor, grateful for the fact it was indeed cold. My skin flushed with heat and I couldn't get out of my jacket and weapon sheaths fast enough. Shirt and tank top followed my jacket until I was nothing but bare skin on the floor. I let out a sigh of relief and flung one hand over my eyes.

Alex had said my heart sounded funny; could I really be sick? Had giving some of my Immunity to Liam broken down my own defenses? I rolled to my side. None of that mattered right now. I had more than enough on my plate, like I was at a buffet of bad shit and someone kept heaping it on even though I'd had more than enough. No need to add to it myself with worry about something that may or may not even be an issue.

None of that was helping me decide what I was going to do and I knew it was just my brain trying to distract me. "Faris answer?" I called out from my place on the floor.

"No," Pamela said, her voice soft. "He didn't."

I sat up and slowly pulled my tank top back on, forgoing the shirt. Weapons next, then leather jacket. I stood and checked my face in the mirror. I looked like shit and the splash of water didn't really help much.

Leaving the bathroom, I headed straight to the motel room's door. The one downside to John's motel was that none of the rooms had a phone. He, John, said he'd had too many go missing, people ripping them right out of the walls. "I'm going to see if anyone picks up the phone at Jack's. Assuming that is where Faris took everyone." I didn't wait for anyone and waved Erik to sit as he started out of his seat. "I'll just be a minute, wait for me."

Alex, though, didn't listen. "I come with you."

He no longer wore his collar that hid him from human eyes, but no one had said anything. "Yeah, that's okay, buddy." I dropped a hand to his head scratching him behind his ears. I wondered if there was a chance he would ever be able to shift into human form. In the last few months, he'd come a long way, losing his submissiveness and becoming more self-aware. Hell, he'd stopped talking in the third person, which in itself was a fucking achievement.

I opened the office door to see both John and his wife Mary talking in hushed tones. They looked up as we stepped in.

"Was wondering if I could use the phone?" I asked as Alex tucked in behind me, peering at the elderly couple. Mary's jaw dropped and even John looked a bit taken aback.

"That dog, he don't look so good," Mary whispered.

"Not a dog. Part wolf," I said, and then Alex blew it.

"Yuppy doody. I is Alex. Werewolf. Demon killer." He puffed out his chest and grinned at them, which was not a pretty sight.

Mary fainted, and John barely caught her before she hit the floor.

"Sorry, John," I said, helping him lift Mary and take her to their room at the back of the motel.

"Well, I knew you had some strange friends, but Mary didn't believe me."

We laid her on the bed and left her there. John was taking Alex's revelation better than I would have thought.

"Have you been around creatures like him before?" I pointed at Alex, who then pointed to himself with his eyes round and innocent looking. John scrubbed his fingers under his hat before answering.

"Not sure. But I always believed there was more than we knew out there." He gave me a smile and clapped a hand on my shoulder. "Always knew you were one of the good ones, though."

He led me into the back room of the office. "Use the phone. You're always welcome here, Ry. You and your . . . dog." He smiled and shut the door behind him, giving us privacy. Alex grinned up at me.

"I likes John."

"Yeah, I do too." I dialed Jack's place and listened as the phone rang and rang. Fucking hell, this was not going the way I'd hoped at all. As I moved to hang up, a soft "hello" came through. I jerked the phone back up to my ear. "Hey, who is this?"

"Rylee? It's Frank. I think there is some serious fighting going on. I think Thomas might be dead."

I pinched the bridge of my nose. That was not good news. "Where's Faris? Is he around?"

"I don't know. He left."

Shit on sticky toast, this was going downhill fast. "Frank, I need to know if you can open a slash in the Veil, are you able to do that yet?"

"I can, but I'm not supposed to."

"If Thomas is dead, then you may not have a choice. And if he's dead and one of the vampires killed him—"

"No, Faris tried to save him."

Well, that was a fucking shock. "Who killed him?"

"Berget. It was like her eyes went wonky and then she attacked Thomas, strangled him and . . . it was bad. She seems to be herself again, but she's pretty upset."

I was betting that was a mild understatement on all counts. "Anyone else right there I can talk to?"

Turned out that Frank was the only one not in the middle of the fight that was still ongoing. My heart sank with each word he said, knowing that Berget's control over her adoptive parents, the old emperor and empress, was slipping. Far sooner than we'd hoped for. If she was going to die, though, I couldn't let it be by someone else's hand. I was responsible for her—she was my sister—and I would be the one to make sure she didn't hurt anyone else.

"Frank, first of all, are Liam and Blaz there yet?"

"No, they aren't."

My heart thud hard in my chest. I had to believe Blaz would look after Liam. The big-ass lizard knew I'd remove his hide piece by piece if anything happened to my wolf.

"Okay, I'm going to ask you to do something very hard." I closed my eyes and pressed my head to the desk as tears slipped from my eyes.

"What do you need from me?"

"At sunset my time, which is"—I did the math in my head—"eleven your time, I want you to get close to Berget, and open the Veil to the farm, right in front of the barn. Can you do that?"

He didn't even hesitate. "I can do that."

We hung up and I let out a breath I'd held too long. Alex butted up against me, putting his cold nose right into my face, though I kept it on the desk. "Rylee, why are you sad?"

I wrapped my arms around him, hugging him to me, hiding my eyes from the world.

"Because I have to kill my sister."

6

The flight to the farm would take less than an hour, but I wanted extra time to prep. Pamela would grab Berget with her magic and hold her down while I took her head. There would be no other way and we'd have to do it fast. If the opal was failing already, we had very little hope of extending Berget's sanity long enough to actually help her.

Of course, as my plans normally did, this one tracked sideways. I stepped out of the hotel room, Erik and Pamela ahead of me, Alex a step behind.

Erik stopped short and I bumped into him. He reached over and tugged Pamela back. "Rylee, do you feel that?"

For fucks sake, what now? "What should I be feeling?"

Alex bumped into my hand. "A disturbance in the force." That was the second time Alex had quoted *Star Wars*. But he was right; there was a disturbance in the energy around us. Like something was sucking the light and life out of the very place we stood.

That couldn't be good. "Erik, is that demons I'm picking up?"

"Yes. And not like the ogres. These will be one of the packs. Stronger, faster. Meaner. How the hell they found us this fast, though, I have no idea. They don't have a way to Track like you do."

I wasn't up to snuff, my body still catching up from everything. "Fight or run?"

The demons took the decision away from us as they burst out of the motel's office, John wrapped in web that covered his whole body except his head. But that wasn't what really caught my attention. No, it was the demons themselves. They were human looking if you just considered their torsos and initial limbs. Not so human if you counted the wings on their backs, giant rat heads sitting on their shoulders, and the extra sets of arms sprouting from their sides.

Alex let out a howl, stopping them in their tracks.

"Hey, where the fuck do you think you're going with John?" I pulled my whip with one hand and a sword with the other. There was no choice; there would be no running if they were taking my friends. The demons said nothing, just dropped John and advanced toward us. I counted thirteen of the rat faces. "Eve, stay put!" I yelled knowing the harpies would want to be a part of this showdown.

And did they listen? No, of course not. They dove on the pack, plucking two out and cutting our enemy's numbers a little. The demons saw the harpies and changed formation, closing ranks completely, making it nearly impossible for any more of their members to go skyward. Eve and Marco harried them, but weren't able to get their claws into any more.

Erik took the point, and the fight was on. The rat pack surged toward us, hissing and shooting some sort of nasty smelling goop from their mouths. I dodged the first splash, saw it stick to the pavement. "They shoot their web from their mouths!" I yelped as I snapped my whip toward the rat closest to me, thinking only of keeping my friends safe.

The whip sizzled as it wrapped around the rat's throat and I jerked it forward, ramming my sword into the demon's belly. The actual demon expelled from the human host, leaving me staring at what the demon had been possessing.

A child.

Younger even than Pamela. I screamed and had to fight the rage that spooled up through me. They'd possessed children, those very souls I'd sworn to protect above all others. How didn't matter, only that they had.

"Rylee, they know your weakness. They did this on purpose, to stop you from being effective," Erik yelled as he took down a demon and another child lay dead at his feet. A little boy with ginger hair and a smattering of freckles across his cheeks.

I couldn't stop the anger, couldn't control it as I lashed out at the demons. Their bodies took the hits and they snarled and giggled as they circled around me. Screaming my rage, I fought with everything I had, but none of my blows did anything. I wondered where Pamela was in all this; there hadn't been a single blast of fire from her.

"Rylee, control it!"

But I couldn't. There was nothing in me that could handle this with anything but rage, with the righteous fury that billowed through my body. Distantly, I knew I was going to pay for this.

If only I'd understood just how bad it was going to be.

A demon hit me from behind, stunning me, as he slammed my head to the ground. Alex leapt between me and the demon and with a snarling swipe was able to push the rat faced monster back.

I managed to get to my knees, and I tried to use my magic. But nothing happened. The power slid through my fingers the way Milly said would happen if I got hit in the head. It was one of the few things that could slow down a witch, and I wasn't to ever tell anyone about it. But it looked like someone had told the demons.

I grabbed my head and tried to stop the spinning, tried to slow the out of control beat of my heart as the sounds of fighting pounded in my ears. Alex stayed close to me, but the demons lost interest in me as soon as I was down.

They had surrounded Rylee, making a solid ring of bodies between her and Erik. He was yelling at her and she was screaming at the demons.

One of the demons reached out and grabbed her from behind, pinning her arms to her side. I lurched to my feet, my short sword in my hand, grateful for it. I swayed as I tried to run to them, and tears trickled down my cheeks. This couldn't be the end of things.

Not for my family.

I fell forward with my blade, driving it between the shoulder blades of the demon who held Rylee tight. He let out a howl and dropped her. I had their attention now and they seemed to recall they were trying to take all four of us prisoner.

Two of the demons advanced on me and I stepped back, fighting to grab onto my magic. Like pouring olive oil on my hands, I could feel it, but couldn't contain it. I took up a fighting stance. "Come on then," I beckoned and they laughed, high-pitched squeaking giggles that made my blood run cold.

Alex lunged in first, hamstringing one of the demons. It went to its knee and I slashed with my blade, the steel sliding through the monster's neck—at least, most of the way through. Its head hung from a strand of bone and cartilage, flopping and dangling forward. But it didn't die. It advanced on me, all of its monstrous hands outstretched.

Biting back the scream that swam up my throat, I slashed forward, taking off one of the hands, forgetting about the other demon.

The one I backed right into.

Its arms circled around me the same way it had done to Rylee. "Now we has you," it hissed, the sound of its rat tongue flickering beside my ear. It lifted me over its head and I stared at the scene, unable to comprehend.

There was an opening in the Veil and a woman stood there with long grey hair that didn't seem to suit her face, which was very young.

"Talia, don't do this!" Rylee screamed and my eyes found her. She was held by two demons as they ran toward the opening in the Veil.

"NO!" I drove my elbow down, smashing the face of the demon that held me. Stunned, he dropped me, and Alex tackled him. "Alex, get Rylee!"

The werewolf spun and we ran toward the circle of demons protecting the opening in the Veil.

"Rylee, let go of the anger," Erik yelled as he fought and disposed of another demon. It slid to his feet, a child emerging as the demon's essence dispelled.

I understood then why Rylee couldn't stop the anger.

Yet, that didn't help us save her now. I could just see the top edge of the Veil as I pushed forward, reaching for my magic, desperate.

And there it was. I didn't hesitate, just lashed out with my hand and pointed with my short sword. The power ripped out of me, sending the demons sprawling in every direction, clearing our path to where Rylee was.

Where she had been.

The opening to the Veil was gone. The woman with the grey hair was gone. Worse than that, Rylee was gone.

I couldn't stop the cry that clawed out of my throat. Around me, the demons slowly started to get up and I pinned them to the ground, slamming them over and over again, their bodies breaking under my assault. I didn't care they would look like children once the demons were gone. Didn't care that Erik was telling me it was done, that he was trying to slow me down. My breath came in ragged gasps as I fought the panic and sorrow overwhelming me. The sorrow was quickly replaced by a rage so dark I couldn't see, an anger so deep, I felt it all the way through my bones into my very soul.

They'd taken Rylee into the Veil, the deep level of the Veil.

Orion had her and we would never get her back.

The rat-faced demons dumped me onto the floor in a room that looked like a throne room. They did their squeaky-assed giggling routine as they backed away. Everything in the room was done up in black and white, shades of grey and not much else in the way of color. I knew where they'd taken me.

The deepest level of the Veil was not a place I thought I'd be visiting again. I was so royally fucked.

Talia stepped into view. "I'm sorry. I did not want to bring you here. But it was the only way."

I got to my feet, didn't bother to put my sword away. "Yet you did."

"Rylee, Talia is right. She had no choice. It is the way of the binding Orion has on her."

I turned to see Milly walk toward us. Her hair was bound back in a tight braid and her eyes looked haggard, as if she hadn't slept in days. A blood red, floor-dragging gown hung from her body, the empire waistline accentuating the fact she was hugely pregnant. One hand cupped her belly, which had grown by leaps and bounds even in the short few days since

I'd seen her last. She glanced down. "Orion has found a way to speed up the growth of my baby." Her green eyes slowly lifted to mine. Despair echoed the horror I knew was in mine.

"You can't stop him?"

She shook her head. "No."

I glanced at Talia. "Why did you bring me here; what does he want with me?"

Yeah, I know the obvious would be he wanted to kill me, but he had an opportunity on the other side of the Veil. I wouldn't have been able to stop the rat pack from tearing me apart. Yet they'd waited on Talia to open the Veil and bring me through.

"Come on, we don't have much time," Milly said, striding past me. "Orion didn't expect us to bring you in so quickly. If we make haste, you can be gone before he even knows you are here."

I had no choice but to follow her since there was no one else I could trust. "What are you saying?"

Milly let out a sigh. "You didn't read the papers I gave you, did you?"

To be fair, I'd kept meaning to. Only I'd never found the time. "No. Why?"

"If you'd read them, you would have known what was coming." She started off again, her dress dragging through the skim of dust and dirt on the floor. Like the queen of a hovel.

"What did it say?" I jogged to catch up, swayed and ended up leaning against the wall.

Milly's hands were on me in an instant, a flood of healing washing through me. "Rylee, how have you survived without daily healings?" Her voice held a thread of laughter and I couldn't help but smile up at her.

"Well, I'm getting better at letting people help me."

She snorted and rolled her eyes. "Come, we are almost there."

I felt refreshed like I hadn't been in a long time, the cuts and bruises from too many fights evaporating as if they'd never been. I jogged to her side, and Talia followed at a slight distance.

"What's going on?"

"You need the violet book of prophecy, the book written by the Blood of the Lost. You need it so you have all the steps to stop Orion. That is where all the answers are. But he has it in a spelled room I cannot unlock." She blew out a sharp breath and clutched at her belly. A groan slipped between lips. "Gods, not yet."

Fucking hell, was she going into labor? The sound of fluid dripping onto the floor made me think that was exactly what was going on. "Milly, tell me you aren't in labor."

"Hurry." Was all she said as she used the wall for support. I slipped my hand around her waist and helped her walk. Her belly where it pressed against my side contracted and flexed and something hit me. I gritted my teeth to stop from freaking the fuck out. Like an alien life form, her baby kicked and fought to break free of his mother's belly.

We made our way to the top of a set of stairs that curled up out of sight. Narrow and tight, they would make a perfect bottleneck for someone coming after us. "You sure you can do this?"

Milly nodded, though there was sweat on her face and her eyes were strained at the edges. She gulped in a breath of air and let it out in a slow hiss. "Let's go."

The stairs were just wide enough for me to walk beside her, supporting her as we worked our way up, flight after flight. Milly kept moving though, and I was fiercely proud of her.

There were five floors to be exact, without a single landing to pause on, just a doorway marking the level we were at, until we neared the top. There, on the fifth floor, we found a landing that was about ten by ten and bare, except for a single window that let in a dull, weak light.

"At the top," Milly whispered, "there is a doorway with no door. It looks like you could walk through with no thought, with no consequence." She dragged in a gulp of air and let out a low moan, sliding to the floor. I lowered her down so she could lean against the wall. Talia came up and crouched on her other side.

"The baby will be here soon."

Milly grabbed my arm. "Rylee, there is someone you will have to face within the room. I can't see who it is, I don't know if they would see you as friend or foe. But the spell, you should be able to walk right through it."

"And if I can't, what will happen to me?"

Talia shook her head. "You will be bound to Orion."

I rocked back on my heels. Bound to Orion if my Immunity failed. "Got it. You wait here."

Milly let out a soft laugh that turned into a whimper as she clutched her belly. "Hurry."

Without looking back, I ran up the last flight of stairs. At the top was an open doorway as she said, but it was fuzzy. Like one of those stupid tricks people do when they put cellophane across a doorway and then they put something appetizing on the other side.

The tease for me, of course, was the violet-skinned book of prophecy. I could see it on a small, wooden table in the middle of the room. I walked right up to the edge of the doorway and stared at it. Rimmed in symbols, I knew what some of them represented. The black-skinned book had a lot of them.

Power. Obedience. Violence. Nothing good, of course.

"Piece of shit," I snarled and forced my feet forward. The spell that held the doorway slid over my skin and I felt the daggers of it try to dig in. The black snowflake on my chest burned with a fire that made me want to gasp out loud, but I held my breath and took another step, the spell dragging hard over me, leaving welts. I stumbled and went to one knee, and the spell finally gave up and slithered back to where it had been. I turned to look at the doorway. The spell hadn't stuck to me, but it hadn't been dispelled, either.

The sound of a sword being drawn snapped my head around. An older man stood between me and the table where only moments before the room had been empty. He wore tight black pants and knee-high, black leather boots and a white shirt that was buttoned all the way to the top. Dark hair streaked with grey at the temples accentuated his eyes, which where a bright silvery tone. He reminded me of the three Musketeers. Minus the ridiculous hat and feather. "It seems you must face me now."

"Are you a guardian?" 'Cause if he was, there was no way I could beat him, I'd have to out maneuver his ass, grab the book and make a run for it.

"I am not a guardian. I am the last pureblood."

I arched an eyebrow up. "Well, la-dee-fucking-da. I'm the last Tracker. Want to compare notes on being the last of our kind?"

His lips arched upward into a smile. "I shall enjoy gutting you, Filthy Tracker."

He launched his attack, but I met him from my knees, drawing my swords in time to block his swing at my head. Like I would go down in the first round.

"Come on, let's see what you've got, bitch." I stood and slid around to the left, keeping my eyes on him.

I'll give him his due; he was good. His skills were honed and every move he made was textbook, the forms perfect, the angles superb. But he didn't fight dirty.

Something I most certainly did.

As he lifted his sword arm for what would be a bone-jarring hit, if I caught it on my crossed swords, I leapt inside his guard and drove my knee into his man junk. He lost his air and started to bend over. I snapped my elbow up, into his nose, breaking it. His fingers went limp around the sword and the weapon fell to the floor with a clatter as his eyes rolled back into his head.

"See? You stink, you filthy pureblood." I spit at his feet as I backed away. Just because he was down didn't mean I would take my eyes from him. I slid one of my swords into its sheath and then reached back as my hip hit the table. Blindly, I groped for the violet-skinned book. The leather was smooth under my hand and I thought of Sas. She was the only violet skinned ogre I'd ever met. I tucked the book under my arm, holding it tight.

"You cannot take that book. It is for the one who would save the world from the demons," he gasped out and I stared at him. How much info could I get from him? And would it help me or would he deliberately try to deceive me? I was betting on the deception side of things, but still . . .

"And who is that?"

"The child of prophecy, the one who will face the demons. She will save the world. You cannot take that book." He rolled to his knees and reached for his sword. I jumped forward and kicked it out of his reach. It skittered across the floor coming to a rest near the doorway.

"I am that one," I said, feeling the truth center within me. I was the one who would stop Orion. "I need this book. I don't know everything I should if I'm going to kick his ass into oblivion. So if you are really on my side, stop trying to fucking well kill me."

He lifted his eyes to mine. "You cannot be her. She was to be pure of heart, the last of our bloodline."

A chill swept through me. "I don't know about pure of heart, but what do you mean the last of our bloodline? I am the last of the Blood of the Lost. Is that what you mean?"

His eyes widened and he slid back against the wall. "The Blood of the Lost. That is what we are known by now?"

Shit, he was like me, the ones who'd created the Veil. "I guess so. But what did we start out as? And how can I be the last if you're here?"

His smile was pained. "If you do not know, you do not need to know. The Blood of the Lost is a fitting title. And you are the last, if that is true, because I am not really alive. I have been dead for a thousand years."

Frustration made me bold, and I stalked to him, holding my sword out. "What. Am. I?"

"You are a being that has the ability to create as well as destroy. Your power is miniscule next to those of us who are of pureblood." He shook his head from his position on the floor. "If your blood hadn't been so diluted, I would have recognized you right away."

"You're not even going to try and be helpful, are you?"

A laugh trickled past the blood on his lips. "It isn't a matter of being helpful. At some point you may discover the truth of your family history. But it doesn't truly have any bearing on what you must do. You must stop the demons. So go and do what you were born to die for."

I stepped back from him as my blood chilled for a second time. "I'm not going to die. Orion is."

His smile slipped and I didn't like what I saw on his face. "Yes, he will die. Of that you *must* be right, and I pray to the gods you are successful. Go. Before he knows you are here."

A cry slid up the stairwell, one filled with pain. Milly. I didn't look back at the man who may or may not have been my past, as I ran toward my friend. The doorway's spell knocked me to my knees and I struggled to breathe as I hit the stone floor. Again, the snowflake burned, searing my chest. Milly had set it up so I would gain immunity from demons through the hoarfrost demon's poison—though at the time I'd thought she'd just been trying to kill me. Apparently it was still working in my favor, helping my natural immunity keep me safe.

Book in my arms, sword in my hand, I ran down the stairwell to the level below and the small landing. Milly still leaned against the wall, but Talia was between her legs, hands on her knees.

The necromancer glanced up at me. "We only have minutes before he's here."

"Please tell me you mean the baby."

Talia shook her head as Milly let out a cry and then bore down. Shit, this was not good timing.

I dropped to a crouch by Milly's head, putting the book at her side. "Milly, you can do this. But you have to push the baby out now."

Her green eyes were filled with tears as she blinked up at me. "You'll take my baby with you. Protect him from Orion."

I nodded, stroking her forehead. "I promised to, didn't I?"

She bit her lower lip and a sob slipped out. No more words came from her, no more cries.

"I see the head," Talia said, her voice soft.

Licking my lips, I did something I never wanted to do.

I Tracked Orion.

His threads blazed with darkness that circled around me and his voice whispered inside my head. *You are here?*

I didn't answer him, just worked out how close he was. A hundred feet at best.

I shut down the threads to him with a deep shudder. "Hurry, Milly. You have to hurry."

There was going to be no choice here. I stood and faced the stairs that curled up to us. Orion was coming and I was going to have to deal with him, at least long enough to get me and the kid out.

I pulled my whip loose, wishing I had my crossbow with me. A distance weapon would have been particularly nice. A cry shattered the air, the sound of a baby's first bellow.

"Shit, your kid's got lungs." I made the mistake of looking over my shoulder, seeing the baby pressed against Milly's chest, wrapped in a swath of her red dress. Something slammed into my upper body and drove me back. I tumbled ass over head until I was up against the stairs leading up to the top doorway.

Orion stood looking down on the three of us. He was as big as I remembered him, muscular, completely bald with red eyes that pierced me and made my blood chill. "Three little pigs, did you think you could escape the big bad wolf?"

From the corner of my eye, I saw Milly clutch the baby against her. "You can't have him, he's innocent."

Orion threw back his head to laugh, a move I'd seen him do before. I took advantage of it. I snapped my whip out as I thought about Milly, about her love for her baby, about my desire to protect them. In that moment, I let the anger go, and embraced my heart and all it knew.

My whip curled around Orion's left arm, just above the wrist. He let out a roar as the flesh curled and blackened, but he didn't fight it. Nope, not that asshole. He grabbed the whip and jerked it out of my hands, stopping the connection. I stood and faced him, confidence filling me until I saw his hand.

The charred skin flaked and fell off, revealing an arm that was as unhurt as it had been only moments before.

"You didn't think it would be that easy to take me on in my own realm, did you?" He smiled and took a step toward Milly, as if I were of no consequence. "The child is mine. You have always known that."

With his back to me, I leapt toward him. I drove my sword forward, through his heart as I pulled my second blade and slashed it through his back, nearly severing his body in half. "Heal that, asshat."

He glanced over his shoulder at me, a smile on his lips as his body healed around my weapons. "You truly think you can kill me, don't you? You are a bigger fool than I'd thought. Stay there, Tracker, I will deal with you in a moment."

Just like that, he dismissed me as if I were no longer a threat. Was I that weak?

Erik said hands on was best, that going through my weapons was a weaker version. For Milly, for the baby, I had to try and stop this monster now. If I didn't, and he possessed the child, he'd be free to walk in the world.

With a scream, I leapt onto his back, wrapping my hands around his face. His head went up in a black flame that consumed my hands, but I didn't let go. The heat sung along my nerve endings, a pain that tore at me, worse than any of the injuries I'd ever incurred, even putting them all together.

He tried to buck me off, his hands grabbing at my legs, his fingers digging into my flesh. "Will you fucking die already?" I yelled as the flames began to travel down his neck.

"Rylee, let go!" Milly screamed, and I wanted to, damn, how I wanted to. But I knew that the second I did, he'd heal again.

"Can't."

"You can't kill him! It isn't possible."

That was Talia and my eyes found her next to the doorway on the landing. It was open and on the other side . . . shit, the other side opened up to my farm in North Dakota.

"HURRY!"

Timing was everything in a fight, and this one was no different. Gripping Orion's face even harder, I drove my fingers deep into his skull through the fire softened flesh, and put my feet up into his lower back. With that leverage, I pulled as hard as I could, my jaw tight with the effort and the enormous pain writhing up my hands.

A scream slipped out of me, merging with Orion's as his neck snapped backward and his howl of fury slid into bits and pieces of gurgling mess.

I rode his body to the ground. Talia grabbed me and jerked my hands from Orion's burning flesh. I couldn't look at them, could already feel muscles and tendons tightening into crippled digits that would be next to useless.

"Milly hasn't the strength to heal you," Talia said as she slipped the violet-skinned book into my arms and then a small, mewling bundle wrapped in red silk. I could barely stand; the pain reverberating through my hands and arms was so bad.

"How long will he be out?" I whispered, though whispering hadn't been my intention. I coughed. The smoke I'd inhaled had scorched my throat and lungs.

Talia guided me and I tried to see where Milly was. "I don't know. If we're lucky, days. Not so lucky, hours, maybe minutes."

My brain struggled to function around what had happened, how fast everything had come together. "Milly."

The necromancer let out a heavy sigh. "She has to stay, you know that."

"I want to see her."

Talia moved to the side so I could see Milly slumped against the wall, her green eyes unseeing, a pool of blood blending into the red dress. So much blood.

"No." I couldn't see past the tears that filled my eyes. This wasn't how it was supposed to end. Not with her like that, splayed out in a demon's realm like a broken doll—dying as she gave birth.

"Go, you have to." Talia gave me a push in the right direction, but her voice was thick and heavy with tears that slid down her face. She tucked my whip into my arms beside the baby. "She wanted you to save her child, above all else."

I knew what Talia was saying was true, that Milly wanted her baby to be safe. "Goodbye, my friend," I whispered as I backed through the doorway. The bite of the winter wind was a blessing against the burns arching from my hands almost to my elbows, but the relief was only physical. Talia stood in the doorway, and then shut it so I stared at nothing, not even an empty door. She would tell where she'd sent me the minute Orion questioned her.

A soft cry from the bundle in my arms drew my eyes downward. Brilliant spring-green eyes stared at me, one tiny hand reaching up as if he would touch me. I bit my lip and headed toward the barn, the only structure left intact on the farm. I had nothing to feed the little boy, and I couldn't even touch him, my hands were so badly burned.

There was nothing to do but wait and pray. And hope this time, someone rescued me.

7

Lucky for me, I had good friends who knew when I needed them. Well, at least one good friend.

"What the fecking hells is this?"

I rolled to the side, the baby asleep in my arms, for which I was grateful because if he'd been upset, there wouldn't have been much I could have done. We were half buried in the hay, the insulating factor keeping the winter cold at bay. "Charlie? How did you know I was here?"

"Everyone's looking for ya . . . what happened to yous hands?" He gasped as he limped toward me, his wooden leg obviously giving him grief. He held out his hands to me, but I couldn't do the same. My skin had toughened, already to the point where moving anything made it crack and bleed.

"I need a healer. And food and clothes for this guy." I awkwardly held up the bundle of baby wrapped in my jacket.

"Sweet mother of the gods, Rylee, that be a baby." Charlie's eyes were wide. "Is it yours?"

I barked out a bitter, pain-filled laugh. "No. Milly's. We got him away from Orion."

He stared at me, sadness and pain filling his eyes. More than any of my friends perhaps, he knew the loss of loved ones.

"Ah, lass, I see it in you. She's gone, isn't she?"

I nodded, my lip trembling as I fought the tears. Charlie made a face. "I'll gets Pamela. She'll heal you up right."

He ran back toward the door and slipped through. I tipped my head back and watched the light filter in through the barn slats. We were only an hour or so from sunset, and then Frank would be trying to send Berget across the Veil to me. How the hell was I going to take her head when my hands were so royally fucked up? Never mind the emotional toll I was looking at for finally becoming my sister's murderer.

My family, adoptive mother in particular would finally be right. I would finally be the one to kill Berget. I wanted to vomit.

The how of it, with my hands as they were, weighed on me as I waited for Charlie. How was I going to fight Orion with messed up hands? Was Liam still alive? What was going on at Jack's that things had fallen apart so fast?

Ten minutes, and a thousand questions in my head later, Charlie was back with a bundle of cloth, a bottle, and a heavy wool blanket. Without asking, he took the baby from me, dressed him in the clothes that the bundle of cloth turned out to be, and popped the bottle into his mouth. The little guy latched on and sucked hard, and noisily.

It was easy for me to forget that Charlie had a family at one point, that they'd been killed. He rocked the little boy with a practiced ease while the kid sucked at the bottle greedily.

"Pamela be on hers way. I found thems already on their ways here. Shouldn't be long now. You sleeps, I'll be watching over yous both," Charlie said and, feeling a little guilty, I Tracked him, Tracked demons and evil spirits just to be sure.

Charlie was clean, and there was nothing close by. I Tracked Pamela and felt her moving toward me at a good clip. "She'll be here soon. No point in sleeping."

The violet-skinned book poked me in the thigh as I sat up. "So much death, Charlie. Is it worth it?" I stared at the book, unable to not see my hands. They looked like something from a horror movie, like a prop made to scare little kids. Blackened and charred, nausea rolled through me at the thought that perhaps I couldn't be healed. Perhaps this was part of my destiny.

"The world might not be worth it," he said as he rocked the little boy. "But there is enough good in the world that I thinks yous has to keep fighting." Charlie handed the baby back to me, setting him carefully into my arms above the burns. "Whats yous going to be calling this little tyke?"

That was a good question. He needed a name, one strong enough to carry him through his whole life, however long it would be. I thought of those who'd passed, my friends who'd given their lives for the fight against Orion. Jack and Dox were at the top of the list.

But Milly wouldn't want her baby named for either of those two.

Dark lashes rested against milky skin as his lips puckered and he started to suck in his sleep. "Milly had a brother who died when she was very young. His name was Zane. I think she would like it if her baby was named for him."

"Zane, good name fors him." Charlie leaned over and touched the boy on the forehead. "Looks like his mammy."

That he did; the resemblance was strong both in his coloring and the shape of his face, right down to his eyes which were already green. Unusual for a baby, at least from what I understood.

I leaned back in the hay, biting the groan of pain that bubbled up with the movement. Zane snuggled against me and I couldn't help but love him. Shit, I was turning into a sappy mush. But Milly knew me well, better probably than anyone but Liam. She'd known I would protect Zane with my life, if need be. I let out a sigh and closed my eyes. Protecting him was all well and good, but only if Pamela could heal the mess of my hands.

I rode on Eve by myself as we flew for the farm. Erik and Alex rode Marco. I couldn't stand to have anyone touch me. Anger and rage still flowed through me like hot lava, making my magic burn inside.

"Charlie said she's hurt bad, but that there is a surprise too," I said as Eve dipped low, avoiding a cloud.

"Surprises can be good, Pam," Eve said.

I snorted, unable to keep the bite from my words. "Not usually in our world."

Giselle's words came back and swirled around in my head. *You will face darkness, and you will have to fight through it.*

At the time, I hadn't understood what she'd meant. But now I was starting to see. I couldn't stop the anger that flowered and grew within my heart. All I wanted was to wipe out those who would hurt us. I wanted to rip them apart, piece by piece, with no thought of what would come after. The darkness of those thoughts grew each moment and I worried I would turn into someone bad. Really bad.

I swallowed hard as Eve spiraled down to the farm. With only the barn left intact, the place was a strange sight. The burned remains of the house had crumpled and were partially covered with snow, leaving bits and pieces sticking out like lumpy bones.

Eve landed lightly and I slid from her back, running toward the barn. I burst through the door, ready for an attack, for the surprise to be bad. So when I took in what I was seeing, I couldn't understand it at first.

Rylee was holding a . . . baby?

Then I saw her arms and hands and I couldn't stop the gasp that slipped out. "Rylee."

"Yeah, I look like shit. Don't need a mirror to see it this time."

Charlie took the baby from her arms. "Do yous stuff, young witch."

Healing was not something I was good at and that normally only frustrated me. I'd been better at it when I first learned, and slowly, my skill with it had slipped, though I didn't know why. I swallowed hard, then went and sat beside Rylee in the hay.

"I have to touch your hands." I didn't want to, not just because I didn't want to hurt her, but they looked awful and smelled like burnt meat.

"It's okay. Just do it." She closed her eyes and I carefully wrapped my fingers around hers, the skin under mine flaking away. Rylee sucked in a sharp breath and I closed my eyes, focusing on the parts of the healing I needed.

Water, air, and earth blended to put the pieces back together, but fire was needed too and I was afraid to use it. Afraid I would somehow make the burns worse.

"What if I can't, what if I make it hurt more instead of heal it?" I whispered.

"Then we'll find someone else. You can't make it worse, Pam." She said those words with confidence, but I saw the sweat break out on her forehead.

Before I started, Alex and Erik came into the barn. Erik sucked in a sharp breath, but Alex was oblivious. He ran to Rylee's side and curled up around her, hugging her tight and almost pulling her from me.

"Alex!" I snapped. "Not now."

He cringed and his lower lip stuck out. "You is not the boss of me."

I let go of Rylee and flicked my hand at him. He flipped over once in the air before adhering to the wall, like a fly to sticky paper. "I am right now. Now stay out of the way."

Rylee stared at me, the three colors in her eyes swirling. "You okay?"

I didn't really know how to answer without getting into the whole darkness thing, so I just nodded. "I'm fine. He's just in the way."

I took her hands again and slowed my breathing. Healing took all four elements and then something from myself as the healer, a piece of my essence. Not a lot, but it was the binding between the elements to make the healing take place. I plunged in, tying the elements to Rylee's form and threading them through her essence. I fought not to let go when she cried out as the skin sloughed off and broke away, as her tendons relaxed and the muscles rebuilt.

A minute passed and I'd done all I could. I looked down at her hands. They were pink in patches, like she'd had a bad sunburn, but the worst of the damage had been dealt with and her fingers were no longer charred sausages, nor were her arms black to the elbow.

Then she tried to flex her hands.

Her fingers barely moved, creaking with the effort. She grimaced and tried again. More movement, but it was slow and obviously painful. Rylee turned her hands back and forth several times, flexing only at the wrist. "It'll just take some work. Bad injuries are like that."

I stood and brushed hay off my pants and shirt, feeling tears well up. "I'm sorry I'm not as good as Milly."

"That's not what I meant," she said, but I was already walking away as fast as I could go without running. I was never good enough, not to help Rylee, not to help anyone. But I would make sure one day that I proved I was better than Milly.

That I would be a witch to be reckoned with.

I put my fist to my mouth, opened the barn door, and left everyone behind.

What the hell had that been about? Teenage angst, no doubt; I remembered well enough to know nothing I said would make it better. My hands throbbed and ached like they'd been smashed repeatedly by an overzealous carpenter. At least the pain wasn't consuming me and every thought I had.

Zane let out a whimper and Charlie handed him back to me.

"Whats yous going to do, Rylee girl?"

I rocked Zane in my arms, feeling more than a little awkward. I hadn't been around a lot of babies, never mind one this small. "He needs to be somewhere safe while we deal with the demons. He can't come with us; he'll be too much of a temptation for Orion and his packs."

Lifting my eyes to Charlie and then Erik, I saw the look on both their faces; they were holding back. "What? What aren't you telling me?"

"There aren't any safe places, not anymore." Erik lowered himself to sit beside me in the hay. "But you're right; you can't take a baby into battle."

Alex crept forward and I put a hand out to him. Pamela flipping him ass over tail and sticking him to the wall had thrown both of us for a loop. It wasn't like her. I made a mental note to sit her down and have a talk. A good, long chat about dealing with anger and fear. But first thing I had to do was get Zane to safety.

"You're telling me there isn't a place anywhere in this whole freaking world that could provide even a temporary safe haven?" I couldn't believe that was the case.

Charlie cleared his throat. "Perhaps I can be of helps with thats."

Erik picked up a long piece of hay and stuck it between his teeth. "It would put you in danger. You willing to do that for a child that is not one of yours?"

With a deep puffing of his chest, Charlie crossed his arms. "Yous don't know me."

"What are you two talking about?"

The two men looked at one another then to me. Erik spoke first. "Brownies don't live on this plane; they live on the first level of the Veil for the most part. And while it isn't perfect, it would provide something of a temporary haven that you are looking for."

"Charlie, you can take the baby with you? I thought you couldn't cross the Veil with anyone." That had always been my understanding.

The brownie limped to me and touched Zane on the cheek. "It bees more of a size matter. I can't be taking a big one like yous or the wolf here, but a wee babe, him I could take." Charlie's eyes were soft as he looked down at the baby. No doubt remembering his own children when they had been alive.

"Are you sure?"

"Yes, I bees sure. Give him to me, sooner the better thats I gets going."

I handed him Zane, something in me lurching. I didn't really want to say goodbye to the baby. He was the last piece of Milly I had, and probably the best piece.

"See you later." I lifted my hand as Charlie slipped through the doorway, crossing the Veil. Alex gave a soft woof.

"I likes Milly's baby."

"Yeah, me too."

"I feeds him tiger ice cream next time." Alex grinned at me, his eyes wide and hopeful. I didn't answer, just rubbed the top of his head.

Erik tapped me on the knee. "Things to do, Niece."

He was right, but I had to know something first. "How did you know where I would be, I mean, before Charlie found you? He said you were already on your way here."

"Pamela grabbed the papers from your room before we left Doran's. Milly's message was there, that you shouldn't fight too hard when you next ran into a demon or two. That way she and Talia could get the book to you." He tapped the violet-skinned book of prophecy sitting beside me in the hay. "Said she would drop you back at the farm when it was all done."

I shook my head, disbelief flowing through me. Milly had kept her word, had fought Orion from his side of the Veil. It had cost her life . . . emotions welled up in my heart and I struggled to put them away. Worse was when Erik slid his arm over my shoulder and tugged me close.

"Grieve her, she was your family."

A sob escaped me, but I forced the next one back. "Let me go."

"It's good to let it out." He half shook me.

"I said let me the fuck go!" I jerked away from him, taking solace in the anger that coursed through my veins. Erik didn't seem surprised, nor upset. He just gave me a sad smile and shook his head. "One day you will have to learn to allow yourself to grieve, to feel."

"Well, it isn't going to be today," I snapped. I reached into the hay and pulled out the violet-skinned book. The cover was slightly pebbled, not smooth like I knew Sas's skin was. Maybe it was an older ogre that had lost its hide to cover this book. I shuddered and flipped it open, going for a random search.

My eyes skimmed along, not really catching on anything at first. I flicked the page and in the middle of the paper was a picture that made me hold my breath.

Three figures were depicted in the center, a little girl, and two young boys who were older, but not adults. Under the girl was "Spirit Seeker." Under one of the boys was "Witch," and under the third boy was "Human." That wasn't the worst of it.

"When the three shall be bound to demons, the four horsemen shall be ready to come forth and seek the Tracker's heart. Stop the possession and the end days shall be displaced for a time."

Erik leaned over me and looked at the picture. "Those the three kids who are missing?"

"Motherfuckers," I whispered as I nodded. They could have taken any human, but whoever had done this at Orion's bidding had chosen to take those who were closest to me, those they knew I would go after.

"Doesn't make sense. Why would they take kids I knew, if they read this?"

Erik took the book from me and looked at the page. "I don't follow."

"Why not take random kids, like Simon, that I would probably never know they took? This is more like bait than trying to make something happen."

He frowned and stared harder at the page. "They weren't expecting you to know this would happen. Didn't you want this Kyle kid," he tapped the picture in the book, "to come to you? To help with keeping an eye on things? Would you trust the spirit seeker if she came to your front door? And if a young male witch came to you for help, would you give it?"

He had a point. I wanted to scrub my hands over my face, but I didn't want to deal with the reminder my hands were not yet up to snuff. "Yeah. Either of them I would trust and help without thinking. Both of them could have gotten close to me with ease. This is just another type of trap. Fuck, I hate Orion."

Erik grunted. "He's a demon and will do everything he can to fool you."

There was no choice but to go after the three kids, even if they were bait for a trap. I Tracked India, feeling her threads steady and even in my head. I Tracked Kyle and, though he was terrified, he was physically okay. The other kid, Simon, was curious, but not hurt and not even that fearful. I wasn't sure how I felt about that. It always worried me when a salvage was curious, but not afraid. Spoke of possibilities I didn't like to imagine. Like a child being convinced they were better off with their perps.

"What would it take to make for possession of three kids at the same time? How many witches?" I took the violet book back from Erik and flipped it open to the front. Since it had taken a full coven to try and possess India that first time, I had a feeling I already knew the answer to the question, but I had to ask, to be sure I wasn't jumping to conclusions.

"Three covens."

I nodded as my oversensitive fingers touched the pages, the words flowing under them.

Why, oh why did I have to be right about that? A small part of me hoped it would only be one coven. One coven would be far slower in having the demons possess the kids. Which, in turn, would have given us more time to get to them.

I Tracked witches as a whole, hoping we were wrong and it really was only one coven. Nope, there they were, lighting up inside my head like a pinball machine gone wild. A massive cluster of witches wound their way around the three threads of the three kids I still held.

But for the first time, something new kicked in with my ability to Track.

More than just the general direction the kids and witches were, I knew exactly what city.

My home. Not the one I'd lived in for the last ten years in North Dakota. No, my other home, the one I was raised in with Berget.

Boston.

Shock rippled through me. I'd never been able to pinpoint a thread so accurately, down to the city. Usually, I had a pulling sensation either north or south, east or west, and a vague distance.

But this time it came through loud and clear, the place visible in my head as if I were looking at a picture. Boston. Shit on sticks, if we were going to deal with Orion's black covens once and for all, I would have to go to my hometown.

Where my adoptive parents were, and the chance, with my luck, I would end up having to deal with the past, as well as the present. I slumped into the hay, my head swimming.

Erik touched my elbow, getting my attention. "How bad is it?"

How bad? Fuck, it couldn't be worse.

Nope.

Wrong again.

8

The darkness had swallowed him whole and there was no way back. A whimper slipped out of his muzzle and a voice rippled inside his head.

Stay with me wolf; she will peel my hide and eat me for breakfast if I let your furry ass die.

He tried to focus, to put the pieces together.

Demons, unicorns, ogres, and a dragon. Everything was so fuzzy. There was a witch; she'd tried to heal him. . . .

Pamela tried to heal you, that's true. But she is battling something on her own right now that is getting in the way of her ability. Witch hormones are the worst, almost as bad as Tracker tempers.

Another time, that would have elicited a laugh from him. He tried to open his eyes, gave up when they proved too heavy and the darkness curled around him. He struggled against it; not his time, it wasn't his time yet. There was too much left to do.

Rest easy, wolf. The druids should have a way to heal you.

Rylee.

She is waiting for us in London.

Louisa was closer, though. The shamans should be able to heal him.

Excellent call, wolf. We go to Louisa first. Keeping you alive will keep us both in good standing with Rylee. Better that she sees you all put back together.

Blaz banked hard, and the world lurched around Liam. A relieved sigh rippled out of him. That would have to be enough for now.

Liam was going to be pissed when he figured out we weren't following him. At least, not right away—we'd catch up as soon as we got the kids out of the black coven's witchy hands.

With the violet-skinned book strapped to Erik's back under his cloak, we headed out of the barn. Sunset was only fifteen or so minutes away and I marked it in my mind. On instinct, I reached back and touched my hand to the grip of my sword. My fingers curled around it, but the pain was bad, enough that I knew I'd never hold up in a fight. Fuck, this was seriously not good.

Alex moved quietly beside me, more demure than I'd ever seen him, and it pulled me out of my own thoughts.

"Buddy, are you okay?"

"I feel funny."

I stopped and cupped his face, looking deep into his eyes. "What do you mean by funny?"

He gave a roll of his shoulders. "Twisted up inside."

What the hell did that mean? "Let me know if it gets worse, okay?"

"You gots it."

Of all the people in my life, Alex was one of the few constants I could depend on no matter what. I ran my hands down his cheeks and scratched his neck.

He grinned up at me and gave me a wolfy wink. "I is good. No worries."

Nothing I could do other than keep an eye on his behavior and hope it wasn't anything serious.

Outside the barn, Eve stood at the edge of the burnt outhouse, her head lowered almost to the ground. A flutter of long blonde hair in the wind gave Pamela away.

Zorro, or Marco as he insisted his name was, ruffled his feathers. "Your young witch is going through a hard time."

"Funny, I didn't pick up on that," I said as I walked toward the two girls. One feathered, one full of magic with no one to train her. Shit, even Milly had Giselle to guide her. With Milly dead, who did I trust to continue Pamela's training? Deanna could do it, but there would be no training in the ways of fighting. It would be healing and growing plants and shit like that.

Marco stepped in front of me, blocking my way. "You need to help her deal with it before you go further."

I glared up at him, would have liked to pull a blade and have him at the end of it to make my point. "Listen, we are all dealing with shit right now, every single one of us. She's going to have to just figure it out."

He shook his head, feathers literally ruffled. "You can't ignore this. This darkness will grow in her until there is nothing left."

Jaw tight, I stepped around him. Fucking bird brain, what did he know about witches?

A soft voice, one that sounded suspiciously like Giselle's, whispered to me. *And what do you know? Not much, other than what little we gleaned from Milly.*

I stopped and put my hands on my hips, feeling the pain in my fingers and for the moment, relishing it. Pain had a way of clearing out emotions, of making everything simple.

Pamela needed help. And the only person I had was Deanna. Fucking hell, I did not want to send Pamela off on her own. Not when I needed her to help me get the other kids out.

"How long before this is a crisis?" I asked Marco without turning around.

"I do not know. Not long."

I strode to where Pamela sat on the edge of the house's foundation, her legs dangling over the burned and hollowed-out shell. Crouching beside her, I stared into what had been my home, the one place I thought I'd always be safe. "I need your help, Pam. We have to go after those three kids."

Her eyes never lifted. "I'm not strong enough to help you."

"That's bullshit and you know it," I snapped. "You're almost as strong as Milly right now, and you've been doing this only *five months*. Experienced? No, you aren't. But you are a fucking powerhouse."

Her back slowly stiffened. "You aren't mad at me for not being able to heal you fully?"

I blew out a breath. "Look, it was some sort of funky magic fire to do with Orion and me being a Slayer. I don't think it has anything to do with you."

Her eyes, rimmed with tears, finally made contact with mine. "I don't want to let you down."

"You never have." I brushed hair back from her face and gave her a smile, though I had no doubt it was rather fatigued looking.

Her lips trembled, but she fought through it. "Okay. Let's get those kids."

Eve gave a happy squawk and flapped her wings. "Where are we going?"

"Boston. But not yet. There is one task I have to do first."

Everyone looked at me and I struggled to put the words into a sentence that wouldn't leave me gasping for air around tears. "Berget's opal is failing. Frank is going to open the Veil when the sun sets here, and get her across the Veil." I didn't make eye contact with anyone, chose instead to stare at the barn, right where I thought she'd come through. "Pamela, I will need you to hold her. I don't think she'll fight you. I'll take her head."

No one said anything, no one questioned me, and a part of me so badly wanted them to. To say that maybe there was another way. But we all knew that once Berget's opal failed, her adoptive, psychotic parents would be fully in charge once more and we might not get another chance at eliminating the threat they posed. Even if it meant ending Berget's life.

Pamela moved beside me as I stared at the barn and Alex slid up to my other side, butting his head into my hand gently. I focused on breathing slow and even, not thinking about what I was going to do. I'd fought so fucking hard to keep her alive, to save her, and to have it fail now . . . I closed my eyes as the sun set. The twilight darkness fell swiftly and seconds ticked by. Maybe I'd done wrong by Frank, maybe the kid wouldn't be able to pull it off. What if Berget killed him too? Fuck.

The tension rose, and when I thought I'd for sure sent Frank to his death, the air in front of the barn door shimmered and opened. Berget stepped through, Frank right behind her.

"Rylee said she wanted to see you," Frank said, his eyes flicking up and squinting into the darkness as he searched for us. Behind them, the Veil closed.

Pamela lifted her hand and Berget stiffened as the spell took hold, pinning her in place. I walked forward. "Thank you, Frank."

Berget's eyes were on mine, full of tears. "Rylee, I'm so sorry. I thought I had them under control. But I went too long between feedings. That was why they got out of hand."

"How can I trust that? How can I know you will be safe around our allies?" I whispered the questions, wanting there to be some way out of this fucking mess.

She shook her head. "They are not truly loose; they got away just that one time."

I exploded. "And you killed Thomas. He was an ally, a powerful one! We needed him, Berget!"

"I can control them!"

My hands flexed and the pain soared through them. No one else needed to hold the burden of having to kill her. But how the hell was I going to do it when I couldn't even hold a sword?

"What happened to your hands?"

"Orion."

Her head lowered. "If you shared blood with Doran, he could heal them the rest of the way, you know that."

Shit, she was right. But that would mean taking another side trip to London, then back here and, without Thomas, I wasn't sure how much Frank could do. "How much juice do you have left, Frank?"

He cleared his throat and ran a hand over his hair. "One jump, maybe two if I have a rest."

"Talk about a fucking quandary," I muttered. Then again, I knew in my heart I was desperately looking for a reason to not kill Berget. I did not want to make my parents right, to become the murderer they'd accused me of being all those years ago.

The best I could do was keep Berget close and hope to hell I could handle her and any other blow ups she would have. A part of me knew I was being delusional, that eventually it would come to that. But I would put it off as long as I could.

Erik cleared his throat. "When did you last feed?"

Berget shook her head. "I don't remember, it's been too long and they wouldn't let me feed once my parents went on a rampage. I am holding them tight right now, and they are behaving, I think because they know our lives are on the line."

There were not a lot of options, and I was seeing only one way out of two major problems. So I did what I always did and didn't think too much about the possible consequences. I stepped close to Berget, cupped the back of her head, and pushed her mouth toward my neck. She fought me at first, but her hunger won out and her teeth sunk into my neck.

A rush of adrenaline coursed through me, the first time I'd ever felt anything other than pain or disinterest (as with Doran) when being bitten by a vampire. I realized, as she drank my blood, it was the power she held humming just under her skin that I felt. I knew she was strong, but I'd had no idea just *how* strong until that moment. It made me realize how much Berget had been fighting even when her parents were in control and how much she'd slowed them. If the three ever decided to work in tandem . . . I couldn't help the shudder that slipped through me. We'd be royally fucked up shit's creek with no paddles and crocodiles coursing alongside us.

"Enough." I stepped back.

"It won't be, not if it's been a long time," Erik grunted as he stepped up and let Berget bite into the crook of his elbow.

I went to Frank while Berget fed. "Thank you. I know it was dangerous what I asked you to do."

He shrugged, his face visibly pinking, even in the darkness. "I want to help. And I don't think she wanted to kill Thomas. But Doran is going to be pissed at me. I'd like to stay with you."

He was scared of Doran? Looked like the age-old adversary thing was already coming into play. "Did he say something to you?"

"No, just . . . I don't know, he's a vampire. And he said that no one was to go near Berget."

"He had her locked up?"

Again, he shrugged. "Just in one of the rooms; it wasn't hard to get her out."

I glanced over my shoulder to see Erik step away from Berget. "Pamela, hang onto her a minute more." I put a hand on Frank's shoulder. "Thank you. And yeah, you can stay with us. I think you can help with this next salvage."

Frank gave me a tentative smile. "I'd like that."

I went back to Berget, holding my hands up to her. "Okay. Let's see you do your magic."

She gave me a smile and a tingle rippled along my arms and through my hands, the last of the pain evaporating under her temporary bond to me as the healing progressed at a rapid pace. I flexed my hands, the aches and pains of fighting Orion completely gone. There was only one thing left to do.

I pulled a sword from my back and whipped it forward stopping a hairsbreadth from removing her head from her shoulders. "You two, inside Berget, listen up. I will take her head and end all three of your lives if you force my hand. I hope you understand that."

A voice rumbled out of her lips that was most definitely not hers.

"Crystal clear, Tracker."

Berget gasped, her eyes widened. "I didn't know they could do that."

I lowered the blade and gave Pamela a nod. "Let her go." I put my sword back. "I'm not surprised, they have been holding back, I think, letting us all get comfortable with the idea of them being trapped. We have to find a way to separate you from them in a more final way."

Like so much though, that would have to wait.

One freaking disaster at a time.

9

"Frank." I touched his arm and he spun toward me, eyes unfocused. Shit, this was not a good start. "Pull it together, would you?"

He stared through me and I knew Berget was standing behind me without even Tracking her.

"I really don't like vampires, but I don't understand why." Despite the tremor in his body, his words were clear.

"Long-standing family feud, I think, but it doesn't matter. You have to deal with it. Thomas couldn't; be better than him," I said, making sure my body blocked his line of sight.

Blinking, he finally focused on me. "I will do my best."

Alex and Pamela stood off to one side, or rather, Pamela stood and Alex sat, scratching at his ears with his back feet. Neither seemed particularly worried about this upcoming adventure. Hell, I was struggling with this, but I wasn't the only one.

"Rylee, what will Marco and I do? Where should we go?" Eve was worried, and she wasn't trying to hide it.

"Head to London. Tell them what we are doing and make sure Liam knows I won't be long."

For a moment, I wished Blaz were with us, maybe him and Ophelia, even if she was a bit off her rocker. They were Immune to magic like I was, and with that many coven members turned to the dark side, there would be a serious amount of magic thrown around.

Then again . . . I could just see two marauding dragons wiping out half of Boston in an effort to kill the black coven. Yeah, how would the humans explain that one away? No, as much as I would've liked him to be with us, there was no way we could take Blaz or Ophelia.

"We need to be quick with this salvage." A trio of covens against me, Alex, Pamela, Frank, and Erik. I couldn't pin any hopes on Berget. She could end up being as much of a liability as a help.

I scrubbed a hand over my face to hide the sudden flash of doubt that crept through me.

Erik stepped up and then pulled me aside. "It's not just the coven you are worried about, is it?"

No, it wasn't. My parents were in Boston, and I had a bad feeling fate was going to allow them into my life one more time. Even with Berget with me as proof I didn't kill her, I was still afraid to see them. Afraid it would stir up all the weakness in me, something I really didn't need. Not now, not with the future riding on my shoulders. "No, my parents live there. The ones who adopted me."

My uncle gave a slow nod. "The chances of you seeing them are slim at best. Boston is a big city. They won't even know you are there."

Erik did his best to soothe me, but I couldn't get past feeling like I was sixteen again. Watching my parents tell the police to take me away, that they didn't ever want to see me again. That somehow they would know how close I'd just come to actually killing Berget. Making their accusations the truth.

I centered my breathing as Pamela and Alex moved closer.

"Are we going?" Pamela asked softly, the sound of her voice breaking through my anxiety.

I cleared my throat. "Yup."

Frank gave me one last look over his shoulder and then opened the Veil with a slash of his hand. Through the cut in the air we looked into a darkened room with only a single light and a window illuminating the place. Where it was, I had no idea.

"You sure that's Boston?"

Frank grimaced. "Yes. Hurry, I can't hold this very long."

Berget, Alex, Pamela, Erik, and Frank stepped through the Veil, but I paused on the threshold to look back, feeling a tug on my heart. Ten feet behind me, a shadow stood, watching us go. Our eyes met and a stroke of pain sliced through me. If he'd been solid and not some figment of my imagination, I would have run to him and let him catch me. No words, nothing could truly define the emotions rushing through me. Love, fear, worry, the safety of his arms when he held me, the way he smiled from just the corner of his mouth.

I didn't want to think about what it meant that I was seeing a specter of Liam when I knew he was across the ocean with Blaz. "Eve, please hurry. Make sure Liam is okay."

She squawked and launched into the air, Marco right with her.

I nodded, more to myself than anyone else, and turned from where we'd all come through. Time to deal with what was at hand. "Berget, how are you feeling?"

Her eyes slid to half-mast for a split second. "They are sleeping now. You do not have to check on me every few minutes. I will tell you if something changes."

"Did you feel that change before you attacked Thomas?" I wasn't trying to cause shit, but seriously needed to know. She flushed and the dim light of the building didn't hide the color from me.

Bingo. That was what I was worried about. If she couldn't feel them sliding up and taking control, we could be in serious trouble.

I ran my hands over my weapons: both swords, a whip, and a multitude of smaller blades here and there. "Pamela, you have your short sword?"

"Yes."

I stared around the room. Where the hell were we? The night was full on in Boston, and the sound of cars zipping by and flashes of headlights were the only indications we were at least somewhere near a main road.

The short winter days were a boon to us, even if the weather was shit. The room we stood in was bitterly cold with a damp bite that made me think of England. I'd spent too many years in Boston; my body immediately recognized the cold. North Dakota was far preferable to this.

It didn't take me long to put together the rudiments of a plan. Liam would be proud. "Frank, you got enough juice to raise the dead?"

He pushed his glasses up his nose. "For sure. How many do you want?"

I let out a slow breath. "Enough to piss off three covens, so really, as many as you can. They will be a good distraction. I'm thinking if we can keep them busy long enough, maybe we can slip in and out without them knowing we are even there."

Pamela, though, was already shaking her head. "They could pick up on me as I get closer, though. Milly said witches with experience can sense other witches."

"We don't have a choice. Besides, with so many witches there, you think you are going to stand out?" Maybe I was missing something.

"Everyone has their own magical signature," she said, her eyes narrowing like I'd pissed her off. "They won't recognize me as one of theirs."

I let out a sigh and Tracked witches as a whole. I got a ping off Pamela, but I worked around it, looking for the central mass of witches I'd felt earlier. Tying that to the threads of the three kids, India, Kyle, and Simon, I had a perfect bead on where they were. If I knew where *we* were, that would help, though.

"Berget, any idea where we are?" I took another look around the room.

"Near the Colonial Theatre," she answered, moving silently to my side. "This is one of the few buildings that still stands from the early 1900s and has been a safe house for my kind for as long as it has stood." Her words were soft and I heard the echo of her parents behind what she said. She knew only because her parents, her vampire parents, had been here before.

"Great, didn't need the history lesson." I did my best to soften the words as they shot out of me, but I was nervous as hell. Berget's eyes met mine in a silent communication.

"I'm sorry. I take much from them."

"Wasn't them I'm worried about. They know I'll kill them if they step out of line again." I gritted my teeth and then Berget seemed to get what I was really worried about.

She moved to my side, her eyes worried. "They won't know we're here."

"Still too fucking close for my taste," I muttered, my hands going to weapons out of sheer habit, the feel of them soothing my anxiety only a little.

Pamela cleared her throat. "Well, we are trying to get there without them noticing, aren't we?"

Of course, Pamela didn't realize I was referring to my parents, mine and Berget's, and not the coven.

Berget covered for me. "Yes, of course that's what we're trying to do."

I looked at our group. Erik and I were pretty much bristling with weapons, Alex didn't have his collar anymore, which meant it was fucking good it was dark out. Frank, Pamela, and Berget looked the most "normal" of the six of us.

"I'll take the lead with Berget. Erik, you and Alex bringing up the rear. Frank, you stick close to Pamela and listen to her."

"She's younger than me," he muttered, but I heard him.

"She's also a hell of a lot more experienced with this kind of shit than you are," I snapped, my temper and nerves getting the better of me. Again. Perfect. I grimaced. "Let's get the fuck out of here then and get this over with."

I started toward the side of the empty building, assuming I would find a door at some point. Alex trotted beside me, disappearing in the darkness, only a faint glimmer of his eyes giving him away. Pamela lit a small globe of fire above her hand and I cringed. Pamela and fire were a bad combination.

She saw my flinch and frowned at me, her face in shadows from the flame. "I can do this better now. Milly taught me how."

I hoped to hell she was right. The last time she'd helped with a little fire she'd burnt down a house. With me in it.

This time, we made it to the door with no major issues other than a softly whistling Erik.

I pushed the door open and into the wane light of a weak looking moon. Dark storm clouds hung distended over the city, thick and ominous, which made the night even uglier than it normally would be. The wind was not strong, not like North Dakota, but the bite of the air was damp and heavy.

The street we were on was fairly quiet. A side street with a dead end and no active stores, dirty and abandoned. At the other end of the dead end, traffic zipped by; no one even looked our way as the humans rushed about their lives. Like watching a movie, we all stood, staring at the flash and blink of traffic, the constant flow a perfect foil to the nearly silent alley in which we stood.

"It's like we don't really exist," Pamela said softly, echoing the feeling that rippled through me. The humans were blind to the world around them; I could only hope that would include my parents.

"Let's try to keep it that way." I paused, checking the traffic before preparing to cross the lanes.

Alex took that moment to act like a bucking bronco, laughing and jumping about, arching his back and throwing his body every which way for no apparent reason. Not unusual for him.

"Alex, not now," I snapped, my nerves twanging at the high end of the stress meter.

He stilled midair, dropping to all fours. "Sorry."

Doing my best to not snap again, I jogged out of the alley, Berget beside me and everyone else lining up like I'd wanted. I wondered what people would see when they looked at Alex or if they would even see him in the dark night. Probably not, or at least, I was banking on that.

There were no screeching tires, no honking horns as we jogged down the sidewalk. So I assumed whatever the humans saw didn't bother them.

Score one for us.

I held tight to the threads of the black coven members, let the emotions the group was feeling keep my mind busy, and for a split second I wished I hadn't. My throat tightened with horror.

The black coven members were running on a high of elation that could only mean one thing.

They'd managed to bring a demon through.

Which meant one of the kids was done.

"Fucking hell."

10

Boston hadn't changed much since I'd left and I found myself retracing steps I'd taken years past. At a major intersection, my feet stilled. To the left was Beacon Street, and from there we were within a few minutes of being in front of my parent's house.

My heart pounded as I thought about how long it would take. No more than ten minutes. I could spare that. Berget put a hand out. "You don't have to, Rylee. You don't owe them anything."

She was right, and she was wrong. Where would I have ended up if my life hadn't played out they way it had? Would I have found Giselle? Would I have Liam in my life? As horrible as my parents had been, I had to see them. Just one more time.

"Do you want to see them?"

She shook her head, almost violently. "No. I don't want anything to do with them."

That made this easier in some ways.

"Stay here." I pointed at the intersection and didn't wait for the others to answer as I bolted down Beacon Street at full speed. My guts churned and a pang started to wind its way through me. I wasn't sure if I wanted to puke or if my heart was just trying to explode.

This was fucking ridiculous. We were in the middle of a major battle, of fighting for the world's safety, and I decided I needed a detour into the past. What the hell was wrong with me? My rational mind told me to turn around, what was done was done and there would be no changing it. I knew that. But the little girl from my past, the girl I'd been so many years ago, who huddled inside me, the one who was afraid and weak, the one who cried for her parents when no one was looking, she wouldn't be denied. Not this time.

I had to see the ones who'd raised me, the ones I'd loved more than any others in the world, even after they'd turned me out. Even after they believed the worst of me.

I pushed all that away and ran as fast as I could. If I was going to do this, I was doing it fast. And with that decision, the anxiety fled, and I knew I'd made the right decision. I had to reconcile this part of my life before I fully committed myself to being the one to stop Orion.

The buildings around me took me back to my childhood, the expensive homes, the money that was as abundant as the air we breathed. Brownstones for the most part and the occasional fancy custom-built house were everywhere, but I didn't hesitate in my footsteps. Didn't pause in my run. My feet knew where they were going and they took me home unerringly, with a spooky déjà vu that washed through me.

I stumbled to a stop in front of the building I'd grown up in. Made of brick, there were units on each floor. Third floor was where we'd lived. The fence was wrought iron and the gate was keyed, there was no way I should have been able to get in. Except for the fact I could short circuit electrical devices just by touching them. I lifted my hand to the keypad, wondering if the pass number would be the same. My fingers hesitated as I stared at the top floor. Behind me a car pulled up, slowed, stopped, and then a door slammed. My hearing slowly came back online and it was only then I realized I was nearly hyperventilating.

"Oh, my dear, isn't that your daughter?"

I didn't recognize the voice, but I turned and the world slowed to a halt. A limo had pulled over and four people were stepping out, two couples. One set I vaguely recognized, friends of my parents, they'd been over for dinner a number of times during my childhood. The woman of the couple, she stared at me with her mouth hanging open and her hazel eyes wide with shock. Her trim body and meticulous makeup made her look far younger than she was. Leanne was her name, if I remembered right. She'd been friends with my mother since I was a child.

The other two people, they were far more familiar.

Amelia and Robert Adamson.

My parents.

Fuck, Amelia looked like Berget, even more so now that Berget was older. Nearly white blonde hair, bright blue eyes, and features that would make angels weep for her beauty, even now. Dressed in a pale blue dress, it peeked out from beneath her long white woolen coat. Robert was slim, had his light brown hair slicked back; he was every inch the professional businessman in his Gucci suit. Her eyes widened and then narrowed like a set of shutters.

"No, our only child was killed, you know that, Leslie," Amelia said, brushing past me so close I caught a whiff of her perfume, a sweet musk, a scent that made my knees buckle with longing to be a child again. To be held and kept safe from the monsters waiting for me in the dark.

To have my mother love and protect me.

Pain, sharp and intense, flared through my chest seeming to rocket through my soul. Robert, my dad, met my eyes and there was sadness there, and I thought for a minute maybe he would say something.

But no, not against Amelia. I held my hand out to him unable to stop myself from trying. His lower lips trembled and a glimmer of tears shaded his blue eyes.

"I can't. I'm sorry, Rylee."

Amelia whipped around, her face no longer one angels would weep for. More like run from, with the way her lips contorted and her eyes burned with anger.

"Don't you speak to her! She is not our child, she is a murderer!"

Robert took his eyes from me. "Amelia, you're wrong, she didn't kill Berget. Not Rylee."

The tears that had been hovering in my eyes flowed down my cheeks. He believed me; my father believed I hadn't killed Berget. That made this worth it, to know one of them believed.

"Rylee, will you come in?" He held his hand out to me and Amelia choked back a sound that seemed caught between rage and horror as she slapped his hand down. Not that it mattered.

"I just—" I shook my head and slid a hand over my hip my finger brushing against my back pocket. "I can't right now. I just wanted to see you," I said, feeling awkward and unsure, like I was a teenager again.

Robert gave me a small smile, reached out and took my hand. "When you can, come and see us. There are a lot of years to catch up on. A lot of things that need to be worked out. Apologies to be given."

Amelia spun and stormed toward the house, her back rigid, head held high. None of that mattered as my father pulled me gently into his arms, somehow holding me around all my weapons.

"I should have stood up for you then, Rylee. It is my only regret in life, that I let you go when we lost Berget," he whispered into my ear and I all but collapsed against him. His arms supported me and I clung to him as the tears flowed and the pain that had been with me for so long eased. He patted my back and kissed my cheek. "I am sorry, Rylee. Truly and deeply sorry. We can make this better, though, if you are willing."

The words were those I'd wanted to hear for the last ten years. That things could be better, that I could have my family back.

I lifted my head and stepped back, swallowing hard, and fighting to speak normally. "I'll come back when I can."

His eyes flicked over me, seeming to finally see my weapons, the leather jacket, the hard lines of a body that had been trained to work beyond natural limits.

"Be safe, my girl, whatever you're doing, be safe." He kissed the back of my hands like he'd done when I was a little girl, when I'd done something smart or right.

I backed away sliding my hands from his, knowing if I didn't I would never leave, that I would break down on the doorstep of my home and let the world go to hell in a poorly woven basket.

Lifting one hand to him in a weak wave, I said nothing more. Couldn't talk past the lump in my throat. With quick steps I spun and headed away from them.

When I hit the corner and was out of sight I broke into a jog and it wasn't very long before I was back on the street corner with a very nervous looking Pamela, Frank, Alex, Berget, and Erik.

"What the hell was that, Rylee?" Erik asked, his eyes narrowed as if that would somehow make me spill the beans.

"Sorry." I shook off the emotions tangling up my heart and mind, or at least tried to. Already, the guilt of taking the detour was eating at me. A demon had been brought through and was possessing one of the kids, and I fucked off for a family reunion. Not really good form, no matter how you looked at it.

Pamela peppered me with questions, but I evaded them, finally going silent. I knew I was probably freaking them out, but I couldn't talk about it.

They followed me as we worked our way through town. Berget never said anything, never even asked if I'd seen our parents. She knew me well enough not to push, which was funny because we had been apart for years.

That didn't slow the others, or more pointedly, Pamela.

"Look," I finally barked, coming to a standstill on the south side of the Charlestown Bridge. "It was personal. It has nothing to do with any of you or this fucking salvage or whatever the hell this is."

I started across the bridge, my eyes taking in the heavy utilitarian girders, focused on everything but my team ranging in behind me. Near the middle of the span I stopped and let them catch up.

"I went to see my adoptive parents."

Pamela's breath caught and I knew that she, of all those who stood with me, would understand. Her own parents had handed her over to a handful of overzealous priests to have her "exorcised" of the "demons" in her.

"What did they say?" She slid a hand over one of mine as the first flakes of snow dropped from the sky.

"My father wants me to come back to see them," I whispered the words, still unsure how I felt about that. Happy, freaked out, uncertain. Erik said nothing, but there was understanding in his eyes. Family was important to him too. Berget was unreadable, and for that I was grateful. I wasn't sure what she thought about our parents. I wondered how much she even remembered of them.

Frank was the last one I thought would have anything helpful to say. But he shocked me. "Parents love you, even when they are afraid of you. They can't help it; they will always want to believe the best of their kids. Even my mom was like that, with me raising the dead when I couldn't help it; I scared her so badly she passed out on a regular basis. But she still loved me. Even when she asked me to move in with my uncle."

I turned to look at him, and in his young eyes I saw a wisdom that shouldn't have surprised me. "Thanks.

You're right, I guess." I blew out breath, catching a few flakes of snow and spinning them away from my face. "That being said, we still have a job to do. We have to take out the covens and get those kids away." I refrained from mentioning that one of those kids was already lost to us. "To be safe, we'll stake them out for a bit."

"We aren't going in right away?" Pamela asked as we headed over the last half of the bridge.

"No, we need to see if we can figure out the best way in and out, where Frank will place his friends, and see if we can find out where the witches are exactly."

The threads of the coven were growing stronger, getting closer with each step we took. There was very little time before we'd have to go in and face the black witches, rescue the two kids who hadn't been possessed, and kill the one who had been taken over by a demon.

Yup, good times ahead.

Tracking the witches was easy. Simple. And we found them at the Navy Shipyard.

Contrary to the name, there was no navy waiting for us. A shipyard for repairs and construction on big boats. Yeah, I know, not very technical but I was no boat buff. The docks were not active; the night had cleared out most of the humans. Good and bad, it was harder for us to blend in when it was just us walking the docks as compared to say the bustle of mid-day.

"How close are we?" Erik asked, breaking the silence.

I stopped and looked to the far end of the docks, an old navy ship in the farthest berth bobbed lightly in the water. I squinted, using my measly second sight, and could see the lay of spells on the hull. They shimmered and danced in the blowing snow. If I didn't know that it was black magic and witches, I would have thought the boat almost pretty. "That one, at the end. Why?"

Erik didn't answer me. Instead he asked Frank a question. "How many dead can you sense?"

The kid cocked his head to one side, as if listening for voices only he could hear. "There's a lot of dead people around here."

But I had a suspicion I knew what he was talking about.

"In the water?"

He nodded and pointed to a rope ladder that spun down to touch the dark water. "Yeah, there are a lot in the water, but to get them up to the dock might take a bit of work. Zombies aren't known for being coordinated."

"I can lift them if there is a part of them dry from the salt water," Pamela said. "But like I said, the other witches will be able to sense me working my magic, so I don't know if it's a good idea."

Berget tipped her head. "If there was something solid for me to stand on, I could throw the zombies onto the boat."

Neither option looked good.

Crap, without a secure way to bring the zombies out of the water, I wasn't sure it was going to be worth it.

"Frank, are there any dead bodies closer? Some from dry ground, perhaps?"

He rubbed his forehead. "No, sorry there aren't."

I wanted to groan and beat my head against the dock. "Well, we'll just have to run with it and hope the gods are looking out for us."

Frank and Pamela nodded and Erik lifted an eyebrow at me. I lifted an eyebrow right back at him.

"Let's get closer, find a spot to hunker down and get a good look at these fuckers." I led the way, finding a small alcove about a couple hundred feet from the boat. A part of my brain was ticking away at a small problem, one that no one had pointed out.

"Why the hell would they be on a boat?" I muttered.

Alex lay at my feet, his eyes glowing in the darkness. He tipped his head up, and mimicked Frank, cocking it to one side. "So they can go swimming easy."

Erik laughed softly, but the laugh on my lips died. "Fucking hell, he's right."

"What?"

"Salt water nulls spells. If you were raising demons and running spells that could end your life if you weren't careful, wouldn't you want a big-ass amount of salt water around?" I crouched, elbows on my knees and hands under my chin. "This is their fail-safe, the harbor could save their asses and they know it."

Pamela's mouth dropped open. "How did Alex know?"

Alex grunted and rolled to his back, tongue flipping out between his teeth as he grinned up at us. "I is smarty smart now."

Whether or not he knew didn't really matter, I was sure it was the reason behind them being here. I stared at the big boat, eyed the only gangplank onto it. It looked about three feet wide and wasn't secured on either side; just a piece of wood going across a slim portion of water between the dock and the boat.

I gave them all a hard look, one at a time. "You all stay here. I'm going to get a closer look. Frank, if I give you a thumbs up, you start raising your buddies. Let them just float to the surface of the water. Pamela, I'll give a closed fist for lifting them out of the water and onto the deck of the boat. Berget, you see if you can circle around, come in from a different angle."

Frank pushed his glasses up his nose and then rubbed his arms. Pamela gave me a grim smile. Some days I thought maybe she enjoyed the fighting a little too much. One more thing to discuss when we finally had our little heart to heart. Berget gave a short nod and with her spooky-ass speed, ran around to the other side of the docks, disappearing as she leapt onto the boat with a single bound.

"I'm going with you, Niece."

I didn't argue with Erik—no point—and I didn't really mind. He was a good man to have at my back. Crouching, I scooted forward until I was behind a set of crates about ten feet away from the gangplank, Erik tight on my heels. From there, I peered around the corner without exposing my body.

Fifteen minutes passed with no movement on the boat, and no feeling of much of anything from the witches or the kids. Everything was pretty quiet. It made me nervous.

The waves splashed against the dock below and I looked back toward my group. On the dock, the snow had accumulated and, fuck it all, Alex crept forward, leaving large footprints in the snow. I glared at him, but he didn't slow until he was at my side.

"Boss says watch over you." He sat, wagged his tail and looked up at me. "I keep you safe."

Nothing I could do now.

The minutes passed and the snow fell, coating everything around us. That would make the plank slick, and even more deadly to cross. I signaled to Frank, giving him a thumbs up.

I didn't feel anything, didn't sense a disturbance in the force, as it were. A loud splash from below drew my eyes down. There, to one side of the boat, bodies floated to the surface. And damn they were nasty.

"Stinkers," Alex grumbled. That they were. The zombies had not been well-preserved, and I wondered how so much flesh remained when they'd been in salt water for hell knew how long. Bones stuck through in a lot of places, flashes of white in the water, dark pits for eyes. I shuddered, remembering the old vampires we'd faced in the Australian desert. They'd started out with dark pits for eyes too.

The zombies floated along, like lazy vacationers, as the clouds above us opened up and icy cold rain poured around us. At least that would serve Pamela well in raising the zombies out of the water, rinsing portions of them clean of the salt.

A scream erupted from the deck of the boat, a woman's voice letting out the sound of sheer terror across the docks, and I froze. Slowly, moving so I could see around the crate, I peered up at the deck.

"Fuck me," I whispered.

A flash of a blue dress and a dark   aught my eyes.

I didn't know how the witches managed to grab them and beat us here, but the black coven had my parents.

11

At some point, the darkness began to fade and he knew he wasn't going to die. He lay on the cold, bare ground, the sharp winter wind coursing through the night air, ruffling his fur. But he could feel the discomfort, and that meant he was alive. Hands wrapped around him, the scent of a woman filling his nose. He recognized her and the wolf in him identified the pack bond between them.

Voices floated in his ears and around his head.

"You can't move him until I finish the healing. It was started, but there was too much hate in the one who did the healing. Too much anger."

His wolf took another deep breath, scenting the two women who were arguing. Neither was his mate, both were shamans. A growl slipped past his lips and the hands on him increased in pressure in response.

"Be still, Liam. I can heal you, but this will take time."

That was Louisa, her name floated to the front of his brain. Louisa was in New Mexico . . . he forced one eyelid up. It was like trying to lift a truck with one finger, but he managed.

The movement around him was a blur of bodies and faces. He caught sight and scent of a few he knew. But not Rylee.

He tried to whisper her name, forgetting he was still in wolf form.

"It's okay, baby, I'm here."

He rolled his one eye to see a panel of long dark hair swing down and brush his face. Her hand reached out to take something from under him. The copper knife that had caused him so much pain, that had almost killed him.

Something he didn't want anyone else to have.

Snarling, he drove her back, his body barely able to lurch forward. She squealed and dropped the copper knife. The scent of burnt wood curled around him and then Blaz's voice was there.

Get away from him, bitch. You are not his mate.

The woman backed away, her teeth bared at them both. "He is mine. He just doesn't know it yet." Liam struggled to understand how she had gotten here. Wasn't she supposed to be in London? Not on the cold dirt outside of Louisa's house.

With Blaz beside him, he lowered back to the ground. Louisa moved to his head.

"This may hurt, Liam. Try not to bite me, I like not being hairy." Her hands smoothed along his jaw, down his neck and settled over the wound in his chest.

Pain was not the word, nor was agony. It felt as though the copper knife was being dug into the wound while on fire; acid burning his flesh couldn't have hurt as badly.

A howl ripped out of him, but he kept his mouth away from Louisa. She would heal him; she had to.

Otherwise, how could he die for Rylee?

There was no time to wait. I made a fist and raised my arm; Pamela ran to my side. She snapped her hands in front of her and the zombies, dripping wet and covered with seaweed and barnacles, were lifted out of the water. She moved them toward the boat, dropping them on the deck as fast as she could. I did a head count. Fifty, and they were already going to work, disappearing into the depths of the boat.

But no witches came out to inspect who was using magic. Not one.

"Let's go," I barked out and then pointed at the gangplank.

Frank ran to catch up with us as we crossed the gangplank, one by one. The fucking thing shuddered underneath us and as Frank crossed, it slipped and fell, taking him with it.

I dove back, catching his hand before he fell far, though his eyes were wide and startled.

"Pam, little help here."

She grunted. "Can't, not with you touching him."

There were moments my immunity to magic really sucked ass. This was one of them. Putting my feet against the edge of the boat, I pulled hard, Erik reached over and helped me haul Frank onto the deck. I didn't give him time to be freaked out about what had almost happened.

"Make sure your zombies only go after the witches."

Frank gasped a breath as he nodded, his hands on his knees. "Yeah, doing my best."

Now came the fun part.

I led the way, Tracking witches and the three kids, but also now Tracking my dad. He was alive, but hurt. The threads of so many lives tangled inside my head and I struggled to keep it together. It had been a long time since the emotions of a salvage ran rampant through me, longer still since they had caused me to slow down.

One thought rose above the rest. How in hell had the witches known about my parents? Had they been following us? It was the only answer that made sense. They knew we were coming.

Which also meant they knew we were here.

Fucking hell. "They know we're here. We go in guns blazing. Got it?"

Frank and Pamela nodded in tandem, and she pushed her sleeves up her thin arms. "Everything we've got?"

"Everything. We have to kill them all."

Frank paled. "What about those who don't fight?"

"Use your discretion, Frank."

Erik locked eyes with me. "There are at least two demons in this boat."

Crap. I knew one of the kids had been possessed, but had I missed one of the others going under? "How can you tell?"

He tapped his head. "Different than Tracking, but you should be able to sense them as we get near. I'll explain later."

Of course, that was assuming we'd all have a later.

I locked onto the threads of my parents. They were the bait as much as the three kids, and I would take it. Hook, line, and sinker. Only the witches were the ones going to do the sinking.

With a quick twist, I had my sword in one hand, my whip in the other. No more words needed. I ran forward, navigating the narrow halls of the ship, taking us on a direct route where the trap was most likely set.

The halls were tight, grey, and empty. Good and bad. Meant we would be able to get where we needed to go without much problem. We rounded a final corner and the hallway opened into a huge room that had tiers of walkways descending to the lower level. Four levels of tiers, and all empty. I looked at the bottom floor, over the edge of the railing.

A pentagram was carved into the metal and inside the protective bubble of the spell being spun, a witch was on her knees, bound and gagged, a collar on her neck with a large ruby in it visible even at this distance. The collar was like the one Milly had been caught by, and it would force the witch to do what the black coven wanted. That must have been how they had so many members pulled together in such a small area. There was another figure inside the pentagram, but I couldn't get a good look at that one.

My gut twisted as I looked over the coven. There, to the left was my mom's friend, Leanne, a smile on her face. Suddenly the answer to "how did the coven know I was here and that taking my parents would draw me in" was answered. Fuck, fuck, fuckers. I would have come for the kids either way, but my par-

ents—the witches must have wanted insurance that I
would show.

But why? Why want me there if they knew I was
going to try and stop them?

Around them were most of the black coven, if I was
reading things right. They stared up at me, some with
malice, others with apparent glee. Leanne waved, the
stupid cow.

Well fuck them, too, and the brooms they rode in
on.

"Frank and Pamela, you stick together, fight from
here, run if you have to. Erik, you go after the demons. Alex, with me." I didn't wait for them, hated
that I had to ask so much of them, but it was the way
of things.

I ran for the guard rail, grabbed it, and swung over
and down, snapping my legs at the last instant so I
landed on the level below. I didn't feel like trying my
luck at flying through the air all the way to the bottom. Something zipped by my head as Alex landed
beside me. It looked like a large bullet, about a foot
long and pointy, making holes in walls and bodies.
Maybe something left from the ship's fighting days.
Didn't matter, it could still take me out, and the coven
obviously knew it. The joy of everyone knowing I was
an Immune was that they knew magic could hurt me
only through indirect means.

"Fun stuff, Rylee." Alex danced in place beside me,
his golden eyes sparkling.

"Always fun with me, buddy."

He snickered and we repeated the process of using
the momentum of our fall to flick our bodies onto the

level below us. Again, things flew our way, but then the coven was somewhat distracted by a shuffling, groaning, stinking mob.

The zombies had arrived. They fell over the railings and onto the floor below, not even bothered by the four-story drop. I caught a glimpse of the zombies as they moved en masse toward the black coven, surrounding the one woman in the center of the pentagram.

If the witches stopped their spelling now, there was a good chance the demon couldn't be brought through and, from what I understood, it was a hell of a lot of work. Not to mention the backlash, which could be ugly if the spell suddenly went wild and out of control.

The witches held their ground while the zombies bit and grabbed at them. Alex and I hit the floor at the same time, my feet stinging with the impact. There was no hesitation though, there couldn't be.

There were at least two dozen black coven members and I could see four witches with collars. The black coven had taken the few good witches left and forced them to help by the looks of things. Bad, bad juju.

The first coven member had his back to me and I didn't wait for him to notice me, I just drove my sword through his heart. Normally I'd take his head, but with Frank up top, I was hoping he could make use of a few more bodies. Sure enough, the second the witch died, Frank brought him back and he lunged for the coven member closest to him.

Alex dove into the fray, biting legs and taking people out at the knees before grabbing them around the neck. He hit hard and fast, and they barely had time to lift their hands to lay a spell on him.

"Alex, with me!"

He listened, ranging behind me as I cut into the co-ven members. Though they may have been expecting us, they sure as hell weren't prepared.

Or so I thought.

The woman in the center arched her back and I dove through the bubble into the center of the pentagram with her. While it would keep me safe for the moment from the witches outside the circle, it brought me face to face with—

"Oh fuck," I whispered, for the first time really see-ing the woman at my feet. Her long blonde hair and tattered blue dress.

I bent and grabbed her arm as the demon started to pull itself through the pentagram.

"Amelia, get up!" I yanked her hard, unable to be kind in that moment.

"Rylee, this is a dream. What's happening? Don't touch me!" Her blue eyes were confused, but I didn't have time to explain anything, certainly not that her world was about to be flipped upside-down.

"Stay back." I didn't recognize the demon, but it was ugly, like a hound with three sets of wings sprout-ing from its back and the jaws of an alligator. Fucking hell.

I stayed between Amelia and the demon, and from the corner of my eye I saw Alex get to those witches with collars. He knocked one down, ripping the collar off. He was thinking about the long term, which was good. If we could get the captive witches un-collared, then they might be able to help. Or at least, they wouldn't be forced to attack us. Alex was thinking, unlike my idiotic self.

The demon hound lunged at me and I spun to one side, coming down hard with my sword at the base of its neck. The blade dug deep, but the hound just laughed as the sword stuck and ripped from my hand.

"Stupid, stupid, little Tracker. Your hate is sweet on my tongue." To emphasize, he flicked his tongue out and curled it up and around his nose, dipping it into the oversized nostril.

I didn't hate my mom. But my mom sure as shit hated me, and that hatred was feeding the demon.

"That's not me you're tasting, you fucker." I pulled a short blade from my lower back and held it out in front of me. "That's her hatred, and that's why I can do this."

I dropped the knife and put my hand out like Erik had done, laying it on the demon's face. Every good memory I had of my mom, the sweet moments in the past, I relived: baking with her, the feel of her hands on my hair as she braided it, the joy of seeing her smile at something I'd done well.

The demon hound howled and curled back from me, scrambling to get away, but it was too late, the damage was done. He lit up from within, like a lightning bug, going still as a statue and then exploding into nothing more than dust. Red and bone-colored dust, but still just dust.

The bubble around us dissolved and the sounds of fighting beat down on my ears—blood-curdling screams and the groans of the ship as it took stray hits.

"Stay out of the way," I yelled over my shoulder at Amelia as I bent to scoop up my blade. Or at least, I tried to.

My second sword was jerked out of my grasp, the blade skittering along the floor and into the hands of a witch I didn't recognize. He was of average height, bald, and he wore a very nice suit. Not Gucci, but nice, the cut flattered his body. A bubble of fear trailed up my throat. The witch didn't scare me, but the demon possessing said witch, that one I did know all too well, and he was more terrifying than any coven. Of course, that didn't stop my mouth.

"What the fuck, Orion, you thinking you can speed things up?" Shit, shit, shit. Bert had been wrong, Orion wasn't going to wait on killing me, and we were going to end up dying because we stupidly believed the gods-be-damned doppelganger demon. I faced him, the chaos raging around us, Amelia cowering behind me.

"No, no, not at all, my dear. Things have changed. I'd like to help you survive a little longer, though you do seem intent on pushing the boundaries of your life at every possible turn. You see, you have something I want very, very badly. Especially since you have spirited away little Zane. He would have been perfect. But I think the irony of what I have planned now is much, much better." He smiled, perfect white teeth that could only have been gained through expensive dentistry and thousands of dollars flashing at me.

"Go fuck yourself." My hand gripped my whip and I wished to hell I hadn't dropped my smaller blade. Sure, it wasn't much, but it was something. Better than nothing, which at that particular moment I wasn't far from.

Orion let out a sigh. "I can't stay long to play, that is the downside of being me, I suppose. But"—he lifted a finger—"I realize this coven is no longer working for me as I wish, and I no longer have a use for them. Too unruly. Unlike our precious Milly."

"Don't you fucking well talk about her!" It was stupid of me, but I couldn't help it, I couldn't just let him talk about her. Behind him, I saw Erik appear, but a witch knocked him back, held him against a wall.

Orion shrugged. "Milly is biddable as always, more so now that she is no longer with child."

Horror flickered through me. "She died."

"I brought her back from the brink. Demons *can* heal, you know." He winked at me like he'd given me some super secret handshake. But all I could think about was the fact that Milly wasn't dead. That she'd survived and was still bound to Orion.

Before I could say anything, his hands swirled upward, clapped above his head. A wave of magic blew out from around him, a boom resembling thunder close on it's heels. The magic ripped through the ship and the metal groaned with the invisible impact. A crack in the floor below me ripped along a seam, bolts twanging out with a speed I couldn't follow with my eyes, and salt water spewed up in a spray. "I will save you the trouble of killing them all."

The water plastered my hair over my face and I pushed it away, frantic to keep my eyes on Orion. What the fuck was he up to? It almost seemed like he wanted to help me, but how could that be?

"Why would you do that? They're your allies." I carefully circled around to where my smaller knife lay on the floor and scooped it up. Amelia stuck close behind me and the coven seemed oblivious that their benefactor was about to do something very, very bad to them.

Orion tipped his head to one side. "You have a precious gift and I want it. They would kill you with no real care of what they would take from the world. From me."

A witch ran behind him in an attempt to get out of the spray of water. He reached out and touched a finger to the back of her head, like a gun. Hell, he even made a shooting noise with his mouth.

The witch's forehead exploded, blood and brains splattering out in front of her. Amelia started to scream as the witch's body fell to the metal floor, her blood mixing with the sea water.

Through the water droplets falling in a briny rain, I stared at Orion. Did I dare try to take him out now? No sword, no magic on my side, nothing but what I'd learned from Erik, and my knife. My hands ached at the thought of doing that again. Of the pain that would rip through me.

"Yes, that was unpleasant, wasn't it?" He let out another sigh. "I must say, I was surprised you had the gumption to do that . . . considering."

I frowned at him. What the fuck was he talking about?

Orion's eyes widened and then he laughed. "Ah, I see you are, as always, somewhat oblivious. Then I will not tell you; far be it from me to steal your secrets away."

Fear thumped through me, the pulse of my blood and heart in tune with the primal understanding that I couldn't kill Orion. I didn't know how and I was too afraid to try again, even though he stood there threatening me.

"What? No 'thank you'?" he said softly, stepping toward me. I stepped back, stumbling over my mother who had fallen to the floor, sobbing.

"You aren't helping me, not really. You're doing whatever the fuck you want just because you can," I snarled as I scrambled back to my feet. Without looking, I grabbed for Amelia and again hauled her behind me. I couldn't even look where we were going. I was too focused on Orion, on his face and eyes, which seemed to suck me into them.

And he was so close.

His face was right in front of mine and a distant part of my brain knew he'd caught me in some sort of thrall, but it was too late, I couldn't stop him. Didn't know how.

"You will come with me, Rylee. I will care for you and when it is time, I will end your life mercifully." He reached up and stroked a hand down my cheek, wiping away tears I'd not even known I was crying. "No more fear; no more fighting; you can finally rest. You can finally be free of all this. I will save you from it, from the pain and hurt." Leaning close, he brushed his lips across mine, drawing a shudder from me. I swayed on my feet, unable to detangle my eyes from his.

I couldn't think, couldn't make my brain function around what he was saying and his touch, how it made me feel. Safe and unafraid. Like with Liam.

With every ounce of willpower I had left, I struggled to pull myself out of his thrall. I wanted to Track Liam, and use his love for me as an anchor. Of course, he would be too far away. So I Tracked Erik. Tapped into his emotions, felt his strength flow through me, felt his love for me as his niece wrap around my heart and . . . fuck this shit.

I snapped my hand out that still held my knife, upward and across Orion's throat. His eyes widened as he tumbled to his knees.

Breathing hard, my chest heaving, I stepped away from him, feeling as though my heart would indeed burst with the effort it was taking just to draw air. "I will never go with you willingly."

A snarl curled his lips as his stolen body fell back with a splash into the pooling water. The shakes took me as I realized how fucking close that had been. Clinging to Erik's threads, like a child clinging to the belief that under the covers was safe from the monsters, had been a close call. I forced myself to look around.

Every single coven member was dead, both those collared and un-collared. Their bodies were blown apart. That's what Orion had done with a single clap of his hands through a witch of power. How much stronger would he be if he took possession of Zane?

"Erik, are you okay?"

My uncle nodded and peeled himself from the wall. "We still have a demon to deal with. One left. And the two other kids."

I Tracked them and had to fight the well of frustration in me. They were another level down and the water was spewing up.

"They are further down. I'll get them. You get my mom out of here."

From three flights up, I finally registered Frank yelling for me. "She's hurt, Pamela's hurt!"

My feet feeling as though lead had been poured into them, I stumbled as I forced them to move. Grabbing Amelia, I hauled her to her feet, her dress and hair soaked through from the salt water. "We have to go. Right now."

She nodded, her eyes blank with fear. "Where's Robert? He tried to stop them from hurting me."

I pushed her ahead of me as I Tracked Robert—my dad—, felt what was left of him on the other side of the room. I sloshed over to where he lay face down in the water, my guts churning.

With one hand, I rolled him over. His neck had been slit, a gaping wound like a second smile grinning at me. I squeezed my eyes shut for split second, the pain of what could have been washing over me. He'd invited me to visit, wanted to make amends for the past and now there was no chance of that, not ever. "I'm sorry, Dad."

But, again, there was no time, no time to grieve. I made my way back to Amelia and again grabbed her arm. I would tell her later what had happened to Robert, but not right then. "Alex, we've got to go."

"Yuppy doody, I is coming." He bounded through the water to us. Hauling my mother behind me, I circled the room. There were no doorways out. "Fucking hell!"

"Rylee, she's not doing well."

Fear for Pamela replaced the pain arching through my body. Whatever Orion had done, it had burned through me when I'd forced his power out, teasing my newly healed synapses. "Sister. Get those two out." I didn't want to use Berget's name and have Amelia have a melt down. I took off my coat and put it around my mom's shoulders. It wasn't much, but it would help keep the chill somewhat at bay.

Erik took my mother and dumped her over his shoulder. "I'll get her out, get the kids."

He set off at a jog to the doorway he'd come through. I bent and scooped up my one sword I could find, sliding it into my back sheath, then followed him. There were steps going up and steps going down.

Down was dark and the water sloshed up from the bottom.

One of these days, it was going to be a beautiful, sun-filled, cookie factory that I had to rescue someone from. I smiled, thinking how fucking ridiculous that sounded even in my own head, and started down the stairs.

Deadly, gloomy, and dangerous, here I come.

12

The stairwell lights flickered as I ran, one hand on the railing. Alex leapt from the top and landed in the water at the bottom with a splash. He ducked his head once and came up slopping wet.

"We have kids to find, Alex." I Tracked all three of them, and found two together. India and Kyle were to the left. The water was up to my knees and I ran as fast as I could, the pull on my muscles dragging at me. It still didn't seem fast enough as the water rose noticeably with each minute that passed. The threads of the two kids were close and seconds later I stopped in front of a door with a large lock. Hadn't thought this through. Fuck.

"India!"

There was a muffled yell from inside the room. "Rylee!"

I kicked the door once, out of frustration more than anything else. How was I going to get them out?

"The answer to the question you are undoubtedly asking is, you aren't getting them out."

I spun to face the direction of the voice. My eyes met those of Simon, the supposed young Tracker, and my heart sank. His eyes should have been swirling with blues and greens. Instead they glowed a steady, dull red as he stared at me.

"You know, I've heard that kind of shit before from other bad guys, and you know what happened?" I pulled a sword from my back and pointed it at him, swirling it slowly.

"Tell me." He smiled, like he knew a secret I didn't.

"They always end up in pieces." I lunged toward him and he dodged my first strike. His hands came up with a speed that screamed "demon" and knocked my blade back as I went in for a second hit. He lost two fingers and a huge slash opened up on the back of his wrist. Alex tried to work his way around, to knock the demon off balance, but it was hard to be stealthy with the rising water.

"Come on, demon," I snarled, knowing I needed to calm the rage in me, but struggling to do so. I was too worried about India and Kyle.

Simon, or what was left of him, looked at his fingers, and then looked at me. His eyes were no longer red, but a single blue tone. He was no Tracker, just a kid pulled into this to make me go where the black coven wanted me to go. Fuck. The prophecy said they needed a Tracker and I'd shown up for them.

They'd used the kid and my parents to get me here, only the whole thing had backfired on them. I'd laugh only if it weren't for the kid in front of me that I was going to have to kill. He was going to pay the price for the coven getting me to show up.

Simon's eyes were full of pain and confusion. "Why?"

Oh shit, I didn't think he'd be able to come through with the demon in control.

"You're possessed by a demon." I lowered the tip of my blade. How did I explain to him there was no way for him to come back? I knew it, but shit, I didn't—

He dove for me, his eyes glittering with hatred as they slid back to a solid glowing red. With my sword down, he hit me in the chest and drove me under the water. The icy cold slid over my head as I dropped my sword, knowing he was too close for me to use it. Damn it all. Even with my eyes open, the dark water was too murky to see through and fuck, his hands were around my neck. I grabbed for a knife, but couldn't reach any of them. Fear and anger raced along my synapses and I fought them both as I tried to keep the panic at bay. My lungs burned as I held my breath and the little bastard's hands tightened around my neck, cutting off blood flow. There was a heavy thump and then I was pushed all the way to the floor. I could almost see Alex jumping on the demon's back, trying to help, but instead pushing me even further down. Fuck, this was bad.

I wrapped my hands around his and tried to pry his fingers open, but they were like vice grips around my neck. Skin to skin, I knew I had no choice but to do things the way Erik had taught me.

Love is not an easy thing to think about when someone is choking you under water. I thought about protecting India and Kyle, about Pamela and Alex. But mostly about Liam. The anger and panic slid away from me and my hands tightened on Simon's, but not fierce and digging in—like I didn't want him to let go.

Power rushed through me, stemming from my heart, from the love I had for those in my life. Without warning, his hands were gone and I sat up in the frigid waters, gasping for air. Simon stared at me as the demon expelled from his body. Like pull taffy, the demon's essence yanked and dragged the kid a few steps before letting go with a pop, fading into the air.

Simon looked at me for a split second, his lips curling into slight smile, his simple blue eyes never leaving mine. "Thank you, I will help you if I can." His eyes rolled into his head and he fell backward into the water with a splash. I gritted my teeth against the hurt that swelled in me as I struggled to my feet. The kid should have had years ahead of him, years where he could've had a life.

And how was he going to help me? He was dead, as much as that hurt. I ignored the hot tears that streaked my face, so at odds with the water that was so fucking cold and rising fast.

I went to the door and put my hands on it. Nothing had changed; I didn't know how the hell I was going to get them out. But neither could I leave them. "Is there anything on our side that could help?"

A muffled no was all I got. Alex whimpered. "Gots to be faster. Water coming."

Of that, I had no doubt. Shivering, I turned to look down the hallway, wondering if there would be anything I could use to pry the door open. I stared at my feet, and my dropped sword stared back at me. The cold must have been getting to me, freezing what was left of my brain cells. I leaned down, and had to put my head under the water in order to grab my sword. Shaking so hard I could barely function, I put the tip to the door's locking mechanism. It was thicker than anything else I'd ever cut with my spelled blades. With a hard thrust, I jammed the blade deep into the heavy metal. Resistance met me and I wondered if the door was spelled too. To be safe, I put my hand on the door in order to dispel any lingering magic on it, but felt nothing. Which meant it was just a freakishly strong door. Sawing my blade back and forth, I worked it down and through the lock. A tidal wave wash of water swept down the hallway as the door opened.

As if things couldn't get worse.

"Hang onto each other!" I yelled, hardly looking at the two kids as I watched the hallways swell with water that would leave us no room for breathing. Alex dug his claws in around my belt as I reached out and grabbed blindly for India, who had done as I said and grabbed Kyle. She took my hand and everything blurred as the water hit us full on, sweeping us down toward the stairwell.

There was no way I could hang onto my sword and the kids, which only left me one option. I dropped my sword and reached toward the railing. The metal bit hard into my hand as the water dragged at all four of us, swirling and sucking at our bodies. If I let go, we'd be swept further into the bowels of the ship. Not an option I was going with. With everything I had, I fought the current, tried to find my footing on the stairs. Hands wrapped around me and yanked me, Alex, India, and Kyle out of the water. We gasped for air as Berget dragged all four of us upward. Booyah for a vampire's strength.

"Hurry, we have to hurry," she said as we stumbled up and after her. Her eyes met mine. "The boy, Simon. His ghost told me you were in trouble."

A lump in my throat, I nodded. He'd said he would help, and he did. He'd helped to save us. Or at least, I was hoping that was the case and his efforts weren't in vain. Then again, I realized if it hadn't been him being demon-possessed, the black coven would have come after me. The demon prophecy said it was a Tracker who was possessed.

If between him and me, I would choose to be the one without a demon in my head.

There was no question we were running out of time. I was betting on minutes, at best, before the whole ship dropped to the bottom of the harbor. A place I really wasn't interested in visiting.

Back in the main room, we paused for a quarter of a heartbeat before Berget led the way up the stairs. The whole boat listed without warning and my feet slid on the metal stairs. I fell back, hitting the water at the bottom of the stairs then something latched onto me, dragging me into the main room. Clenching my teeth, I kept my mouth shut, held my breath as I twisted and fought, but couldn't get loose.

Not again.

I was done with people trying to drown me. The hands disappeared as suddenly as they'd grabbed me and I popped up. Berget was at the bottom of the stairs. I waved at her, finding my footing. It wasn't as deep in the middle of the room with the way the boat had tipped. "I'm okay, get them out!"

Berget nodded as I started toward the stairs for a second time.

A splash from across the room snapped my head around. Something was moving in the water. And for some strange reason, I doubted it was anything good.

And both my swords were gone.

Just peachy.

13

Opening his eyes was hard, but this time he managed the feat, to see he was no longer in his wolf form. He was in a clean bed, the scent of sage and incense filling the room. Were they still at Louisa's?

Welcome back. Blaz's voice rippled through his head, loud and clear.

Liam put a hand to his chest, the puckered scar there proof to how close he'd come to biting the big one. "How long was I out?"

A few hours. Once the shamans patched you up, it was all good.

He had a feeling Blaz wasn't being entirely honest, but it didn't matter now. "What about the wolf, the woman werewolf Beauty, how did she get here?"

Apparently you connected strongly with the pack and when they felt you in trouble, they talked Faris into letting them come back to New Mexico. He opened the Veil for them and they came to find you.

Liam was not certain that was a good idea. "Beauty still thinks I'm her mate, doesn't she?"

Blaz snickered. *Yeah, that's going to be fun when Rylee shows up.*

"Not funny, lizard."

Ignoring him, Blaz just kept on laughing. *It will be funny. A good laugh is something we could all use right about now.*

Carefully, Liam slung his legs over the edge of the bed and sat up. His head spun a little, but wasn't too bad. "Where am I? Still at Louisa's?"

No, they moved you to another of the shaman's for some reason. Crystal's, I think. I didn't argue, since they were all about healing you.

That was strange. Why wouldn't Louisa have kept him at her place? Something tickled along his spine, a worry he couldn't shake. Orion had infiltrated nearly every aspect of their allies, could he have gotten to the shamans, too?

Since he was already there, he knew there was something he could, and should, do before they left for London.

"I need to speak to the other guardians. Or at least speak to those we know about. If something is off, then they will know." Eagle was gone, his blood used to shut the Veil. Would the other guardians still be alive? If nothing else, they should be warned of the danger. It would give him a chance to check out the shamans too. Then he would go to London as they'd said they would.

Anything to keep his mind busy, to keep from worrying about Rylee. Then again, she had Erik and Pamela with her; she should be fine. Except he knew Rylee, knew how often trouble strolled into her life.

Wrapping a sheet around his hips, he padded out of the bedroom. While the house was done up in a southwestern motif, not unlike Louisa's, it was much smaller and far less tidy. Again, he wondered at the reason he was brought here and again, he got an unpleasant shudder. Something was off; his wolf gave a low rumble deep within him, instincts warning him to be careful.

There was no one in the house, no sound of breathing or steady heart rate, so no need to call out. He opened the front door and dropped the sheet, shifting into his wolf form.

Be careful, Wolf. Death stalks this world like it never has.

Liam gave a short bark in understanding, projecting for Blaz to wait for him there.

I don't think we should split up, and we need to get you to London.

Frustrated, Liam shook his head, thick fur ruffling. With a single bark, he did his best to impart that he was going alone, then, using the tools Peter had given him, impressed on Blaz that he was to stay behind.

Wolf, that is dirty pool. Blaz shook his head, and then curled up on the ground. *But you know I cannot go against you, jerk.*

With a snort and a nod, Liam loped toward Louisa's home, hoping Blaz would forgive him. He just didn't think taking a dragon along would be a good idea. He remembered all too keenly where Louisa lived, and how prickly she could be about unannounced visitors. The last time he'd been there was with Rylee and she'd nearly died, her broken ribs puncturing her body. The time before that, Louisa had allowed Bear, her guardian, to attack them and in the process turn Liam into a guardian himself.

His ears flicked at the soft sound of padded feet on the hard-packed dirt and slush around him. Within moments, the pack had swept up, flanking him. He pointedly ignored them; they were not his friends, nor were they his family. Beauty rubbed herself against him and he snarled at her. She gave him about two hairsbreadths of space, but it was better than her shoving herself on him.

He had their loyalty, could feel it humming along his skin, the power and control that came with binding them. This was what Peter warned him about, the strength of his own power and what it would do to other wolves. How they would submit to him so fully they would barely know themselves, if he wasn't careful.

And he hadn't been careful when he'd taken the pack from Beauty. He'd used everything he had because he hadn't thought of anything but stopping her. Shit.

They loped together as a unit, moving with him, heading straight into the rural lands. The pack's footsteps were almost perfectly in sync with his, a steady thrum that wormed its way through his body and brought him a sense of peace that shocked him.

Rylee was his mate, and the others were his pack. But this . . . this was different. This was a void he hadn't known was missing.

He could have run for hours like that, only too soon, they were at Louisa's home. If he shifted he'd be walking in naked, and while it didn't bother him so much anymore, it still could be a shock for others. With a sharp bark, he made the pack stay behind as he trotted up the steps and then scratched at the door.

From inside came the sound of footsteps, not Louisa's. Heavier, and a longer stride between each step than the shaman could have ever pulled off.

The door opened and Bear, Louisa's guardian, looked down at him with long black hair and a tanned upper body, wearing only a thin pair of khaki pants and the silver eyes that marked every guardian.

"Hello, Wolf, I see you are hale. Louisa is sleeping yet, it took a great deal out of her to heal you."

Liam shifted and within seconds, stood eye to eye with Bear. "I'll wait."

Bear's lips twitched ever so slightly. "So it would seem my blood chose wisely when it took you to be a guardian."

Liam followed Bear in, his curiosity piqued. Though he'd gained a lot of knowledge from Peter, it would be interesting to see what Bear had to offer him.

"What do you mean by that?"

Bear tossed him a pair of pants and t-shirt. "A guardian doesn't choose who they create, like with a werewolf. Your blood chooses who will become a guardian. The Wolf has been gone a long time, and so I suppose it was time for him to come again to this world."

Liam, clothing on, stood in the middle of the living room, seeing a vision of Pamela curled up on the far side of the couch, her eyes wide and full of fear while they waited to see if Rylee would live or die. He shook his head, clearing the image. "So it had nothing to do with Alex drooling into the wound?"

Bear grunted. "No doubt that was part of it; you would have become a werewolf regardless, but getting swiped by me, that only made you a guardian because it was time. The world needs the Wolf again. He has always been the one to tip the scales in times of dire straits." A light chill seemed to fill the air as Bear lowered himself to a wooden chair, his movements smooth and filled with barely restrained strength. "The Wolf doesn't generally have a long life span, a few years at most, usually less than that."

How was he not surprised? "Yeah, I've been told more than once my time is coming."

"And did you listen? Did you hear the unspoken words of how you will die?" Bear was serious, there was no joking in him.

"I will save her."

Bear's eyes were grave and he leaned back in his seat. "Yes, I do believe you will. But I think—"

"Bear, who are you talking to?" Louisa stepped into the room, stalling the conversation between the two guardians. Liam wasn't sure if he was happy about that or not. The premonitions, prophecies, and readings he'd been getting lately, none of them spoke in his favor. So one more didn't really bother him. Or at least, that's what he told himself.

"Louisa, I need to speak to you and the other shamans about the guardians."

Her dark eyebrows rose and she pursed her lips. "What, no thank you for saving your life?"

"I am grateful, but my life will mean little if I do nothing with it. The shamans and their guardians, I need to speak with all of them."

Her eyes flicked toward Bear almost imperceptibly. He was sure Bear hadn't caught the look, but he had.

She put her hands on her hips. "That is not your place, Wolf, you need to leave."

His wolf shot upward, anger flooding him, and he didn't even realize he'd grabbed her until he had her lifted off the floor. "The guardians are all in danger, and you will call your sister shamans here so we can figure this out."

"Bear." Her voice was ice, but her eyes were a mixture of emotions. "You would let him lay his hands on me?"

Bear let out a snort. "He's not hurting you, and if my brothers are in danger then I want to hear what he has to say."

Her jaw twitched and the indignant fury leached from her eyes, but there was something else there too. Fear. And Liam wasn't sure if it was fear of him, or of something else. "Fine. Put me down. Now."

Liam dropped her to the floor and she stumbled back, straightening her long flowing white nightgown.

Without another word she left the room, stomping all the way. Liam watched her go.

"She hasn't been sleeping well. It makes her moody." Bear sat completely relaxed. "The guardians will get here well ahead of the shamans."

"How many are there?"

"Besides me and Eagle, only two others, Coyote and Hawk."

Liam thought about what Rylee told him when they'd tried to go through one of the doorways in the castle with Faris.

"What about Spider?"

Bear stiffened in his seat. "How do you know Spider?"

"Rylee."

The other guardian slowly stood, unfolding himself bit by bit. "There are guardians that help, and there are guardians who hurt. And then there are some like Spider who sit on the fence."

Liam lifted an eyebrow. "From what Rylee said, Spider wasn't exactly helpful."

"Yet they survived her."

Her. That was interesting. "I thought all guardians were male." He chose not to mention the water dragon Rylee and he met in Russia during their vacation.

"All but Spider and one water dragon. Spider is rather bitchy, but she keeps to herself, spins her webs and tells her tales. The water dragon hasn't been heard from in years; so long I can't even recall her name." Bear pointed at the kitchen and Liam followed. This was seeming so ... mundane. Was this how life would be without Rylee setting things in motion? Quiet. Mellow.

Ordinary.

"How many guardians are there?"

Bear poured and handed him a cup of coffee without asking. Liam took it, but didn't drink.

"Some for each continent." Bear didn't elaborate and the conversation died after that. But Bear was right, it didn't take long for the other two guardians to show. Hawk walked in without knocking, Coyote right behind him.

They looked as though they could be twins, both with long hooked noses, shorn dark-brown hair and deep tans that came from hours and hours in the sun. They stood shoulder-to-shoulder inside Louisa's home, a few inches shorter than Liam and Bear.

"So, this is our Wolf?" Coyote's voice sounded as though he barely restrained himself from a bout of laughter.

Liam gave him a nod but said nothing. Coyote let out a howl, his head thrown back. "Always the same, stoic and not much for fun. Good thing you'll be dead soon."

A threat was not something his wolf took lightly. Without thinking, he leapt at Coyote, pinning him to the floor. Coyote didn't seem bothered by it, though, he just winked up at him as he was slammed into the wooden floor. "Ah, see, there it is, your lack of humor shining through like a ray of sunshine." He reached up and patted Liam's cheek affectionately. Liam fought not to bite the smaller man's fingers.

"Stop poking at him," Bear said. "He has information we need."

"Like how Eagle died? That Harpy was too busy sobbing to get much information out of her," Hawk said, his voice cutting and sharp.

Liam got off Coyote, but didn't offer him a hand to help him up. "Eve was very attached to Eagle. He was her mentor."

Hawk shrugged. "Doesn't matter who he was to her. He was a guardian first. What killed him?"

The three guardians looked at him and he nodded. "You don't want to wait for your shamans?"

"No. Tell us," Bear said, his voice growing deeper, as though he were close to changing forms.

Even with Bear being on edge, Liam hesitated. How did he explain everything that happened in a condensed form?

"Say what you must say, Wolf," Hawk snapped.

"Tears in the Veil can be closed with guardian blood. That's what killed Eagle. A group of demons came through, kidnapped some of our people, and used Eagle's blood to close the tear in the Veil behind them so they couldn't be followed."

Coyote snorted. "You're shitting us." Interesting. Coyote spoke in a much more modern way than Bear or Hawk, who both spoke in a more formal, old school style.

"I saw his body. I believe he was killed with the same copper knife that nearly ended my life." Liam folded his arms, suddenly wondering where the hell that knife was. It was not the kind of weapon they needed floating about. "He was cut, badly, and bled out."

"Guardian's can't be killed by mere cuts," Hawk said, circling around. "But they can be killed by other guardians. How do we know you aren't the dark Wolf?"

Now that was a new one. He chose not to ask what the dark Wolf was. He could guess. "Why would I kill Eagle? What purpose would that serve?"

Hawk shrugged and Liam could see he wasn't much better than Coyote when it came to poking at things he shouldn't. "Just pointing out the obvious. You showed up; Eagle gets killed. Not a coincidence in your favor, my friend."

He had to fight not to roll his eyes. "I came to warn you there is a good chance the demons will come after you with a weapon, or weapons, that can kill you and you want to play games? Not to mention there is at least one coven of black witches, and if they get a hold of you, they have spells that will bind you, and they could force you to carry a demon. And your blood and mine can be used to hide the evidence of tears in the Veil. You really want to point fingers at me right now? Maybe instead we should be working together to stop this before it gets any worse."

Silence flowed through the room, the tension between the four guardians high. Even so, Liam never saw it coming. Couldn't have guessed what was about to happen.

Hawk and Bear launched at him at the same time, shifting midair, the red glimmer he caught in their silver eyes meaning only one thing.

They'd already been possessed.

Oh, hell no.

So much for his theory that Rylee was the one at the center of all things chaotic.

He hit the ground and scrambled away, Coyote on the floor with him. "Run!"

They bolted for the front door, nearly ripping the hinges off as they blasted through.

"What the hell?" Coyote barked out as they bolted into the front yard. Hawk and Bear weren't right behind them, though.

Louisa.

"They'll kill her," Liam said and let the change take him. Coyote didn't need any prompting, just shifted beside him.

The pack crept forward and Liam flicked his head for them to stay back. They would be slaughtered if they got in a fight with the guardians.

A piercing scream from inside shot through the air like a gun going off. Coyote followed him as he ran toward the house, his mind racing. Two guardians, both possessed. But they could be killed and now had to be, there was no choice.

His nose saved him as he skidded through the doorway and he flattened himself to the floor as Bear swiped a paw over top of his head. Liam rolled, then sprung to his feet, paws scrambling as Coyote dodged toward Bear, snapping teeth at the larger guardian's legs. Blood flowed and Bear roared. Coyote let out a yipping laugh and Liam took the distraction to scent the air. Hawk was still here, but it was Louisa he worried about.

Following his nose, he found Hawk battering at a door, the frame shuddering under his blows. Even though Hawk was huge, almost on par with the size of Eagle, his wingspan easily twenty-five feet, he was having trouble knocking the door down. With his wings and body, there was no room left in the hallway to get enough speed to beat down the door.

Nor did he seem interested in anything but the door. Liam didn't hesitate, just leapt forward, aiming for the back of Hawk's neck.

But his luck had run out. Hawk spun at the last second and ducked out of the way, his talons coming up to rake Liam across his right front leg.

As Hawk's legs went by, Liam snapped at them, catching one in his mouth and snapping it like a chopstick.

Hawk screeched, his beak flashing forward, heading straight for Liam's face. He dodged and managed to grab Hawk's right wing. Using his body weight and gripping fiercely to the feathers and cartilage in his mouth, he jerked Hawk off balance, throwing him into the wall with a house-shuddering blow.

Stunned, Hawk slid to the floor.

One stride and he was on top of Hawk, the guardian's neck in his mouth. He chomped as Hawk began to struggle, tasted the sweet blood, the pulse of life fading as he yanked at the spine. He had to protect Louisa; this was not personal in the least. Removal of Hawk's head; that would do it, much as he wished he didn't have to.

Three hard jerks with his teeth tearing through the flesh was all it took. Hawk's head rolled away, shifting back to a man, as the rest of his body convulsed once, twice, and once more for good measure before stilling. The shimmer of a demon's essence curled around him. Like a ghost it floated, eyeing him up and down. Liam snarled at it.

"We are not done yet," the demon whispered, lifting its hand. "We will have this world. The doorway is open, and you cannot stop what is coming." The demon faded as it laughed.

A high-pitched cry of pain snapped his head up. Bear would not be as easy to take as Hawk had been.

He bolted out of the room to see Coyote on the floor, his back bent at an impossible angle, his eyes staring toward Liam.

Bear stood on all fours over Coyote and let out a roar. Liam growled back, letting out a howl he couldn't help. This was it; he could feel the finality of it in his whole body. Bear and he would go down together, and that in itself would keep Rylee safe. A guardian possessed; there was nothing that could have stopped them, short of another guardian. And there was no doubt that Bear would have gone after Rylee at some point for Orion; it would have been just a matter of when.

His heart and mind settled into a steady thrum of acceptance. His only regret was there had been no true goodbye between him and Rylee.

Slinking forward, his belly to the ground, ears flattened to his skull, he bared his teeth. Bear had been a friend of Wolf's for many years, but the demon in him . . . that could never be changed.

They circled one another, but before either could attack, the scrabble of claws on hardwood floor met his ears.

The pack slunk into the house, mimicking Liam's stance, ears flattened to their heads, rumbling growls echoing his.

A rush of emotion flooded through him. Loyalty was something wolves understood, and even though they would die, they would fight for their alpha.

After that, the melee turned into a bloody mess. Bear didn't hold back, but neither did the wolves and they were as tough as only werewolves could be. Dodging in and out, they took shots at Bear while Liam did the same, always working toward where he could get in a deathblow.

Minutes passed and the house filled with the stink of death, blood, and broken bowels. Half the pack had been killed in that short time, and Bear looked no worse for the wear other than the few bites Liam had gotten in. Coyote lay at his feet as he paused between attacks and the guardian shifted his head to look at Liam. "Hamstring him."

Liam took the advice. Using the remaining wolves, they taunted and teased Bear until Liam could dive in, driving his teeth into Bears legs, ripping and tearing at the flesh. Bear roared, and from within the house the sound of a woman crying out nearly stopped him. Nearly.

They had to finish Bear off, no matter the pain it brought Louisa. She'd known something was wrong, but didn't have the strength to stop it.

Tackled to the ground, Bear was held down by the wolves and he shocked the hell out of Liam by shifting back to human form.

"I can see I'm done in, Wolf," he rasped, the backs of his legs shredded to nothing more than mincemeat. "But I have a message for you, from my master. Orion wants you to know you cannot stop him; he won't settle for Milly's child now. He knows about you, about what you've done to the Tracker."

Everything in Liam stilled, but he didn't shift, just trotted to Bear and put his muzzle next to Bear's neck. There were no words anyway. With an efficiency born of months of practice, and a millennium of instinct, he snapped Bear's neck and wrenched his head from his body. The demon's essence floated away, sucked back through the Veil as it laughed.

If only that would still the fear spiking through him, the fear that Bear wasn't just making idle threats.

The fear . . . that Orion knew his secret.

That Orion knew Rylee's secret.

14

Louisa was, to say the least, shaken. It took Liam half an hour to convince her to come out of the bathroom. It wasn't until Crystal, the youngest of the shamans, showed up that they talked her out.

Crystal took the lead, helping Louisa to the couch and then getting tea made. "Here"—she handed Louisa a cup—"drink this."

He didn't really want to wait around, but with Coyote in rough shape, he also didn't want to leave them without any protection. The wolf in him didn't like leaving allies to be killed.

"Bear, I thought something was off with him, but I couldn't figure it out," Louisa said, her lips touching the rim of her cup, but she didn't sip any of the hot liquid. On her lap lay the copper knife. Liam itched to take it from her, but restrained himself. Any sudden moves would have the two shamans on high alert.

Coyote still lay on the floor, no longer contorted but very still, all his previous humor gone. "I can't believe Hawk was possessed."

Liam wasn't surprised by anything now. "They may come for you yet, Coyote. Whether to possess or to kill for your blood, it doesn't matter." He thought for a moment. "Where are the other shamans?"

Crystal looked up at him, her eyes soft with sorrow and tears. "Dead. We are the only two left."

That didn't bode well. His wolf urged him to act, to pin Crystal down and force the truth from her. With his time running out, feeling it slide away with every passing second, he agreed, and before he thought better of it, grabbed Crystal and jerked her to him. Reluctantly, he tightened his hands on her arms and squeezed hard enough that the bones ground together. He put his face close enough that their lips nearly touched, though his teeth were bared.

"You did it, you killed them."

She shook her head frantically as Louisa shrieked at him to let the younger woman go. But there could be no way to be sure that Crystal hadn't been possessed too. Louisa threw her tea at him, the hot water burning his bare chest, but he held on, waiting for Crystal to do something, anything to give herself away.

Crystal was frantic, her eyes wild with fear. "I didn't, I swear I didn't kill them! I don't know who did it!"

Louisa stood, the copper knife pointed at him, and though it shook, he knew she would use it.

Crystal's eyes rolled and as she slipped into a faint, so he let her body slide to the couch once more. "She would have fought back if she'd been possessed."

"You bastard, you can't just go threatening people!" Louisa screeched, the edge of hysteria in her voice making the words crack and break.

"I'm not Rylee, I can't Track people and figure out if they are hiding things. There is no other way for us to know." He kept his voice even and firm, business-like, more than reminiscent of his FBI days.

Louisa crouched beside Crystal, stroking her cheek. "She's breathing, I thought—"

"If he'd thought she was a danger, he would have killed her, shaman," Coyote said from the floor. "You don't remember Wolf, but I do. He always does the right thing, no matter the cost." He took in a shuddering breath. "Let me guess, before you became a guardian, you were a cop of some sort?"

Liam turned toward the guardian. "FBI."

Coyote barked a laugh. "Not surprised."

None of this really mattered, not in the scheme of things. "Louisa, you and Crystal need to go to London. Now. It is where Rylee's allies are rallying."

The shaman stood and folded her arms in front of her. "Why would I listen to you?"

"Because I just saved your ass from your own guardian," he snarled. "And more demons will come for the rest of you."

She paled, and her arms tightened around herself. "Fine. We will go."

Crystal came around, her eyes wide when she took in Liam. He apologized and while she nodded and said she understood, he could see she was nervous about him now. He didn't really care. He just needed them to do as he told them. The two shamans left, though not without Louisa glaring at Liam again for good measure. As she passed him, she handed him the copper knife. No words, just slapped the handle into his open palm with a sniff.

"And what of me?" Coyote asked and then clapped his hands together. "You think I'm possessed?"

"Nah. Too helpful against the other two." Liam sat on the floor beside him. "How long before you heal?"

"Don't know. Never actually fought another guardian before," Coyote said, a grimace working its way across his face as he took a deep breath.

"What about the other guardians, the ones who are on the fence?"

Coyote twisted his head and looked up at Liam, his eyes narrowing. "Not many of those. And the few who have gone rogue, they aren't really bad. They just don't like to be tied to shamans."

Liam's eyebrows rose. "You look at me like I'm one of them."

"In a way, you are. Wolf comes when the world is in trouble and binds himself to a single person, someone who can make changes, rarely a shaman. It depends on that person how Wolf turns out—good or bad." He put a hand to the floor and rolled slowly to his belly. "Give me a minute, I'm going to try and shift. That should speed things up." Coyote didn't actually make a move to shift, though, he just lay on the floor breathing hard.

Moving back, Liam gave him some room, but began to doubt Coyote's strength to make the change.

So being tied to Rylee had dictated whether he would have been good or bad? Thinking back, there had been times of utter darkness, especially with Milly, where he wasn't sure he was even himself.

Yet since he'd been with Rylee, when she'd gone after him, those dark spots in him had disappeared. Gone.

He shook his head. Didn't matter now, not really. At that moment he wanted only to find a place for Rylee that was safe. Where Orion couldn't find her.

"Coyote, do you know much about demons?"

Coyote turned his head toward Liam again. "Why?"

"If there was a place that could be clear of demons, where would it be?"

The guardian groaned and pushed himself to his hands and knees. "Some sort of holy ground, something untainted by the modern world and the revelry in it. I'd say a place with a guardian, but I don't know anymore after this shit fest if we are as good at protection as we once were." He shook his head and Liam helped him to his feet.

"I thought you wanted to shift?"

"Can't. And since you want to talk, this works better anyway." With his arm over Liam's shoulder they left the house. The remainder of the pack, only six werewolves—and of course, Beauty was one of them—immediately surrounded them. Injured and still bleeding, the werewolves didn't hesitate.

"Sometimes I wish coyotes were as loyal. Your pack saved us both."

"I know." Liam shifted his arm so he could take more of Coyote's weight. "Tell me more about a place apart from the world, somewhere safe."

"You going to run off and leave the world on its own?"

"No. But I need to find a place for my mate to be safe. She's going to need it."

Coyote gave him a funny look, but he spoke freely about where he thought would be best, the attributes that would keep demons away.

The final refuge for those seeking sanctuary from evil.

Liam could only hope he was right, and could convince Rylee to go.

15

"**B**erget, are there any zombies still fucking about?" I yelled loud enough that she could hear me. She responded in kind.

"No, they all went down the same time the witches did. Same time Pam did."

I didn't want to face anything in the water, but I doubted it was going to let me get back to the stairs without some sort of confrontation. Let's just call it previous experience.

Reaching for one of the short knives I kept tucked away for just such an emergency, I gripped the handle in my right hand, whip in my left, and braced myself for another fight. The water was over my knees and steadily climbing; the spray floating around me disturbed the surface and made it hard to see what was under it clearly. Something I really wanted to know.

The thing in the water started toward me again, slower this time, its body sliding along, the flip of an iridescent fin catching the light before going under again.

I kept walking backward, slowly, feeling my way with my feet and hoping to hell I didn't stumble over anything. As the water rose and the creature circled, the bodies of those killed floated to the surface, bobbing up like some creepy carnival game of whack-a-mole.

One of the bodies floated close and I pushed it away, toward the creature that was following me. A hand shot out of the water and—shit—a mermaid popped her head out to stare at me. Long purple hair was braided back from her face, but then the braid ended at her shoulders leaving the length of her hair to float freely. Her eyes were a paler color than her hair and they fixed a stare on me that made me bring up my blade.

"You think to kill me?" She slurred her words, sounding like she was still under water.

"Only if you start something." Mermaids were not known for their kindness. They were more known for the shit they would pull when you weren't looking, and their temperamental love lives. If eating your mate after he knocked you up could be called temperamental.

She grinned at me. "Whoever broke the hull broke it just enough for us to get in."

Us. Oh, that did not sound good. "And why would you want in?"

She spread her hands and rested her face on the floating body I'd pushed her way. "A banquet awaits; a feast of proportions we rarely see. The flesh of supernaturals the elementals haven't yet put away, that is something we don't often get."

"Fine, eat away, but leave me the hell out of it."

"Or you'll do what exactly?"

There was a splash behind me and a voice I'd been waiting for whispered, "She'll have her little sister drain your body of every last drop of your sea ridden blood."

The mermaid hissed and dove under the water. I turned to see Berget, her skirts swirling on top of the water, her eyes narrowed.

"I told you to go."

"I'm not leaving you here, Rylee, any more than you'd leave me."

"India and Kyle?"

"Alex is taking them to Erik and Amelia."

Unspoken words flowed between us. She didn't call Amelia "mom" or "mother." I didn't ask her why. Nor did I ask why she didn't help our mom.

I sloshed to her and she put an arm around my waist. She pushed off with her legs and we shot up three levels to where Frank and Pamela sat. Frank's arm was around Pamela's shoulders, helping her sit up, but he nearly dropped her when we appeared at the edge of the railing.

Grabbing the metal railing, I pulled myself over. "They killed Dad."

Berget sucked in a sharp breath and stared down into the water.

Alex, Erik, and Amelia appeared at the far end of the walkway with India and Kyle. Amelia was stumbling, her hands buried deep in the ruff around Alex's neck, no doubt for warmth as much as stability. He waved a paw at me and gave me a grin that showed off his teeth. Nothing ever truly fazed him for long.

Amelia's head was lowered so she didn't see me, nor did she see Berget.

"I have to go. I don't want her to know I'm alive," Berget whispered and in a flash only a vampire could accomplish, she was gone.

Amelia slowly lifted her head, saw me and stiffened. "You couldn't be content with killing your little sister; you had to murder your father too."

"Shut up, you ungrateful wretch," Erik snapped, and I was intensely appreciative he defended me. But it didn't stop the emotions that engulfed me.

My guts clenched and I fought the instant pang of guilt that sliced through me. Mostly because she was right. If I hadn't gone to see them, there was a good chance Robert and Amelia would be home having their nightly drinks, discussing their day.

Teeth gritted, I ignored her, turning my back to her. That had always been the best way in the past. The best way to deal with her accusations.

"That's right, you did it, you killed him," she said.

Alex whimpered. "Rylee not bad."

Amelia jumped as if just noticing her companion was a twisted werewolf who could talk.

Alex, oblivious to her surprise kept talking. "Rylee good, you are bad mom to be mean to Rylee."

If nothing else, I did have my supporters. Ignoring Amelia, I crouched to check on Pamela. She blinked groggily up at me. "What happened?"

"I think you got a backlash that was meant to kill you."

Frank nodded. "I saw it coming, saw it was tuned to magic users. Death magic doesn't bother necromancers, so I—"

Pamela's eyes shot wide and her hand covered her mouth. "He kissed me."

He blushed. "Thomas told me that some sort of exchange would have to happen if I was to stop death magic on someone else. Something like a kiss or blood. I didn't have time to draw blood on her or me, I swear!"

I held up my hand. "Thank you, Frank, for taking care of her. You did the right thing." I reached down and helped Pam to her feet. She wobbled and leaned on me, pushing me back into the railing. I glanced down. Nope, that wasn't Pamela making me sway. The boat listed hard as a rush of water swelled through the broken hull.

"Time to go."

Amelia let go of Alex and I gave a nod to Frank. He stepped close to my mom and let her lean on him, leaving Alex free to move near me and Pamela.

"Mean mom."

"Alex, enough," I said, though there was no force behind my words. I was battered through and through and so fucking confused with what Orion had done that I barely knew what to think. India ran to my side and slipped an arm around me. "There are so many spirits here, Rylee."

"We're going, kid. Kyle, you okay?"

"Yeah." That was all he managed and I wasn't about to ask more at that particular moment. He looked as bedraggled and done in as I felt.

We wove our way out of the ship as it tipped even farther into the harbor. Lucky for us, the boat listed so that once we were on deck, all we had to do was hop across the railing and we were standing on the dock. Solid ground beneath us. Kinda.

Amelia threw my coat at me even though the snow was still coming down. "I will see you in jail for this."

I caught my coat with one hand, but didn't put it on. It was still warm, or warmish, from her body and I wondered if she cared that I'd almost died in there. That all of us had almost died and it was a miracle only Robert, my dad, hadn't made it out.

I knew my brain was stalling, filling with other things so I didn't look at my mom and start crying right there. A part of me was amazed she still had so much power over me, could still cut me to the quick.

And then something shifted in me and my spine stiffened. A memory of the desert and the very first salvage I did on my own surfaced. Reminding me of the strength it had taken to face down someone I thought had loved me when I realized he had been a total shit. That had been the turning point for me; how could I go back to that girl who was still so eager to please that she would give up everything? That's right, I wasn't going there again. Not. Ever. Not even for my mom.

"You fucking well do that, Amelia. I didn't kill Berget, and I sure as hell didn't kill my dad. You saw everything that happened in there, you almost got possessed by a demon and I SAVED YOUR ASS!"

My voice echoed across the docks and Amelia shrunk away from me. But I wasn't done.

"You didn't deserve to have me or Berget." Okay, that was a seriously low blow, but it felt so fucking good to finally say it. To turn on your child when they needed you the most, and give up on the other? No, that wasn't a mother. At least, not a good one.

My ragtag group hobbled down the dock, each passing Amelia as though she didn't exist.

Amelia didn't try to catch up with us, and I didn't really care. At the far end of the dock where the true dry land met with the wooden pilings there was a flash of bright blonde hair. Berget stepped out to meet us just as Amelia ran up from behind.

"Rylee, don't you turn your back on me—"

Amelia's voice died as she spied Berget, who had also gone very still.

Well shit, it really had nothing to do with me now at all. I'd said my peace and for the first time felt the past slide away from me, no longer tugging at my emotions. I ignored Amelia and kept walking.

Berget looked like she'd swallowed a hunk of troll flesh and was about to throw it back up. "I thought she'd be gone."

I shrugged but said nothing, felt nothing as I walked past her. Berget's hand snaked out and she grabbed me. "Don't leave me with her."

As she asked, I stopped. Pamela let out a deep breath. "Let me try and stand on my own."

Letting go of her, I slipped my coat back on, the scent of Amelia's perfume floating up and around my nose. It didn't make me nostalgic anymore, just ill.

"Berget, my baby, is that really you?" Amelia stumbled forward and I felt more than a little voyeuristic, and just a tad bit jealous. I couldn't help it; who wouldn't want their mother to love them?

Berget stepped back and shook her head, drawing herself up, and every jealous thought I had evaporated. "You aren't my mother. My mother would have loved Rylee when she was in her darkest moments. She would have stood by her and kept searching for me. You might be the person who gave birth to me, but it has always been Rylee who loved me best. She was the only one who never gave up on me."

Amelia put a hand to her throat and her body shook. "I thought she killed you." What I found interesting was that she didn't say that she loved Berget, didn't beg for forgiveness. No, she went right to me again.

Berget glared at her. "No, you just wanted someone to blame. Someone who didn't look back at you in the mirror."

With that, Berget turned her back on our mother and took my hand. "Don't let her get to you. She's wrong about everything." Her eyes, though, were clouded. Hundreds of years of wisdom might have been stored in her head, but she was still a teenager, still trying to figure out life and the blows it handed us. Still fighting to keep control of herself.

My fingers tightened over hers. "Let's go, everyone is waiting for us and we have shit to do."

We left Amelia on the docks, on her knees watching her two children disown her as they walked out of her life for good.

"It was for her own good, and besides, she did deserve it," Berget whispered to me as we crossed the Charlestown Bridge.

I nodded and brushed a lock of her hair back behind one ear. "I know." The people we loved, they would be targets, and those we fought, like the black coven, would seek out those targets and use them against us.

The way back was uneventful.

Which was weird. I kept twitching, waiting for something to jump out at me, grab one of the kids, pull us down, and try to kill us.

Call it history, but there weren't many times lately that we'd been able to do anything without running into uglies.

When we got to the safe house, I turned to Frank. "You feeling up to it?"

"Yeah, I think so." Frank stepped in front of us. "Where are we going?"

"London."

He swallowed hard. "I don't know if I can do that."

I scrubbed my face. "Where can you get us?"

"Back to the farm. Maybe to New Mexico." He blushed. "I'm sorry, I just need to rest for awhile."

New Mexico was where Louisa and the other shamans were. Maybe we could rally them while we were there. "New Mexico. Louisa's, if you can."

I moved to his side to watch his face. Severe concentration and a bead of sweat were all he gave away as the Veil sliced open. In the distance, I saw Louisa's house lit up in the dark night. Looked like she was home, at least.

As we all stepped through the Veil, Frank collapsed to his knees. Pamela and I dropped beside him. "Hey, you've overdone it."

He nodded and I helped him stand, though he was wobbly. Pamela put a hand to his forehead and frowned. "I don't think I can heal this. It's fatigue, nothing more."

"A night's sleep should do it," he mumbled.

If only we'd known we'd not even get that, we might have stayed in Boston.

16

"**S**tinks like blood and shit," Alex said as we drew close to Louisa's house.

Seriously? "Everybody on their toes." I went to draw one of my blades, forgetting that I'd lost both of them. There was a first time for everything, but did it have to be right then?

Erik took point and I let out slow breaths, taking my whip and uncoiling it. Had the ogres come after Louisa and the shamans?

"Smell any ogres, Alex?"

"Nope. Just wolves. And guardians."

I frowned. "What wolves?"

"Boss's pack."

I shared a look with Erik, who just shook his head. "They should be in London."

And you were supposed to be on your way to London too. Blaz's voice rippled over me and I turned to the left, the direction he spoke from. That wasn't really my main concern. "Where's Liam?"

Alex let out a yip and then took off into the darkness.

"Alex, stop!" Which, of course, he didn't listen to, not for one second. "Fuck!"

In the distance, there was a howl and then a small chorus of howls started up. I Tracked Liam and the tension flowed out of me. He was not far away, and better yet, he was not hurt. Or at least, not hurt like he had been.

"Rylee, what do we do?" Pamela asked me as she lifted her hands.

"It's Liam. We're okay."

For the first time in what felt like days, I relaxed a little, knowing Liam wasn't hurt.

Minutes passed and we waited while the pack and Liam slowly made their way to us. Liam walked next to a dark-haired man who hung from Liam's side. Pamela rushed forward and put her hands on the man. He straightened up within seconds.

"Good job, witchy woman." He gave her a wink and then lifted his eyes to take us all in. "Wolf, you going to introduce us?"

"Rylee, this is Coyote. He's the last guardian alive around here."

I sucked in a sharp breath. How could that be? What had happened to Bear? Liam didn't elaborate, just headed straight for me. I didn't hesitate, either. Too many close calls, who the hell cared what other people thought of what was going to be a seriously public display of affection?

A large wolf darted in between us and shifted. Beauty was really going to be a pain in the ass, one that I was really done with. "Out of my way, bitch."

"Liam, love," she purred. "Who does this human think she is to question me? Doesn't she know who I am?"

Liam love? Oh, fuck no.

"Rylee, meet Beauty." He flicked a hand at her, a twist to his lips like he'd bit on something sour.

I didn't bother to even try to restrain myself. These were wolves after all, not some pansy-assed human. Mates were taken seriously. "We've met. Am I going to have to kill her, or is she going to play nice and acknowledge that I'm your mate?"

Beauty's jaw dropped, though she caught herself quickly and within seconds charged me.

Mistake number one. My whip was in my hand and snapping toward her before she took two steps. A thin line of silver filament was threaded through the leather and as it curled around the naked flesh of her legs, she let out a scream.

I jerked the whip hard, dropping her to the ground. "Now, did you have something to say to me?"

"He's mine!"

I burst out laughing and flicked the whip so it uncoiled from her legs. "Liam, this is your territory. You want to deal with her, or should I? I really don't want to kill anyone else. At least, not tonight."

Liam moved beside me so we faced her together. She let out a groan as her eyes flicked over me, pausing as she took in a deep breath, her nostrils flaring as she scented the air. Her eyes widened with understanding, and a wicked glimmer crossed them. "Oh, I see what this is. Liam, you should have told me about her. Shameful, so very shameful between a wolf and a human." Her eyes flicked up and down my body. "You know it will kill her, when the time comes."

What happened next couldn't have shocked me more if Faris had put on a dress and said he was marrying Doran. Shit, I didn't think Beauty's words hadn't been *that* bad.

Liam lunged forward as he shifted. She scrambled backward, her eyes wide, but no one shifted as fast as Liam, and Beauty was no exception. His teeth closed around her neck and she scrambled to push him off. A sharp twist, the crack of vertebrae, and she stilled with a last single gasp of air. Even in death her body was stunning, her hair fanned out around her head as the blood dripped down her pale neck and over her perfect chest, her hands open in an artful gesture.

Didn't seem to affect Liam, though. He threw her body away from us and into the night where the lights from Louisa's home didn't touch. The werewolves around us sunk even lower to the ground, their teeth chattering in a creepy, clacking unison that brought Alex running from the back of the pack.

He skidded to a stop when he saw Beauty's body and clamped his oversized paws on his muzzle. "Oh, shitty dips."

Liam didn't glance at him, just shifted back into human form. "She was bound to cause more grief than either of us need right now."

I couldn't keep my eyes from widening further, if that was possible. That did not sound like Liam.

He glanced at me and just shook his head. "We have to get out of here, you know that, right? The ogres aren't going to take long to figure out where we are. The other guardians were possessed, and I've no doubt that they have some sort of connection with those possessing the ogres. "

Well, wasn't that just peachy. Explained what happened to Bear and the other guardians, though. "What about Louisa?"

"I sent her and Crystal on to London. They were clean."

I choked a little. "All the other shamans?"

"Dead."

What the fuck, we were losing allies left and right. But that was what Orion wanted, he wanted us cut off and fighting on our own.

"The only doorway on this side of the world that we know will still let us into the castle is back home." I turned to look in that direction. It wasn't close, but ultimately it would be faster than trying to get to London via Blaz. The old mineshaft had become a veritable highway for us when it came to crossing the Veil.

It didn't take much convincing on my part. Frank was still done in and even if he could open the Veil directly to Jack's, Liam would still be stuck in New Mexico.

"Liam, you wait here with your wolves. Blaz, are two trips going to be a problem?"

Don't insult me. His voice boomed through everyone and, of the newbies, it was Coyote who let out a laugh.

"Does that mean I'm coming with you?"

"You don't have to." I looked him over. "But I'm thinking that being on your own at this point probably isn't the best idea."

Coyote bobbed his head once, his silver eyes serious, though he had a big grin on his face. On the outside, he might look like this was all just fun and games, but there was a lot going on behind those eyes of his. "I'll come with you. It's been a long time since Wolf and I hunted together. And he is rather fun to poke at." He winked at me as Liam snorted.

The werewolves backed away into the darkness waiting for Liam. He came to me, touched one hand to my cheek and bent his head to mine. "We need to have a long talk, as soon as we get to London. No more distractions, no matter how bad they are. Promise me."

Shit, that didn't sound good. "If it's that bad, tell me now."

"Not bad, but we have to sort some stuff out that won't wait." His eyes never left mine, as if trying to impress something important on me.

My stomach clenched. He was talking about the secrets he'd been keeping the last few months. I'd wanted to know, pestered him about them, and now that the moment had drawn close, I wasn't so sure anymore I had any desire to know what he'd been keeping from me.

He kissed me, quick and clean, and then backed away, shifting. Moments later, a chorus of howls broke the night air; at one time, the sounds would have sent shivers down my spine. Not anymore. Though I couldn't tell them all apart, I could hear Alex and Liam adding their voices to the mix, and their voices soothed my fears. I had my boys; they would stand by me no matter what.

Pamela helped Coyote, boosting him with her magic onto Blaz's back, and then followed him up.

Frank and Berget were right behind them, then Kyle and India. I paused, looked to Erik and saw the same hesitation on his face.

"What?"

He shook his head, his eyes narrowing. "Something big is coming."

"Yeah, four horsemen, end of the world, all that shit." I said the words, but in my heart I knew he was talking about something else.

"Don't dismiss this, Rylee. You are always going to be the center of things and your intuition is trying to tell you something, isn't it?"

I flicked my hand at him, silently asking him to follow me, and we walked to the edge of where the light touched the night.

"The witches are dealt with. No more demons should easily be able to possess supernaturals. The ogres have been outed. But that damn doorway, it's still open, and we are planning on walking right by it to get to London."

Erik put a hand to the back of his neck, rubbing at the skin. "The horsemen shouldn't be coming through yet, not until the packs do some serious damage in preparation for them. I think we have time in that regards. But there is something else. Like a crux in time, a moment where we aren't going to be able to fix whatever it is that happens."

I swallowed hard. Erik had hit the nail on the fucking head. We'd heard nothing in regards to the demon packs and what they were up to other than the one we'd run into at John's motel. That was not a good sign. Either we were too far out of the loop, or the packs were working on something big. Not good, not good at all.

"We'd better go. The longer we take, the worse this is going to be. We've just got to rip the fucking Band-Aid off." I strode toward Blaz and climbed up, Erik right behind me.

The flight was cold, but easy. No demons popped out of the sky, no explosions sent us spinning into nowhere. The mineshaft was as we'd left it, ropes and climbing gear still set up and waiting.

Will you wait for Liam in the shaft, or in London?

That was a good question. "We'll wait for him at Jack's." It galled me, not waiting for him, but there was no other way. Doran and the others were waiting.

Our group slid down the ropes with ease and Pamela lit up the inside of the cavern with three floating balls of fire. The mineshaft was cool, but the doorway through the Veil felt hot to the touch. I pressed my hand against it. Why the hell would it be hot?

Without another thought, I pushed hard on the door, shoving it open. A burst of flame curled out and I fell back from it with a yelp.

Pamela stepped up and the flames bent away from us, but only by a few feet. Her face turned into a deep scowl. "I can't put it out, it's not regular fire."

"Can you hold it back long enough for us to get through?"

"I think so."

"Then we make a run for it."

Erik grunted. "What about Liam and the wolves?"

"I can wait for them," Pamela said. "I can get you out and then come back here and wait."

I didn't like it, didn't want to see her put herself in that kind of danger, but there was no other choice.

I gave a sharp nod, not happy about the newest twist in events. "Let's do this."

Pamela nodded and her hands clenched into fists. The flames were fucking hot, but we bolted through, all of us.

Except Berget. I stood inside the castle and looked back to see the fear on her face.

"I can't, Rylee. Even from here, the heat is too much. I will wait for Liam and the werewolves, tell them how to get through."

A gust of hot air whipped around me, drying the sweat on my forehead. "I can't leave you again."

"You aren't. I'll find a way to get to London. I can always catch a ride with Blaz." She gave me a soft smile and I knew there would be no changing her mind. Berget was right. There was no way for her to get through the fire without going up in flames. Too damn combustible.

I reached across the doorway and gave her a hug, holding her tight for just a moment. "I'm holding you to that. I expect to see your ass in London, ASAP."

"I love you too, Rylee."

Lips tight, I turned away and ran after the others. The castle was completely engulfed in deep-red flames. They looked like what a child would draw, blood red and towering above us. From time to time as we ran through the castle, they dipped toward us and Pamela fended them off.

"Who would light the castle on fire?" Frank asked as he jogged beside me.

It was a good question, and I was pretty sure I knew the answer. "Orion. If the castle is on fire, how do we close the doorway?"

Erik grunted his agreement and I knew I was right. Not that being right made me feel any better.

The main entrance in and out of the castle onto the open plane burned hotter than the rest of the flames around us and a niggling fear bit at me. None of us had even considered this might be a trap, a way to end us all in one fell swoop. "Pam, tell me you can get us through there."

"If I can't, no one can," she whispered, as she flung her hands toward the flaming gate. They groaned and leaned outward, leaving a small gap, just big enough for us to run through.

The group bolted for the opening, but again, I felt the pause of one of my people. Pamela stood, sweat pouring off her face. "Go, I'll be okay and Liam will need my help to get the wolves through."

I wanted to tell her not to take risks, to just be safe, and get her ass back to us in one piece. But it was advice I would never take myself. I settled for something more subtle. "Don't dawdle."

Her lips twitched and I turned my back on her to run through the gate. The heat singed my face, tightened my skin and made me sweat like, well, like I was running through a furnace.

Leaving my family behind was not something I was comfortable doing, but the last few months taught me I couldn't do it all. I had to let each of those close to me do the things they were designed for, much as it killed me to let them go into danger.

I just hoped I was making the right choice.

17

Watching Rylee and the others run through the gate left me feeling . . . funny. That she trusted me enough to leave me on my own was an amazing high. But being left on my own within the castle reminded me there were demons just waiting to snatch me again. The fear of being kidnapped haunted me, made my blood freeze.

I spun and ran back toward the doorway where Liam would come through. Second floor, end of the hallway. The flames weren't as bad there since I'd already pushed them back. Which was good, because the door to the mineshaft wouldn't open when I got to it.

"No, don't be a wanker," I whispered, jerking on the handle, yanking it hard. Nothing. Despite the heat from the flames around me, a chill slid down my spine. I couldn't wait anywhere else, which meant I had to sit here and fend off the fire until Liam, or Berget, opened the door. Sound didn't travel between the doorways, so I could knock all I liked and no one would hear.

I hadn't told Rylee the fire was more than magical. It was alive. There was some sort of entity running it, making it push hard against me, testing my boundaries even as I held it at bay. I swallowed several times, trying to get saliva flowing. My mouth was parched, dry, and hot, like I'd been sucking on desert sand.

I put my back to the door and stared into the flames. Using a technique Milly showed me, I put a barrier between me and the flames. Like a wall for the fire to hammer at, it gave me some relief. Yet I knew it couldn't last. The barrier drew off my power, like I was a battery feeding it. There would come a point where I couldn't hold it any longer, when I had finally run out of juice.

"Hurry, Liam," I whispered as I slid to the floor and put my hands on the warm stone. "Please, hurry."

The ride to the mineshaft proved difficult only because the wolves would be naked if they shifted to their human forms, since they couldn't retain their clothing like he could, and without clothing they'd freeze in the air. Blaz grumbled the whole way about claws digging into his hide.

You are lucky I like you, Liam.

He just snorted. "Luck has nothing to do with it. You like Rylee, and that's enough."

Blaz echoed his snort. *True.*

The dragon spiraled down to the edge of the mineshaft and the werewolves jumped off Blaz's back in unison. And then the second problem Liam hadn't really considered presented itself. There was no way to get the wolves down the mineshaft. Sure, he could have them shift, but they just weren't strong enough for shifting multiple times, and some of them were still healing from the battle with the other guardians.

They milled around him, and finally he shook his head. "End of the line. Go back to your territory here. I will call when I need you."

The second-in-command, a young male that resembled a pinto horse with black-and-white splotches on his body let out a whine, his eyes full of worry. They'd lost one alpha already; they didn't want to lose another.

Liam nodded. "I know. But for now, you keep things going. I'll be back for you."

The much smaller pack gave out a chorus of howls as they spun in the snow and tore off across the badlands. Liam watched them go, the wolf in him wanting nothing more than to run free, to be wild and not have a single care in the world. But that wasn't his life, nor meant to be.

"Alex, you coming?" He turned and his jaw dropped. Alex had already rigged himself up and was sliding down the open mouth of the mineshaft.

"Yuppy doody, going down, boss!"

Alex let go of the rope and disappeared from sight. A howl of excitement echoed up the mine shaft.

I think it won't be long now, for him, Blaz said, leaning over the shaft and peering down into it.

"What do you mean?"

Won't be long before he remembers how to shift.

"I wondered if that would happen." Liam set to putting on his own harness. "Thank you, Blaz. We'll see you on the other side."

A smart blast of wind curled around them as he said those words and Blaz's eyes narrowed with concern.

Premonitions abound, Wolf. Be safe. She needs you yet.

Nothing he could say to that; he agreed. Rylee needed him and he would fight for her 'til his last breath.

Sliding down the ropes made him think of the first time he'd come down the mineshaft, with Rylee's legs wrapped around him. How he'd come to realize she'd been innocent of the crimes he'd thought she'd committed. Lost in his memories, he hit the bottom of the shaft quickly.

"Vampire here," Alex said softly, his eyes glowing with the little bit of light from the top of the mineshaft.

"Which one?"

"Rylee's sister."

That was interesting. Why would Berget be waiting for them?

Grabbing one of the torches they left at the bottom of the shaft along with a lighter tucked in beside it, he lit the torch and headed toward the doorway that led to the castle.

There, standing quietly with her hands tucked behind her back, still as a statue, was Berget. Her eyes found his and his gut clenched. Something had gone sour.

"What's wrong?"

She shook her head. "Rylee is fine, if that's what you're asking. But I cannot cross the Veil into the castle. There is a fire raging and it is too much for me."

"Fire? If there was a fire when you got here it should be out by now."

"No, it is magical in nature."

He scrubbed his hand over his face. "Orion is trying to keep us from closing the doorway."

"Most likely."

A strange energy rolled off her, one he realized a moment too late. Berget launched herself at him, teeth wide and eyes glazed with madness. He jammed the torch into her face at the last second, and she screamed and fell to the ground with a sob.

"I'm sorry, Liam. They are getting too strong. I will stay here; I can't go to London. They hate her for trapping them in me."

He knew "they" were her adoptive parents and the "her" in question was Rylee.

Taking a chance, he crouched beside her. "Berget, it will kill her to lose you again."

"I'm not safe around her. Not in the condition she is in, especially. They know, they could tell when I took her blood." Berget raised her blue eyes to his. "I wouldn't risk innocent lives for this. I love her too much to hurt her like that. I will stay here and do what I can to help. When the last fight comes, I will be there. That is all I can do."

Her words were too much an echo of Milly's when Rylee had left her in the deep Veil. And that had not ended well. He reached out and pulled her into a hug. "I don't want to leave you here, but you're right. We can't risk innocent lives."

She let out a sob and covered her face. "Tell her I love her. And . . . tell Doran, tell him the same." Her eyes flickered and her face flushed, but he didn't point it out to her.

"Of course." He stood and let out a deep sigh. This was going to crush Rylee.

Alex moved up to his side. "Bye bye, Berget. I will miss you too."

"Protect Rylee, for me, Alex," she whispered and he nodded vigorously.

Liam put a hand to the door and Berget whispered, "Wait."

He half-turned so he could look her in the eyes. "What is it?"

"Days, you only have days left."

She blinked several times, tears streaking her face. "They . . . they just showed me. Days, at best. I'm sorry. Maybe less."

His heart wanted to stutter, but he held it together. "Thank you."

With a quick turn of the handle, he pushed through the Veil and into the burning inferno that was the castle, shutting the door behind him. He stumbled over something at his feet. "Shit, Pamela!" He scooped her up and she let out a mumble.

Alex grabbed at her legs. "Pamie, Pamie, wakey up!"

Her eyes rolled, fluttered, and then opened. "Hurry, Liam. I can't hold out much longer."

He didn't ask what she meant, only picked her up and started to run. Twisting and turning through the castle, it was as if the flames around them were chasing them. Alex yelped several times, and as they skidded into the main courtyard, he let out a shriek as a piece of his tail caught on fire.

"Fucking ouchie!"

"Hurry, Liam," Pamela groaned. There was no waiting; he bolted for the main gate, aiming for the slim opening in it. They burst through and into a steady downpour of rain that soothed his skin. He fell to his knees as he gulped in the fresh, cool air.

Alex poked his nose into Pamela's face. "Pamie, you okay?"

Her breathing was steady and even, and Liam could tell it was just exhaustion. She waited inside that burning castle for him and Alex. He touched her face gently. "Kid, you did good. Real good. Don't you ever let anyone tell you that you aren't amazing."

He knew in his heart it was a little like him saying goodbye, saying the things he should have said a long time ago. The time had come for his goodbyes, and he wouldn't shirk them. As hard as they would be, he would say his peace before it was his time so those important to him would know he loved them.

Going on a hunch, I had Frank open the Veil a half mile from Jack's house. Just to be safe. And as close as we were, Frank was able to open the Veil for that short jump despite his exhaustion and inexperience, completely avoiding the giant who stood on guard at the castle watching the fire rage.

We stumbled through the Veil as fast as we could, every one of us worn out.

I Tracked the unicorns first; they were in the forest around the mini mansion and they watched us closely. I lifted a hand to them. They were safe and that was enough. Eve, Marco, and a whole damn clutch of harpies were on the rooftops and I could see now why the unicorns were in the forest. Sure, there might have been a truce between the two species, but that didn't mean they had to like it.

Coyote was doing well, and he proved it by alternately pissing off Erik and then making him laugh. Frank and Kyle were discussing computer programs, but it was India who held my attention. She was in her own little world, and when I Tracked her to get a bead on her feelings, there was a lot of sorrow coursing through her. The spot where Frank had dropped us would give us a bit of a walk; I hoped that would give me enough time to talk to her.

"India, you know about your parents?"

Her eyes flicked to mine and then away. "Yes, they're with me."

Damn, being a spirit seeker had its pitfalls. I put a hand on her shoulder. "I'm sorry about that. I wish we could have saved them too."

She gave a slight shrug. "It was their time. That's the way it works, you know."

Unfortunately, I did know. Even if I didn't like it.

"I can sometimes tell when someone's spirit is close to crossing the Veil." Again, her eyes flicked to mine and away. Like she was embarrassed.

A part of me didn't want to know. The other part knew it was important. "Someone in our group?"

"Yes."

"You don't want to tell me, do you?"

She shook her head. "I'm not allowed. But it makes me sad. It will change everything. But they won't really be gone. You need to know that."

"What do you mean?"

"They are always with you, the ones you love. They never leave you. They fight for you even after they're gone."

Such wise words from one so young. "You mean like Giselle?"

A smile broke across her face. "Yes, like Giselle. And others too, there is a man named Jack who wants to say something to you, but he's saying very bad words." She blushed and I couldn't help the laugh that slipped out of me.

"That sounds like Jack."

She screwed up her face. "He says he's proud of you, even though he didn't spend a lot of time training you. And that the book of the lost is where all the answers are. And that he's sorry he didn't tell you that in the beginning."

I inserted the f-bomb here and there in her message in my head and it sounded just like Jack. "He can hear me?"

"Right now, yes."

"Thanks a fucking lot, Jack."

She clapped her hands over her mouth, covering a giggle. "He's laughing."

I kept an arm around her as we walked, knowing she needed the comfort far more than I did. At least, that was what I told myself.

The sun wouldn't set for another hour or two, from what I could tell, but to be honest, I was so messed up with all the Veil jumping I just knew I needed to sleep. Fatigue didn't even begin to cover how I was feeling. A roll of nausea swept through me as if to imprint the fact that I hadn't been taking very good care of myself lately. None of us had.

The house was quiet, and I supposed that made sense. No ogres other than Mer were left to keep

Doran and Faris company—if the asshat had the balls to stick around. I Tracked the two vampires, but only picked up Doran. Which meant Faris was across on the mainland most likely. Or maybe even all the way back in the States.

Following Doran's threads, I led the way through the house to the large library. He was slumped in a chair, his back to us.

"Miss us?" I said as I crossed the threshold.

He spun, his eyes wide, and I knew then he really had been worried if we'd snuck up on him. "Rylee, how the hell did you get here?"

"Little help from Frank, Pamela, and a shit ton of luck." I tried to give him a smile, but I couldn't. I was worried about Liam, about Pamela and Berget.

"Where are the others?" He didn't name them, didn't have to.

Erik stepped up and filled Doran in on everything that had happened. The coven, the guardians, the castle on fire. With each word, Doran's eyes narrowed.

"I'm glad you made it out safely, but the danger is far from over. The demon packs are here, Rylee. Three of them, anyway. They are busy tearing up and down the coast, but seem stymied by the water crossing. They are causing some serious problems." He sighed. "Most notably, a new strain of smallpox seems to have erupted. The humans are freaking out, and rightfully so." Doran offered me his chair and I took him up on it. India climbed into my lap and put her head on my shoulder. I thought about Talia and Milly, about how they'd made the fourth demon pack work for them. That must have been how they'd come to our side of the ocean; Talia must have brought them. No matter what help Talia had been, I had to remember she was not on our side, she would always help Orion first.

"Why wouldn't she be made to take the rest of the packs to North America?" I mumbled softly to myself.

India gave a yawn. "Jack says it's because they are waiting for you."

I wrapped one arm around her and looked to Erik. "That makes sense."

His eyebrows shot up. "What are you talking about?"

"The packs are here looking for me, for those who Orion wants to control. He might not want to kill me for the moment, but he'll try and wipe out the rest of my support. And he fucking well knew we were coming here, where else would we go? The small pox breakout though, that is for something else."

I recalled all too vividly our discussion about the bubonic plague, how the demons used it to weaken the human's natural immunity to them. Fuck, that's what was going on. A new plague to open the world to demon possession. The words spilled out of me as the realization hammered home.

There was no argument Erik or Doran were able to come up with. Erik helped me to my feet. "Go get some rest, Rylee. You need it. We all do. When Liam gets here, we'll make a plan."

With India sound asleep in my arms, I headed for the door. "We have to draw the packs to us. You think we can do that?"

Erik nodded, his face grim as he clapped a hand on my shoulder. "I know we can. You see, if you haven't already figured out, demons love chaos. And you, more so than anyone I've every met in my life, have a knack for chaos."

Doran let out a snort and I glared at him. He did nothing but wink and blow me a kiss. "Your uncle is right. You and chaos. . . ." He smacked his hands together as if he were going to clap for me.

Much as I hated to admit it, they had valid points. Frowning, I headed for my old room, the one I'd shared with Liam. Doran agreed to keep an eye out for Liam, the wolves, Pamela, and Berget.

I gave India Pam's room, and Frank and Kyle went off talking still about some sort of electronic thing that was of no interest to me. There was a bathroom attached to the bedroom and I made good use of it, running the shower as hot as I could. The dirt, sweat, blood, and sea salt washed from me and down the drain. I let the water pour over me, wishing it could wash away the feeling I was going to lose someone very close to me. India's words echoed in my head.

They are always with you, the ones you love. They never leave you; they fight for you even after they're gone.

The thing was, I didn't think I could lose anyone else and not lose myself. Too much had been taken from me already. Another loss and I wouldn't be strong enough to fight Orion.

Another loss and I wasn't sure I would care what happened to this world and those in it.

18

Getting out of the castle was one thing. Getting past the big bastard on the outskirts was going to be entirely different. Pamela was out cold, so there was no way he could shift and carry her.

"Alex, don't move," Liam said as he took in the giant standing directly in front of the tree line. Sure, the giant was a mile away, but that didn't mean he wouldn't come after them.

"I is standing still," Alex whispered out the corner of his mouth.

There were not a lot of options; he couldn't leave Pamela and he couldn't do the distracting of the giant himself. "Alex, you think you can tease the giant, make him run away so we can get past him?"

Alex cocked his head to one side and put a claw tip to his muzzle. "Perhaps."

Liam knew he shouldn't laugh, but it was just such a classic Alex move. "Perhaps? That's the best you've got?"

Snickering, Alex swaggered out. "I will rescue boss this time. Rylee loves boss, but I will rescue him this time." With no more than that, Alex set off at full tilt toward the giant. Liam held his breath as the giant took note of the werewolf running toward him.

"Bad dog!" the giant roared out and stumbled toward Alex and it was then Liam saw the giant was hurt. The oversized supernatural tried to take a few steps, but then fell to his knees, and from there, to his belly. A ripple of earth burst out around him. Nothing else after that but heavy breathing and the odd groan of pain escaping his mouth.

Liam took a chance, knowing he held Pamela's life in his hands, but also knowing if someone could kill a giant, then they were in serious trouble.

Alex was barking and yipping at the giant's face, trying to get him back up until he saw Liam. "He's no fun. Pooped out."

The wounds on the giant were enormous and they weren't healing. There were great gouges on his thighs and back where chunks of flesh had been stripped away, bruises littered his face, and it looked like his nose had been broken. The ground shook around them with a heavy footstep and the giant at their feet rolled his eyes toward them.

"Demon giant coming."

"Alex, time to go." He hoisted Pamela in his arms even more and took off at a flat out run, Alex right beside him. They were deep within the forest when a high-pitched scream ripped the air, followed by the gurgle of a creature's last breath. Liam had no doubt it would be the original giant who breathed his last.

At the far edge of the forest where the road met the tree line, they finally stopped. Not because they were out of breath, but because there was a car parked there, waiting for them.

The door flicked open and Doran leaned across. "Thought you could use a ride."

Liam slid in. Alex was not content with just getting into the back seat. He climbed over top of him and Pamela, drawing an "ooph" out of her. She sat up, her eyes ringed with dark circles. "Are we out?"

"Yeah, we're out, you did good."

She smiled and closed her eyes.

Alex spun in circles in the back seat at rapid speed before flopping down. "Time to sleep."

Doran put the car in drive. "Rylee made it with everyone except Berget."

"I saw her. She isn't well and won't be coming to London. She said to tell you she loved you."

A shot of pain slid across Doran's face. "I knew it was a temporary fix, but I'd hoped it would last a little longer."

Liam nodded, not needing to say anything, noticing Doran chose not to acknowledge the younger vampire's affections. A few days was all he had left and he wasn't going to waste it worrying about Berget's madness and lack of a love life.

No, he had far bigger things to worry about.

I thought I was dreaming when Liam's hands slid around my naked body, pulling me tight against the length of him. I whispered his name and buried my hands in his hair and tugged him to me, as if I could disappear in his arms.

Tender and sweet, there was an ache of longing in the way he made love to me. Every touch lingered, as if he would imprint himself on me, every kiss held a breath of hesitation to make it last, every brush of his skin on mine left the sweet burn of emotions trailing along my nerve endings.

It felt too much like a goodbye for my liking, and it scared me. "Liam—"

"Just let me love you."

Such a simple request and yet, it was so damn hard. Loving him and letting him love me wasn't the issue. My fears were the issue. India had seen a death of someone close to me. I was afraid the secret he held so close was that he knew he was going to die. That I was going to lose him.

He fell asleep in my arms and I couldn't stay. For the first time in a long time, I ran from him. Dressing quickly, I made a straight shot for the pond.

Emotions rolled through me, fear and love, grief and confusion. Why was I so certain that it was Liam India had referred to?

I didn't want to answer my own question, though I knew the answer all too well.

Pamela found me, but she said nothing. She just stepped beside me and stared into the dreary night with me.

She shivered and I handed her my coat. "Here. I'm too hot anyway." That was the truth; I was sweating profusely, a flush of heat I couldn't seem to escape even now that I was outside.

"Rylee, do you remember when Giselle said the darkness would make a bid for me?" Pamela's voice was soft and uncertain and my problems were swept away.

"Yes, I do."

"What if I'm not strong enough to hold out?"

Shit, I wasn't the only one facing fears and staring down the inevitable. Some days it was far too easy to forget that.

"Pamela." I slid an arm over her shoulders and tucked her tight against me. "You will hold out. Because you don't give in, and you don't give up. Giselle warned you so you would be prepared, not scared."

Of that, I had no doubt. I didn't worry about Pamela switching sides. If it had been Milly I'd been talking to, that would be a totally different conversation. But not Pamela.

"How can you know for sure?"

I turned her to face me, looking straight into her eyes. "Because I know you, and I know your heart. You faced down a dragon to protect me; you've faced down enemies that would make grown men weep with fear, all to protect those you love. You can't corrupt that, it's too pure."

A tear slipped down her face. "I don't ever want to lose my family, you all mean too much to me."

That I understood all too well. When you loved people, you had something to lose. I hugged her tight and she clung to me as soft sobs rippled through her. "It will turn out in the end, Pam, it always does. Maybe not how we envisioned, but it always turns out. And if it isn't okay, if something is still not good, then it isn't the end."

She sniffled and pulled away from me. "Okay."

"You feel better now?"

A smile briefly touched her lips. "Yes, I do."

"Then go get some sleep. It'll be dawn soon."

She handed me back my jacket and I slid it on, my own fears and worries buried for the moment under hers.

But with her gone, they came back full force.

Love made people strong, but it also gave their enemies leverage. That was what I was afraid of more than anything else. I knew I needed to hang onto the love in order to face the demons; I had to put away my anger and fear. But it was so fucking hard.

Orion knew my weakness; hell, he had already exploited it. He would tear those I loved from me, torture and kill them. My own pain, my own death I could deal with. But not those I loved.

Taking my own advice to Pamela, I headed back inside. Being exhausted wouldn't help me face down Orion.

Liam was awake when I got back to the room, and he gave me a tired smile. "Have a good walk?"

I shrugged and he crooked a finger at me. With his help (not that I needed it), I slid out of my clothes.

The tang of my tight muscles under the insistence of his strong fingers kept my mind from dwelling on anything too serious. Or so I thought, until the words poured out of me.

"Orion saved my life, killed the entire coven to keep me safe. Because he wants something I have."

Liam's fingers faltered, then started up again. "He won't take you. I won't let him."

I smiled to myself at his confidence, but the smile slipped as I spoke. "I know. But what the hell could I have that he wants enough to keep me alive? I'm the only threat to him not succeeding with his stupid-ass plan to take the world for his own. It doesn't make sense."

It hit me like a ton of troll turds. Zane. Of course, Orion knew I had the boy, had him in hiding.

Liam turned me around to face him. "We need to sleep now. If nothing else, you need to rest. For a few hours at least."

I stared at him, saw the fear in his eyes and knew he thought he knew what Orion wanted.

"You'll tell me what you're thinking, won't you?"

He kissed me softly. "Soon. Not yet, but soon."

Curled under the blankets, I put my head on his chest, the sound of his steady heartbeat lulling me to sleep.

Leaving Rylee curled up and sleeping soundly, he made his way to the library. Opening the door, he knew who he'd find there, could smell them clearly. Erik and Doran were leaning over. . . .

"Shit, is that the Book of the Lost?"

Erik nodded, but didn't lift his head. "Yes."

Walking toward them, he lifted his hand and pointed at the book. "Does it tell us how to shut the doorway in the castle?"

Doran dropped into the chair closest to him. "Unfortunately, it does. You know the blood of a guardian can close a tear in the Veil?"

He nodded, feeling his life tie into what Doran was about to say. The vampire flicked his hand at the book. "The guardian's life, freely given, and taken by one who loves him, will seal *all* the doorways through the Veil for a given time. Too bad Coyote doesn't have any loved ones here."

There it was, Liam felt the truth drop through him. This was what he'd been waiting for. Doran was right, Coyote had no one who could take his blood.

But Liam did.

"How long?"

Doran snorted. "We aren't doing this. It isn't a viable option."

"Rylee would never let it happen." Erik closed the book. "Never."

Gritting his teeth, he took a slow breath before asking again. "How. Long."

Doran grabbed his arm. "You don't get it; she will never let it happen. We have to find another way."

Liam wasn't upset, even though Doran's fingers dug into his bicep. "There isn't another way, though, is there?"

Neither of the two men would look at him. He pried Doran's hands from his arms. "Anything to keep them both safe. Do you understand? I would do anything to keep them *both* safe."

Doran's eyes widened and he fell backwards. "You're shitting me."

Erik let out a low groan. "That's why Orion wants her alive. Fucking hell!" He threw the book across the room, and Liam smelled the grief on the older man, the pain of again losing someone he loved.

Liam blew out a breath, knowing this was it. This was his end, and he was okay with it. "I have a plan.

She can't know, but I think we can take out the packs and close the doorway at the same time. Will you help me?"

Erik's shoulders slumped, at the same time that Doran dropped his chin to his chest. They would help; he knew they would. "We just need one more person, though I don't want to include her, she's the only one."

"Sweet baby Zeus, Liam. She's too young."

Liam knew Erik was right. But what other choice did they have? There was only one person who could get him through the fire of the castle to the doorway, only one person he knew loved him as family other than Rylee.

Pamela.

19

Every time I thought I'd get a good night's sleep, something happened. Though, at least in this case, I wasn't waking to someone screaming. Actually, I wasn't really awake at all, at least, I didn't think I was.

Giselle stood in the corner of the room, her figure clothed in armor, weapons peeking out from her back. She was young, younger than when I'd first met her, and her eyes were clear and bright. Fierce.

"Rylee, this is the last time I will be able to visit you. The war grows stronger on this side of the Veil, even though we are doing our best to stem the flow of evil spirits coming through, with the new plague, it won't be long before the demons can enter this world on their own." She sounded tired, as tired as I felt.

"This is goodbye then? No more advice, no more midnight visits?" I was going for sassy, but the words were whispered and sounded like a little girl begging her mother to stay just a few more minutes.

"Goodbye is relative. One day you will be here, fighting beside me, keeping the world safe, just in a different way. It is the way with all of us who would stand between the world and the demons."

I remembered what she had said before, that those who fought the darkness on this side of the Veil continued to do so after they died.

"Any last words of advice?"

She smiled, but her lips trembled. "Not advice so much as information. Milly is not dead, though it may have looked that way. We were wrong about her; the darkness I felt was Orion clutching her close." She shook her head and a tear slipped from her eye. "When it comes time, do it quickly, she deserves that much."

I stared at her, my mind refusing to understand what she was saying at first. And then when it hit me, I balked.

"No," I whispered. "You can't ask that of me, it's bad enough I have to kill my own sister, I can't . . . not Milly too."

Giselle shook her head. "Be strong, my girl, for it won't be me who asks it of you, but Milly. Let your heart lead, always your heart. Love will not fail you, not even in this; your hardest hours are yet to come, but love will save you. It will save all of us. You must believe that, even when you think you cannot go on another step. Even when you think your heart is dead."

I blinked and she was gone. The dream, or vision, or whatever the hell it was, faded.

Of course, I lay their wide fucking awake, my brain unable to shut off now that it had started down the course Giselle had introduced. My hardest hours yet to come? Hells bells, I wasn't surprised, but really? Didn't life owe me a break or two? One night of sleep was all I really wanted. I thought about Milly and Berget, neither a sister by blood. Both bound to me and both putting me in the position where I would have to face them. Liam had told me that Berget had stayed behind, that she wasn't coming. That I'd effectively lost her once more. I reached for the spot where Liam had lain, the heat from his body still in the sheets. Call me needy, but I wanted to be with him, to lean on his strength.

I Tracked him. He was in the house and as I Tracked the rest of my family I felt Pamela, Alex, and Doran with him. It seemed early, but that wasn't unusual for him.

Knowing sleep was not going to show, I slipped out of bed.

Quickly dressing, I made my way first to Jack's small armory. There were only a few blades left and I grabbed two of them, grimacing as I slid them into their sheaths. They were fine, except they weren't mine and they weren't spelled. Not quite balanced the way I liked, they were both a little on the short side for my taste. But they would do.

I made my way through the house, avoiding the library and heading to where I felt Erik's threads. He was outside, near the training grounds we'd set up when we'd been staying here.

Erik sat on the edge of the circular area we used, but he seemed lost in his own thoughts. Fine by me. Taking my two swords out, I settled my feet into a practice stance and started to weave my way through the various movements of swordplay. The minutes ticked by and my mind slowly quieted as I focused on my breathing, the weight of the swords, and the placement of my feet. This was where I would find the plan to take care of the demon packs. In the silence of the morning as my blades cut through the air.

Behind me came the soft scuff of a foot and I spun to face Erik. He held out his hand. "Give me one."

I tossed a sword through the air and he caught the handle with ease. It had been a long damn time since I'd actually sparred with someone who knew how to handle a sword. Not counting creepy-ass dude who guarded the violet book of prophecy in Orion's castle.

He circled around me and then—shit he was fast— he was on me, the sword thrusts and blows coming hard and steady, forcing me back a few steps before I caught myself. Grinning, I pushed back, diving under a hard slash and coming up on his side. I kicked him just above the hip, driving the wind from him and nearly putting him into the fountain.

"Too slow, old man." I beckoned him with my free hand, wiggling my fingers. Laughing, he lunged forward, a wild grin on his face and in him I saw a reflection of myself.

Swords sliding off one another, we worked our way around the fountain for fifteen minutes until he finally backed off. "Enough, enough. You win." He crouched, using the sword as a prop to lean against.

"You fight pretty good." I slid my sword back into its sheath and he handed me the second one. I spun it in my hand, thinking. "I'm going to Track the three packs; I think I can draw them to us." I lifted my eyes to his, but his head was down, chin on his chest.

"Not worth the risk. It isn't."

"And if we can't find them before they've done so much damage we can't rein them in?" Anger leached through my words, though I tried to keep it under control. "We have a chance to beat them at their own game. One chance. I can't believe you would fucking well think this isn't worth it!"

Erik finally looked up and I thought he was going to yell at me. But he didn't, he was calm and cool. "If they destroy you in the process? What then? What do we do when the one person who can save us is dead because the demon packs have fried your brain like an egg on the sidewalk?"

Shit. The image stuck in my head, a drooling mess of a person by my own stupidity and rashness. Not a pretty picture.

"I don't know. I can't sit here and wait for a report to come in that they are demolishing our world. The fact they've been so quiet scares me." I pushed the tip of the sword into the soft, wet ground, the fight blown out of me with his calmness.

He laughed softly. "They aren't being quiet. They are spreading this new strain of smallpox. But you are right; we do need to stop them. You will do whatever you want, with or without my permission. Which of course, you weren't looking for, right?" He arched an eyebrow at me and I flushed.

"No, I was just looking for your opinion."

"Now you have it. You do what you want. Then again, Liam has quite the plan laid out."

This was not how I was used to dealing with a mentor. Jack, I'd been able to curse and swear at; Giselle had always been calm and soothing.

Erik was somewhere between the two, both calming me and giving me reasons to get fired up.

We stood as the sun rose higher, the distant promise of spring in the feeble heat the rays gave off.

"Liam has a plan already?" I frowned. Why hadn't he told me about it? Then again, we'd been busy with other things.

"He just told me. Thinks if we can lure the demon packs to the castle, we can ambush them, use Pamela to pull the castle down on them, and trap them there."

It actually wasn't a bad idea. Not like we could really use the castle anymore with all the doorways broken to pieces and no way to repair them. "What about the doorway, the one to the deep Veil?"

Erik shrugged and looked out over the grounds, his eyes distant. "He seems to think a little of his blood should do the trick. Close the door."

It sounded too easy. "And how are we going to draw the demons in?"

He grimaced. "I'm going to summon them."

"What the fuck?" I couldn't help stepping back, even though he held up his hands.

"Every Slayer can do it, but once I do, there is no turning back. It'll be good for you to see though. Just another tool in your belt as a Slayer, something you need to learn."

They were keeping me out of the line of fire. My jaw twitched, but he wasn't looking at me. "When is he planning this?"

"Tomorrow night, if the summoning works as it should. Blaz should be here by then, and the vampires can help if Pamela can get the fire put out."

There was something in his voice I couldn't pin down, and I didn't like it. "Erik, is this really what's happening?"

His eyes shot to mine, eyebrows climbing. "What are you asking?"

"What's really happening?"

"Liam has a plan to shut the gate and stop the demon packs. It will work, but you aren't central to it. Is that what bothers you?"

Like a slap in the face, his words smacked me. "No, I don't need to be at the center of things. Fuck. I'm just getting a weird vibe is all."

I stomped away from him, jamming my second blade back into its sheath, not knowing what else to do.

The reality was, there was nothing I could do. If Liam thought he had this under control, who was I to question his plan? I could be as difficult as anyone out there, but I wasn't into causing drama if it wasn't warranted. If Liam had a plan, I could trust him.

I found my way to the library. Everyone had left except Liam and Doran, who had their heads together over the violet book of prophecies.

"You two plotting against me?"

Their heads snapped up in unison, telling me they were really not paying attention to the world around them if I could sneak up on them both without even trying.

Doran laughed and shook his head. "Hardly. But this book here, it is fascinating. There is a great deal in here about you facing Orion and beating his ass into the ground."

"There is?" This was what we needed, some good news, finally. I moved up beside them and Liam slipped his arm around my waist as I bent over the book. Doran pointed out a section that I read softly to myself.

"When the blood of the lost shall break on the altar of sacrifice, bound to that which she fears the most, then shall the world be free of the darkness that seeks to devour it. When her eyes shall open, then shall she see."

I lifted my eyes to Doran's. "Not exactly what I'd call helpful."

He shrugged. "Thing is there are clues here. Lots of them. Altar of sacrifice, you're going to have to give up something, which isn't really a surprise. We know blood is involved, and now we know you have to be bound to your biggest fears."

With a snort I poked at the book. "It still doesn't say *how* all that is going to happen. Or even where! It's like trying to understand a different language. Is it all like that?"

Liam's hand tightened on my waist. "Yes. We've been pouring over it, all of us. Just in case it goes missing again."

While it made sense they would all have a look at it, there was a part of me that knew ultimately I had to understand what was asked of me. If I couldn't figure it out, there was no way I'd be able to stop Orion. I picked up the book and went to Jack's chair, sliding down into worn and well-broken-in cushions. Neither of the two men said anything, they just watched me, the weight of their eyes on me a palpable thing.

Ignoring them, I flipped the book open from the beginning and began to skim through, looking for key words. Unlike the black-skinned book of demon prophecies, I didn't feel dirty reading the violet-skinned book. The words were all like the first, a mess of sentences that, while I could read them, made very little sense. Worse than all the other books of prophecy. At least those could be deciphered for the most part.

Sitting in Jack's chair, trying to read my own future in a book written hundreds, if not thousands, of years before, I couldn't help but think there was something else we should be doing. Yet there was nothing but to wait on Liam's plan, a truth that ate at me and my natural inclination to run in, kick ass, and ask questions later.

"Are you sure we can't go tonight?" I asked him as we ate lunch in the kitchen, the violet book tucked in beside me.

Liam shook his head. "No, I'm sure. Besides, Erik said he needs time to prepare. Shouldn't you be helping him?"

That was something I didn't want any part of, but Liam was right. Reluctantly, I Tracked Erik and followed his threads to the rooftop. When I got there, the harpies were off flying, or at least, most of them were. Three roosted with their heads tucked under their wings on the far side of the roof, oblivious to us. Erik sat cross-legged next to a chalk drawing. I crouched beside him. The drawing was a simple circle with two lines bisecting it. "What do you have to do to call a demon? I thought there would be a pentagram involved."

He didn't open his eyes. "This isn't calling a demon to possess their power, this is calling them out."

"Like a bar fight."

"Exactly. Demons are somewhat sensitized to Slayers, so when we announce ourselves, they are drawn to us. The problem is, you can't just call one demon. You end up calling anything within range."

My eyes widened. "Then why would this be something you would even want to learn?"

He blew out a soft breath. "It's a form of suicide for a Slayer, a way to go out with a bang if you will."

I sat beside him. "What do you have to do?"

He finally opened his eyes and tapped the chalk drawing. "This is a compass. North, south, east, and west are represented and the Slayer becomes the center of it. Essentially, you throw yourself at the mercy of the elementals to take your call to all the demons of the world, to draw them to you. If they take your request, they will give us notice."

There it was again, that elemental thing. "You say elementals like they are cognizant of us."

He chuckled. "They are, but they are not allowed to interfere with the rest of the world. They are neutral."

"Why?"

With a shrug, he closed his eyes. "I don't know. No one does. But they will either take my message to the demons that are here or they won't."

I hated to admit it, but the whole thing intrigued me. Though, maybe again it was the mention of elementals. A part of my brain insisted I'd met one, but I couldn't remember that being the case.

"Would it help if I added in a request of my own?"

"Might. Sit quietly and reach for the demons, demand they show themselves."

Well, that was a new one. "That's it?"

"Yes." The way his lips curled told me it wouldn't be that easy, but a challenge was what I needed to keep my mind off the time ticking by. I sat beside him and closed my eyes.

Fucking asshole piece of shit demons, come and get me.

His hand tightened on Doran's shoulder. "A minute, please."

Doran stilled under his grip.

Liam took a slow breath, finding the scents around Doran disturbing and yet somewhat comforting too. "You love her."

"Yes." Doran stared back at him, unmoving for a few seconds before nodding. "But she sees only you. She doesn't have it in her to be any other way. I don't think that will change, even . . . after."

"But we both know what's coming for me." He had to swallow any jealousy, any hurt on his part, and it tore out a chunk of his heart to say it. "Keep loving her, Doran. She's going to need you."

Liam couldn't help but see the qualities in Doran that would pair well with Rylee. Doran's sense of humor, his laid-back way of dealing with things, they would temper her seriousness. His jaw ached from holding it tight, from not snapping out that Doran should stay the hell away from Rylee. The mix of emotions made him sweat and he had to fight to keep his wolf under control for the first time in a while.

"Liam, I don't think she will see things that way. But I will always stand with her. I won't let her fight this alone." Doran's uncharacteristic solemnity eased Liam's anxiety . . . at least a little.

Teeth gritted, he walked out, leaving Doran behind. It was all he could ask now, to make sure those around Rylee would be with her when the time came. Because if there was anything Liam knew, it was that Rylee wouldn't let him go without a fight.

Next, he went to find Pamela, scenting her out and finding her in the kitchen. She was baking, something he'd learned she did when feeling uncertain. The smells filling the kitchen told him she was indeed feeling out of sorts. Alex sat awkwardly on a stool next to her, his gangly legs hanging off the edge, like some sort of unhinged puppet. Just Alex's eyes followed him and in them was a worry that Liam felt.

To ask Pamela what he'd asked of her was brutal. "Pamela."

Her head came around slowly, but she didn't lift her eyes.

He tried again. "Pamela, I'm sorry I have to ask you to do this."

She bit her lower lip as if to stop the tremble that reverberated there. Tears dripped down her cheeks as she lifted her eyes to his. "I don't think I can. Anything but that. You're a part of my family."

His heart and gut clenched into a knot he wasn't sure would ever release, and he pulled her into his arms. She was covered in flour and grease, but none of that mattered.

He kept his voice low. "It's the only way to save Rylee. And she's more important than me. You know that."

Her words were hiccupped out between sobs. "But it will kill her, and she'll hate me."

"She won't hate you. I promise."

There was no choice. Orion had backed them into a corner, and Liam had to give Rylee time, time to deal with the newest twist in her life. The only thing he could do now was pray it would be enough.

And that Rylee would forgive them all.

20

The next night didn't roll around, it fucking well erupted into chaos that we should have seen coming. Erik and I had taken turns calling out the demon packs with no apparent success. Until the sun set.

Erik and I were on the rooftop after dinner. Alex was with us this time, his head in my lap as he mumbled obscenities at the demons. Not that he was adding to the actual call out, but it was funny as hell.

Maybe the elementals also found it funny because there was a sudden break in the air. The tension that had been building around us for the last twenty-four hours snapped.

The harpies roosting launched into the sky with a chorus of screeching and squawking that made me clap my hands over my ears. Erik stumbled to his feet, and looked over the edge of the roof.

A woman, floating on the air rose in front of us. Gauzy and surreal, she gave us a soft smile. The wind picked up, swirling her soft pink skirts out around her. Eyes the color of storm clouds pinned me to the roof. "You have called the demons, and I will take your request to them. Do you wish for the giant demon to be called as well?"

I shook my head at the same time as Erik. It seemed that both of us were a bit star struck. An elemental was the thing of legends. And we were staring at one.

Her smile was soft and full of sadness. "It will be done. They will come with a roll of thunder. Be ready, Slayers."

She clapped her hands and then was gone. I turned to stare at Erik. "Holy fucking shit, was that an elemental?"

"I believe so." He passed a hand over his face.

We sent Alex to warn everyone to be ready. My hands tightened on my crossbow, nerves jangling and adrenaline pumping. We waited, my uncle and me, side by side. Facing the east. The air around us grew heavy, and a boom of thunder shattered the stillness. I felt it in my chest, the reverberation of what I knew was a turning point in my life.

Erik took a few steps closer to the edge of the roof. He pointed to a spot in the distance. "They're here."

I ran to his side and felt the world spin out from under me. Not only had we called the last of the demon packs, but we'd also managed to call out a bunch of demons who'd escaped me at the police station in London. The ones who bred like rabbits. Also known as the ones that, currently, completely outnumbered us a hundred to one.

So the whole thing should have been easy from then on out.

Yeah, right.

"Time to run." Erik pushed at me and I let him as we ran for the stairs. Everyone in the house was ready to rumble. Doran, Pamela, Frank, and Liam waited impatiently at the front door. Coyote was absent. When I questioned that, Liam grunted.

"He has another job tonight." Nothing more, though, and I wondered what Coyote's other job could possibly be.

A unicorn, dark-brown like milk chocolate, stood there, stomping his foot. He was the new leader of the crush, since they'd lost Nikko—at least until Calliope grew up.

Let us see if these demons can keep up.

Liam's plan was simple. Lead the demons on foot to the castle, have Pamela blow the gates once they were all inside and then pull the castle down around them. That was where Blaz came in. He was going to keep any wayward giants at bay, and the rest of us were just bait. India and Kyle would stay behind, with Eve and the harpies watching out for them. Frank was coming with us, seeing as he really wasn't a kid anymore. At least, as far as he was concerned.

I didn't wait, just leapt onto my ride's back. The unicorn reared up and screamed a challenge at the demons, swinging his head and baring his teeth. They responded in kind with snarls and deep-throated roars as they raced across the property.

Those of us who couldn't shift had a unicorn to ride; Liam and Alex were in wolf form and ran ahead, leading the way. My heart pounded with adrenaline as we leapt forward, hooves tearing up the soft ground. The wind whipped around us, drawing the unicorn's mane into a frenzy of tangles. I gripped hard with my legs and hands. Around me were the sounds of drumming hooves and the screech of demons in the midst of mania that came from blood lust.

The demons thought they had us on the run, and maybe if they'd been smarter they would have realized we were drawing them into a trap.

The full speed gallop over the countryside whipped by, and the demons never got close enough to do anything but snarl and snap, and hurl a few rocks and shit at us. Literal shit.

Alex took to yelling insults back at them, and that was the most entertaining part of the whole gambit.

"Shit throwers."

"Rabbit fuckers."

"Stinker heads." That last was followed by Alex sticking his tongue out and blowing a raspberry at the demons.

I glanced at Pamela who rode next to me, expecting to see at least a small smile. Nope, her eyes were focused ahead of us, her body tense like a rubber band pulled taut. I swallowed my own smile. I shouldn't be thinking this was fun at all; it was serious business. But I couldn't help it, if you couldn't look at the world when it fell apart around you and see the funny shit, you would end up hating everyone and everything. Even I knew that.

I turned in my seat and fired a few bolts from my crossbow, taking out the early runners. At least it would slow them down a little. Not to mention it pissed them off and made them even blinder to what we were doing.

We galloped through the forest preceding the open plain to the castle, branches swatting at us, but everyone kept their seats.

Three minutes and we were on the wide open space, the unicorns jumping over the downed legs of what was left of the original giant. The smell of rotting flesh and seriously bad feces rose up. Everyone except the unicorns gagged as the wind shifted, smacking us directly in the face.

Ahead of us, the castle still burned with its freaky blood-red flames and in front of it stood a new giant. This new guy wasn't any bigger than the last. But he was infinitely more deadly. He held a massive club with spikes and his eyes glowed red, the mark of possession clearly on him. He snarled as he started to run our way.

"Okay, Blaz, you're up."

About damn time.

Blaz dropped from the sky where he'd followed us above the clouds. Fire rained down on the running oversized monster that let out a roar as flames wrapped around him. The unicorns turned on a burst of speed as we raced across the open plain, stealing my breath. From my position, I got a clear look at Blaz clamping his mouth around the giant's hand—the one that held the club—and tearing it off. Previous experience told me the arm would grow back, but it would slow the big-ass bastard a little.

"You got him?" I called over my shoulder.

Blaz reared back in the air, his wings fanning the flames he'd started on the giant, his eyes wide and full of rage. *This bitch is mine.*

Good enough. Pamela lifted one hand and the gate to the castle exploded inward, a perfect opening for our party.

That was when the confusion started. My ride spun on his heels, skidding to a stop as the demons swarmed in behind us. I clung to his back as we dodged and ducked through the swarming mass and back out the gate. Erik was on one side of me, and Doran the other. Alex was ahead and I realized something was wrong.

Pamela and Liam had stayed behind.

I didn't think about the consequences, or why they might have stayed, only that I couldn't leave them there.

I swung my legs to the side to slide off the unicorn's back, but Erik's mount slammed up against us. "You can't save them."

My eyes shot to his as the horror of what he was saying overwhelmed me. "No!"

I twisted to the other side only to find Doran there, blocking me. This was not happening. Behind us the castle exploded, sending blocks of granite and stone flying through the air. Our mounts were forced to scatter and I took my chance, sliding off the unicorn. I hit the ground, rolled to take the edge off the fall and was up and running toward the castle. This was not happening.

Not now, not here.

He shifted, grabbed Pamela, and bolted for the doorway that opened into the deep level of the Veil. There was no time to waste. Rylee would figure out what they were doing and then there would be no stopping her.

Pamela clung to him as she kept the flames away. The demons seemed to think it was some great game and continued to chase them up the stairs. And all he could think about was that he wished he'd had one more minute to look into Rylee's eyes. To tell her everything in person instead of in a letter. He'd entrusted it to Doran and it told her everything. Why he couldn't tell her about this, about letting Coyote show her where she needed to go to be safe, and why. About how much he loved her and hated that he had to leave her in her darkest hours.

The castle walls seemed to close in around them as they rounded the final corner and the open doorway loomed. Over ten feet, the gaping wound in the wall vibrated with energy. Behind them, the demons howled, closing in.

"Pull it, Pam."

She didn't question him, just pulled the walls and ceiling down behind them with a mere flick of her wrist. When it came to destruction, she was the one to deal out the blows. There was no stopping her at that point. She slid from his arms and went to the window, pointedly ignoring the opening in the Veil. With her arms over her head she shook with power. The castle around them blew apart, chunks flying everywhere. Everywhere except where they stood.

The demons set up a chorus of howls and screams, trapped under the rubble, and unable to escape.

"Do we kill them first?" she whispered, as she lowered her arms and turned to face him.

"No, we'll leave that for Erik and Rylee. Trapped, the demons won't be able to put up much of a fight."

She nodded and he knew what happened next would be hardest on her. He stood in front of the open doorway. "Hand me the blade."

Pamela moved up beside him and silently handed him the copper blade. He ran it over his left palm, opening up a deep cut. The blood flowed and he smeared it around the edge of the doorway, gritting his teeth as dirt and stone chips dug into the open wound. Behind him, Pamela struggled not to cry, her hiccupped breaths as loud as cannons going off in his ears.

Jaw tight he turned to face her. Her eyes were shut tight and tears streamed down her face. Her lower lip was gripped tight between her teeth, so tight he could see the color fade.

He didn't say anything, just put his arms around her and hugged her. "Pamela, this is meant to be, and you are the only person who could do this."

"I don't want to."

"I know."

He slid the copper blade back to her, wrapping her fingers around the handle. "You can only do it because you love me. I know that, and I will be forever grateful for not only that love, but your willingness to fight for Rylee."

He smoothed her hair back, but she still wouldn't look at him. From the courtyard came a voice that snapped both of their heads around.

"LIAM!" Rylee called to him, her voice filled with panic, and he knew they were out of time.

Wrapping his fingers around Pamela's hand, he placed the tip of the blade against his heart. "It will be quick."

Pamela shoved him away from her, wrapping him in magic so tight he couldn't breathe. Anger rippled across her face. "You can't make me do this."

He lowered his head, chin to his chest. "You're right, I can't. But if you don't, Rylee will die and the world will be lost to Orion."

My heart beat so loudly I knew Liam heard it. Could hear the fear in me. The copper blade gleamed and I twisted it in my hand. Rylee was coming; if I was going to do this, it had to be now. The sudden burst of anger slipped from me and I lowered Liam from against the wall, but he didn't step away, didn't rush at me. I'd hoped he would be angry I used my magic on him, but he wasn't. His eyes were sad and resigned.

He was the brother I'd never had, the almost father figure I so badly wanted, and the friend who never let me give up. And he was asking me to kill him.

Sobbing, I stepped forward, the tip of the blade wobbling as I held it up. No more words were needed. I had to be the one to do it. In that moment, I had to be the strong one for our whole family.

I had to make the tough choice. Because Rylee couldn't.

His eyes never left mine, and a soft smile hovered on his lips, but it was the tear sliding down his cheek that held my attention. I stared at it as I slid the copper blade home, heard his breath catch, felt him slump forward, pushing the blade even further in.

"Thank you," he whispered as he crumpled to his knees, his blood pooling around him, flowing toward the open doorway.

I left the blade, turned and ran for the window. I would climb down; Rylee would never know it was me. She couldn't.

Because Liam was wrong. If she ever found out I'd been the one to kill him, she would never forgive me. I would no longer be family.

Erik fought beside me as I demolished the demons in my path. The only thing I could think of was Liam. The feel of his threads fading inside my head as I desperately Tracked him. I tried to give him my strength, lend him what I had, and he fucking well refused it. My crossbow twanged over and over again pinning demons to the burning walls around us until there were no bolts left and I jerked my two blades out.

The trapped demons were easy pickings, and even though I was afraid, terrified of what was happening to Liam, I managed to send them back. Because under all that fear, my heart was beating for a single person.

Liam.

Finally, I found what would have been the hallway, but it was demolished. "Blaz!"

Out of my way.

He landed beside me, awkwardly balanced on the rubble that was still burning in places. With a swipe of his claw he cleared the path for me.

Rylee, it is bad.

Not what I wanted to hear.

The floor was slick under my feet, and my brain was trying to tell me Blaz was right. Tried to tell me what the liquid was, that it was so much worse than just bad, that I didn't want to see. Not Liam. I would give up anyone but him.

He tried to open his eyes, but even with them closed he knew she was close. So close. Yet even that, he knew it wouldn't be enough. This was the moment. . . .

"Liam." I choked on his name as I fell to the floor beside him, the heat of the flames around us ignored, barely felt around the burning of my soul. "Liam."

Her voice called to him, and he fought the fog that dragged at him, tugged his body into the darkness. "For a little while. Only a little while, you have to trust me."

I gripped his hand, curled my body around his, my lips touching his, tasting his blood, trembling as I tried to think of a way to bring him back. Knowing it wasn't possible. My mind screamed, unable to even process this pain, unable to conceive a world without him, without Liam. Hands dragged at me, tried to draw me away from him, my fingers interlocked with his, the feel of his lips still on mine. "NOOOOO!"

"A little while. I'll come for you. Always. Protect them, do what you must. This isn't about you and me, or even the world anymore." The words whispered out of him, as he unclasped his fingers from hers and his hand settled on her belly. "I love you *both* more than anything."

What was he saying? My own hand trembled as it covered his and he gave me a slow nod. Everything I'd been feeling the last few months came rushing back to me. The fatigue, the emotions, Alex saying my heartbeat sounded funny, Orion wanting what I had . . . I opened my mouth and he shook his head. "Don't say it out loud."

I curled against him, his hand spanning my belly and the life inside of it. "Not now, Liam, you can't leave me, us, now."

A gasp of air escaped with a final promise.

"Love always wins." His body convulsed and he didn't fight the inevitable, as much as he wanted to stay with her, with them. This was his path now, and for a while, it was without her. Just a little while. There was no doubt in him they would be together again. Love like this didn't happen only to be snuffed out.

Everything around us burned, but all I saw was Liam, a dark shape in the flames. The only one who'd ever truly held my heart, the only one who'd understood me. Tears streamed, drying before they reached my chin in the suffocating air. Someone picked me up, threw me over their shoulder, the pain of my wounds crushed under the pain inside. I didn't fight them because I knew.

Not Liam.

Anyone but him.

Please, spare my love. Just this once. Give me this. I didn't know to whom I prayed, only that I prayed with all I had in me.

Someone took her away; that was good. It wasn't her time. She had too much to do. Too much to give the world—a child to save. He smiled, knowing she would understand why he sacrificed himself. To buy her time. To give them all a chance. They would prove the darkness wrong.

He put his hand over his heart, a single tear slipping down his cheek as the darkness swamped him. "Love . . . always . . . wins."

I knew the moment he died, before the flames consumed him. A howl ripped through the air, the sound of hearts breaking all around. Only it wasn't any wolf who let out a howl.

It was only me.

21

The world blacked out for me, there was nothing in me but a dark and painful emptiness that could never be filled. People wandered in and out of my hearing range, and Alex stayed close to me, but I could feel nothing but the exquisite loss of Liam.

Nothing could have ever prepared me for his death, nothing.

"He's not really gone, you know." A soft voice whispered in my ear and I slowly turned to stare into India's eyes. I said nothing and she put her fingers under my chin, lifting my face. "He says you need to read the letter he left with Doran. That it's important. And if you don't, he will keep pestering me until you do."

I didn't want to get up, didn't give a shit if the world fell down around us. What was the point, what was the reason? My left hand drifted to my belly. Liam's child, wasn't that reason enough? That was why he'd done it, why he'd sacrificed himself. Not only for me, but for the life we'd sparked together.

Less than four hours had passed since he'd died and yet it felt like four years, the weight of time pulling me down. Reluctantly, I Tracked Doran and followed the threads to one of the spare rooms. India walked with me, as if to make sure I did as I said.

Before I could lift my hand to knock on the door, it opened and Doran ushered me inside. India didn't follow, and I didn't even realize Alex had been with me until Doran spoke to him. "You wait here. This is for her ears only."

"Okay," Alex whispered, the sorrow in his voice turning me around. His ears were slumped and his eyes never lifted. I wasn't the only one who'd lost Liam. The thought only started a fresh round of tears that I couldn't stop. Doran shut the door behind me, but I just stood there, numb, too numb to take even another step.

"He left you a letter." He pulled a thin envelope from under his shirt. "He asked me to give it to you, after."

His words slowly sunk into my head. "After?"

"Yes, for after he died."

Doran had known what Liam was going to do, and he'd let him. The shock hit me so hard my knees buckled. My first instinct was to attack Doran, to kill him for letting Liam go. As quickly as I thought it, I let it go. There had been too much death, and I wouldn't risk the child, Liam's child, for revenge. Not yet anyway. The envelope waved in front of me and I took it, opened it and stared at the words as they blurred in front of me.

I'm sorry I couldn't tell you. You and the baby are the only ones who matter to me, and you needed time and a safe place to go. The doorway will stay shut for six months; it is my last gift to you, a respite from Orion for that time.

Don't be angry with those who helped me, they did it for the same reason I did.

Because they love you. Because I love you, because you are the only one who matters right now. Coyote knows of a place that will be safe for you and the baby, holy ground protected by the first guardian. That is the only place Orion cannot find you. Please, for me, do this. Be safe for a little while, be selfish, and don't tell people about the child. Already too many who would kill or trap you both know.

I wish I could be with you, wish I could see and hold our child in my arms.

His penmanship grew shaky with that last line, and I couldn't see anymore, and had to hold the paper away from my face in order to catch my breath. The sound of paper fluttering opened my eyes. My hand was shaking and I fought to still it.

You are my world, and I promised you I would never leave you, that we would always be together. Death won't keep me away. I am always with you. I will be there when our child is born. I will be there when you cry in the night. I will be there when you think you are done in and have nothing more to give. I will not leave you.

You are my world, my heart, my soul. Never forget that.

I have one last request of you.

I want you to live, Rylee, truly live. You know what I mean, so don't argue with me. Just live. Love. Don't let the darkness and grief beat you.

Forever yours,
Liam

So easy for him to say. I folded the paper and tucked it into my shirt. "I have to go."

I didn't wait for Doran to say anything, just bolted from his room and headed for the main doors. Outside in the fresh air I broke into a run until I hit the edge of the pond. The dock had never been repaired, and the splinters of it were still scattered around the edge of the water. Fog curled about my feet, hiding the ground and quickly soaking the bottom of my jeans.

I squeezed my arms around my middle, as if I could hold myself together as I stared into the pond. The surface of the water reflected my image back to me. I blinked, unable to believe what I was seeing.

Liam stared back at me.

I whipped around, the last of the night fading and the fog holding just the faintest image.

"I told you I wouldn't leave you."

I reached for him, already knowing my hand would pass through. "How could you do this to me?" The words were broken, tear-filled, and they didn't sound like they could come from my mouth.

Pain rippled across his face. "There was no other choice. But I knew you'd never let me do what I had to, not without a fight. I couldn't risk you, either of you."

He lifted his hand and let it trail down the side of my face, a breath away from my skin.

"How are you still here? You closed the Veil." I stared at him, drinking him in, trying to think of anything I could say just to keep him with me a little longer.

His smile was full. "We bound our souls together, Rylee. Where you go, I go. I never crossed the Veil. I won't, not without you." The smile slipped and his eyes grew serious.

"You have to go. Go now while things are still in upheaval on this side of the Veil. Take Coyote, Blaz, and Erik. Those are the three you need."

I shook my head. "How do you know?"

His lips, those gorgeous lips I would never kiss again curled into a smile. "I know a lot now, more than you can imagine, now that I'm on this side of things. You have to trust me that in the end, this will be for the best. Can you not trust our love is strong enough?"

His words pierced me, through the heavy grief laying on my heart and soul. "I trust you, Liam. With all that I am."

"Then go. And let the grief go. I won't leave you." He began to fade, but his voice stayed a moment longer. "I will always be with you. And call on Charlie."

I stood on the edge of the pond, my heart pounding. Those last words, they were both sweet and not. Charlie had baby Zane. Zane needed to be protected as much as I did.

Time to go again, to somewhere safe. For me, for our child, for Zane. A steady thrum of resolve began to beat in time with my heart. This was a salvage in reverse, stopping the loss of a child before it happened.

I went to my room first and packed a small bag. The fire opal Doran had bestowed on me still held heat in it, a few small knives, a change of clothes, and what else was there? Nothing.

Alex crept into the room. "Rylee is going without Alex."

I sat on the bed so I could face him, knowing he slipped into third person because of his sorrow. The fur on his cheeks was streaked with tears and I knew this would be the hardest of all my goodbyes. "I need you to stay here, to look after Pamela, Frank, Kyle, and India. Can you do that while I'm gone?"

He climbed into my lap and put his muzzle on my shoulder. "You will come back to me?"

I wrapped my arms around him, squeezing him tight, my throat constricting on the words. "You and me, to the bitter end, buddy."

"Yuppy doody," he whispered, his gangly front legs wrapped tight around me. "I watch the others. Keep them safe for you. To the end, Rylee. You and me to the end."

He went with me to find Pamela, and though I could Track her, her emotions were completely off the chart with grief and guilt. I couldn't face her. I chickened out and wrote her a note, leaving it in her bedroom. We still hadn't had our talk, and I knew I was leaving her when she needed me, but there was far more at stake than just her life. I had to trust that she would be strong enough to wait on our chat, strong enough to hang on without me for a little while.

India and Frank were a little easier. I just told them I was leaving for awhile and that they should stay with

Doran. And Doran . . . well, Doran held on a breath too long.

"Try and help Berget. If you can, if you can find her," I said as I pushed him away, anger lacing my words. I hadn't forgiven him yet. Nor did I think I ever would. But I couldn't kill him, either. Liam had done this, had made this choice, and I had no doubt that he'd made sure Doran helped him.

"For you, I will try. But I think we've lost her this time for good."

His eyes were so very full of sorrow, and another bucket of guilt and grief sloshed over me, soaking me through to my soul. All I could do was nod and push away from him.

Another of my loved ones that I couldn't save.

I Tracked Coyote, almost running away from Doran, heading straight for the Guardian. I still had no idea what job Liam had him doing when we were facing the demons. Why couldn't Coyote have been the one to die to close the Veil? I didn't know, and now it was too fucking late. I suspected his "job" was to stay alive so he could take me where I needed to go.

Coyote didn't crack any jokes when I found him in the library, nor did he question me when I asked him to follow me.

Erik was next and he too followed me without a question. We made our way out to the far side of the property where the training building was.

"Charlie." I said his name softly, and within moments he popped through the doorway closest to us. "How do you always hear me?"

He gave me a wink. "If I bees telling you all my secrets, yous might not think me so interesting. Little Zane and I went for a visit to me family in Ireland. 'Tis safe, don't be worrying your head." His smile faded as he looked at me. "What's happened, lassie?"

"Liam's dead." Two words and yet they were surreal to me, like a language I couldn't understand.

The brownie stumbled backward. "No. Not the wolf."

I kept a tight rein on my grief as it surged upward. "I need to know if you can hear me anywhere I go."

He shook his head, his eyes glittering with tears. I had to look away.

"No, I can't. Why?"

"I have a safe place for Zane, so I guess you need to bring him to me now."

Charlie didn't ask any more questions, just disappeared through the doorway, and within moments was back with a sleeping Zane. I slipped the fire opal over the little boy's neck and tucked it against his skin. Flying with Blaz was going to be bitching cold and I didn't want to take the chance on the newborn, no matter how strong a witch he might be one day.

Alex watched us mount, his eyes mournful and hurting as he waved a floppy paw at me. In that moment, I almost let him come with me. Almost.

Blaz leapt into the sky.

Where are we going?

Coyote pointed to where the sun rose on the horizon. "East."

Erik sat in front of me and I leaned forward into his back, blocking the worst of the wind from Zane's tiny face. East, somewhere in the east. The unknown awaited me and it scared the shit out of me. Without Liam I felt adrift, and yet he was right. He hadn't left me, and I wasn't alone.

I took a steadying breath and lifted my head. Our child needed me to be strong, needed a mother who would fight to her dying breath to protect him or her. Erik reached back and touched my hand.

"You are strong enough, Rylee. Even for this."

I squeezed his fingers, a sense of understanding sweeping over me. Giselle always said things happened for a reason, even if we didn't understand them at the time, even if they seemed to be the worst thing imaginable. Well, here we were, my worst fear played out and yet . . . there was hope.

"I know," I said, my voice soft, words carried away by the wind. "Much as I hate to say it, I know."

Rylee left without saying goodbye. Everything in me twisted up; there was only one reason she would have done that. She knew I'd killed Liam. I found my way to my room and fell into my bed. A crinkle of paper brought my head up and my fingers wrapped around a single sheet of paper.

Pam, I have to go away for a little while. I can't tell you why. Stay here with Doran, look out for the others. Be brave, I'll be back. See if you can get Deanna to teach you. I love you, kid. Don't ever forget it.

Rylee

I folded the paper up and tucked it under my pillow. "You wouldn't say that if you knew the truth. You wouldn't love me then."

There was a knock on my bedroom door and Doran stood there. "Even if she knew the truth, it wouldn't change how she feels. You're family; you did what you had to do. We all did."

Doran was one of the three who knew what I'd done, so that was easy for him to say.

Inside my heart, I knew she would never be able to forgive me. The pain and grief turned into a bitter gall I could barely breathe around. Doran left when I would say nothing else, and I turned to the only thing I was good at. My magic.

I made small swirls in the air, killed a few bugs that dared float into my room, and felt immensely better. Their deaths were minor in the scheme of things, but still, I felt better for them having been annihilated.

Winding my way through the old house, I killed every bug I could find. Then the mice and rats, and even a few bats that had taken up residence. With each death, my own grief slid away. No one was safe in this world; the darkness would take everyone eventually. . . .

A distant pang in my heart tried to warn me this was what Giselle had meant, this was what I would face.

This, what was happening to me, was the darkness rising.

Pushing that voice away, I squared my shoulders. No one would hurt me or my family again.

Not ever.

Not even if it meant I had to embrace the darkness.

COMING SEPTEMBER 2017 FROM TALOS PRESS

RISING DARKNESS

A Rylee Adamson Novel
Book 9

"My name is Rylee, and I am a Tracker."

When children go missing, and the Humans have no leads, I'm the one they call. I am their last hope in bringing home the lost ones. I salvage what they cannot.

One last salvage and the final battle with Orion and the demon hordes will be upon me. I don't know the name of the person I'm Tracking, or what she looks like so finding her is going to be . . . impossible. But she is the key to defeating the demons.

The world has been swept with a plague that is killing not only the humans, but every supernatural it touches. While I'm out Tracking, my allies are being wiped out.

Worse than all of this? I am losing Pamela to the darkness with every second that passes.

I'm not sure even I can control any of these outcomes.

But that doesn't mean I'm not going to try.

$7.99 mass market paperback
978-1-945863-07-3

AN EXCERPT FROM *RISING DARKNESS*

The second dragon was black as the night sky and fucking hard to see, that is my only excuse for what happened. The big bastard slammed hard into us. His claws raked down Eve's side, taking feathers and breaking the skin. "Berget, my straps!"

She ripped them with a swift tug, freeing me from my restraint. The black dragon rolled and tried to take Eve with him.

The Harpy dodged the grasping claws, rolling the other direction. I stood, took one step and leapt from Eve's back. I pulled two short blades from my sides as I fell and held them out, gripped in my fists. I'd practiced this move with Blaz while I'd been away. It had better work.

The black dragon didn't see me coming. I hit his side and drove my two blades in deep, using them as anchors. He roared and twisted trying to see me.

Bitch, I will use you as a toothpick.

"Doubtful." I let go, dangling with one hand, pressing the other against his scales. Sounded easy, but it wasn't. The dragon twisted and jerked, and my hand slipped until I was hanging on with fingertips. The demon squirmed under his skin, and beneath that I felt the sorrow of the dragon before he'd been taken over. Better to be dead than a tool of a demon. "Be free," I said. Power rippled through me and into the dragon. A flash of light as he lit up from inside, his body stiffening, the demon expelled.

Thank you, Tracker.

The dragon's eyes met mine as the color and life in them faded. The wings stopped moving, the heart slowed. Frozen now.

We began our free fall, his body spinning slowly until it was belly up. I yanked my blades free and ran with the turn of his body like a log roll. "Eve, hurry up!"

She streaked toward me, snatching me with her claws, and then shot up into the sky hard. "Get me above the green lizard, and drop me."

"You got it."

She had me gripped around my upper body, my legs dangling. The green dragon roared and blew chunks of fire at something on his back.

I squinted. "Berget. Is that what I think it is?"

"Yes, Faris is keeping its attention on him."

Faris ran along the dragon's spine, jabbing it with his cutlass, then ducking out of the way of the snapping jaws. Alex and Marco were pinned together in its claws.

"Rylee, if you kill it, the claws . . ." Eve whimpered and I knew what she was getting at. Death could cause a spasm, making the claws grip harder yet, and Alex and Marco would fall with the dragon.

"Change of plans, go in low and I'll cut the fucker's legs off if I have to."

At least, I was hoping. With a sharp turn, Eve took me toward the dark-green belly, spinning in the air at the last second in order to throw me toward the dragon's foot that held Marco and Alex.

Her aim wasn't so good.

"Shit!" I missed the claw completely and hung in space for a half heartbeat as I contemplated the timing gone terribly wrong. I fell, reaching for the dragon, knowing it was futile but doing it anyway.

A set of clawed hands reached out and snagged me from the air, dragging me to Marco's back. "I has you."

"Holy shit, good catch, buddy."

Alex grinned at me, but the smile slipped into a grimace of pain. His back right leg was crushed against Marco on a weird angle. I didn't have time to free him. He'd have to wait. I pulled my two blades and drove them into the tendons around the dragon's claw. The blades cut through the thick hide and the dragon screeched, a sound that went on and on as I dug deeper and deeper.

"Let go, you fucking overgrown gecko!" I screamed, forcing the blades in as far as I could, feeling them grind against the bones, like metal on metal.

"Pull the blade to the left!" Marco yelled and I didn't ask why, just did it. I dragged the two blades hard to the side and there was a subtle shift in the flesh they were in. The claw popped open and we fell. Alex grabbed my ankle with one claw tipped hand as he clung to Marco with the other.

"Land, just land!" I yelled as the wind rushed around us.

"Not much choice, I've broken too many feathers to climb," Marco replied. We spiraled downward—fast. If Alex hadn't been hanging onto me I wouldn't have stayed on.

Eve followed us, and it was then that I realized we'd left Faris on top of the green dragon. Shit sticks.

I looked up to see the dragon diving toward us.

"And here I was worried we'd have to go back for the vampire." I managed to get one blade into my back sheath as we dropped. I kept the other squeezed in my right hand. There was nothing I could do until we landed and hoped to hell that Faris could get off the dragon's back.

I shouldn't have worried.

We hit the dirt hard, Marco unable to slow himself enough, and so Alex and I were thrown. The three of us tumbled, rolling at least twenty feet before we lost momentum. A tree stump was my stopping point. Eve landed right behind us, a hell of a lot more graceful than we'd managed.

The dragon landed ahead of us, holding its maimed claw up. Faris stayed where he was.

"I'm safer up here," he called out.

"Ass hat!" I yelled back.

He gave me a mocking bow as the dragon roared, baring teeth and flicking its split tongue at us. It looked like they'd worked out their act together with the timing.

I eyed the distance between us, and the limping, raging dragon, as it headed our way. "Berget, think you can toss me up to Faris?"

"I could, but the dragon will just snatch you out of the air."

She made a rather good point. "Eve, get Alex and Marco out of the way."

If the dragon hadn't been wounded so badly, it would have been on us already. As it was, I had a second to think.

"Berget, help me dodge the mouth."

I put my sword into its sheath and ran toward the dragon. Its eyes glittered in the dark, and it opened its mouth wide as it swung its head toward me.

That's right, run into my mouth, Tracking bitch! The voice was distinctly female and seriously pissed if the volume level was any indication. Her fangs dripped with saliva that sizzled as it dripped to the ground.

Berget ran with me, keeping pace, and when the dragon snaked toward me, Berget yanked me out of the way at the last second, spun, and threw me toward the dragon's back, like we were in the Olympic Games.

Disoriented was a fucking understatement. She'd heaved me like I was a damn shot put and I stumbled hard, going to my knees as I landed on the thick scales of the dragon's back. Faris grabbed my upper arms and steadied me. I didn't pause, couldn't. I reached for the dragon and she leapt into the air, throwing me off balance once more. I needed to get at least one hand on her. She climbed fast, her sinuous body twisting and spinning so I couldn't keep my balance, couldn't get my fucking hands on her.

No, I like my demon. He makes me stronger than the other dragons. I will kill you, and the master will reward us both.

"Not going to happen," I yelled as I tumbled down her spine, the ridges slamming hard into my side. Jerked to a stop, I knew it was Liam, and not Faris holding my ankle. I put my hand on the dragon's back and the power flowed through me. Calm, soothing, and so very easy to call on. "Be free." The demon fled, its spirit twisted and writhing in the air above the female dragon. But she wasn't giving up, either. She reared her head toward us, mouth open wide as her belly rumbled with the beginnings of a fireball I knew from past experience would obliterate us.

I may die, but you will die with me.

"Time to go." Faris, or Liam—whoever the hell he was at that moment—grabbed me and leapt from the dragon's back. Flames curled around us, seeming to push us from the dragon as the night sky welcomed our falling bodies. How high were we? I had no fucking idea, but I knew we were about to feel the distance in a very visceral way.

ABOUT THE AUTHOR

Shannon Mayer is the *USA Today* bestselling author of the Rylee Adamson novels, the Elemental series, and numerous paranormal romance, urban fantasy, mystery, and suspense novels. She lives in the southwestern tip of Canada with her husband, son, and numerous other animals.